raves for *Shadow in the Sandpit*

Shadow in the Sandpit by Christine Noyes grabbed me from the first page, dragging me down into the dark depths as we follow FBI Agents Bradley Whitman and Derek Richards through many twists. The characters are exceptionally well-developed. The plot is unique and thrilling. I highly recommend Christine Noyes as a must- read author.

—Anne-Marie Reynolds
Readers' Favorite

Shadow in the Sandpit has an intense plot, a mysterious case, a strong protagonist with a trusted sidekick/friend, and a solid plan. Author Christine Noyes gave me modern Agatha Christie vibes with the intensity of the plot and the hard-to-guess mystery. Bradley has a witty charm to him—intelligent and surprisingly fast at solving puzzles I had to think twice about. Detective stories are either over the top these days or are far too complicated to understand. Not this one. though. *Shadow in the Sandpit* is perfect in every sense of the word.

—Rabia Tanveer
Readers' Favorite

*Shadow in the Sandpit i*s a thoroughly engaging read with an intricately interwoven plot that keeps you guessing. You'll become totally involved with the believable characters. Whether you met Bradley as a precocious teen in Christine Noyes's first novel, *Picture of Pretense*, or are meeting him for the first time as a successful FBI agent, you will be won over by his wit, intelligence, and incredible ability to puzzle out and solve crimes. *Shadow in the Sandpit* is a must read for anyone who loves a great detective story.

—Cynthia Crosson, EdD., author
LICSW therapist
UCC minister

SHADOW IN THE SANDPIT

CHRISTINE NOYES

a Bradley Whitman novel

Shadow in the Sandpit

Haley's

Athol, Massachusetts

Haley's
488 South Main Street
Athol, MA 01331
haley.antique@verizon.net • 978.249.9400

Copy edited by Mary-Ann DeVita Palmieri.

Proof read by Richard Bruno.

Cover designed by Christine Noyes.

Cover background photo by Maurits Bausenhart on Unsplash with
    shadow by Christine Noyes.

Library of Congress Cataloging-in-Publication Data
Names: Noyes, Christine, 1961- author.
Title: Shadow in the sandpit : a Bradley Whitman novel / Christine Noyes.
Description: Athol, Massachusetts : Haley's, [2022] | Series: The Bradley
    Whitman series ; volume 2 | Summary: "The novel follows the efforts of
    wheelchair-bound FBI Agent Bradley Whitman as he and his colleagues
    disrupt and prosecute a crime ring based in Boston"-- Provided by
    publisher.
Identifiers: LCCN 2022011831 (print) | LCCN 2022011832 (ebook) | ISBN
    9781948380607 (trade paperback) | ISBN 9781948380614 (kindle edition)
Subjects: LCGFT: Detective and mystery fiction. | Novels.
Classification: LCC PS3614.O9745 S53 2022 (print) | LCC PS3614.O9745
    (ebook) | DDC 813/.6--dc23/eng/20220317
LC record available at https://lccn.loc.gov/2022011831
LC ebook record available at https://lccn.loc.gov/2022011832

for Al, always
until such time your hand I hold

Contents

RUSTY

A muffled rustling came from behind the overstuffed dumpster in a dank Boston alley. Bradley inched toward the dim corner. Filled with moisture and wrapped in stench, heavy air parted as Bradley wished for a sliver of sunlight to illuminate his path. He halted his advance and listened. Abruptly, the rustling stopped. Heavy breathing intensified from the corner followed by a throaty, intimidating rumble.

Bradley reached for his Glock, but before he could relieve it of its holster, a large shadow lurched from the dark and raced toward him. The throaty rumble grew to a toothy snarl. The four-legged blur closed the gap fast. Instinctively, Bradley held his left arm in front of his face for protection while he fumbled with his firearm.

He felt a breeze, unusual for the air-trapped alley, as the beast fled past him. And then a scream. Not animalistic, but human. He turned in time to see the large dog leap, fangs forward, toward the unknown figure behind him. The man fell in a heap as the dog tore the clothing from his arms and sunk his teeth into the man's flesh. A gun skidded across the paved passage. Bradley retrieved the revolver from the ground and pointed it at the blood-soaked assailant.

"Stop!" Bradley yelled. "Enough!"

To his surprise, the dog obeyed his command and positioned himself at Bradley's side. His brown eyes concentrated on the mass lying in the alley and writhing in pain.

"Just stay put," Bradley said to the would-be assailant, although he didn't think the man much of a threat in his current condition.

The dog's pointed ear flicked, and then he jerked his head toward the street and bared his teeth. Three figures rounded the corner, each with a hand resting on the grip of a handgun. The throaty rumble returned as the black- and rust-colored Doberman placed himself between Bradley and the perceived threat.

"Sit," Bradley commanded. "Stay."

The beast complied but continued to shift his eyes back and forth to each possible danger point. The man on the pavement continued to groan.

"What the hell are you doing here, Bradley? I said we'd take care of it." A male voice spoke, then pointed to the bleeding man. "Who's that?"

"I'm guessing he's our guy, Nick," Bradley said. "He crept up on me. It's a pretty good bet you'll find the murder weapon in this alley. Probably in the dumpster."

"I need a fucking doctor, assholes. I'm bleeding to death over here. I'm gonna own you guys once I get a lawyer," the suspect hollered.

Nick turned to his partner. "Call it in, Mara."

Mara walked to the opening of the alley to make the call. Jim, the third FBI agent, held his gun on the suspect to relieve Bradley of the responsibility. Bradley handed the man's gun to Nick.

"I'm going to have to tell Richards about this, Bradley. He's not going to like it," Nick warned.

"He'll get over it," Bradley replied without conviction.

"Who's the sidekick?"

"I don't know. He came out of the corner over there. He ran right by me and jumped the guy. Pretty smart, too." Bradley took a good look at the dog who saved his life. The jet-black Doberman Pinscher bore a rust hue around the eyes, on his snout, and on the lower portion of his legs. He returned Bradley's gaze. His tail bobbed and his ears cropped, the animal must have belonged to someone, but he did not have a collar or tag, and he looked thin for his size. He still sat by Bradley's side.

"Well," Nick said, "I'll get a team down here right away. We'll do a thorough search. Richards isn't going to be happy with you. You might want to work up a convincing story."

"Yeah," Bradley sighed.

"Get out of here. Unless you want to climb into the dumpster with us."

Bradley chuckled. "I'm gone."

He reached for the throttle on the right armrest of his chair and pushed it forward. The near silent electric motor kicked in as the nubbed rear wheels engaged. Bradley rolled out of the alley and toward his white Silverado pickup truck. The Doberman followed.

Facing in the same direction as the pickup, Bradley parked his wheelchair on the driver's side. The dog sat beside him and looked forward.

"Where do you live, boy?" The animal looked at Bradley and cocked his head slightly. "Where's your collar? Go home!"

The dog didn't budge.

"Go. Go home."

Nothing.

"Look, I appreciate what you did for me. You're a smart boy.

But it's time for you to go home."

The Doberman's deep brown eyes peered into Bradley's royal blues. Bradley began to imagine the dog speaking to him. *I don't have a home. Can I come with you?*

"Okay, Rusty. But just until we find your owner." The name just rolled off his tongue.

Bradley pushed the remote on his key fob and the single panel comprising the front and rear door pulled straight out from the vehicle. Rusty turned and watched curiously. A platform, attached to the panel, lowered to the ground.

"Okay, hop in."

Rusty leapt into the truck and made himself comfortable in the passenger seat. The usual space for the driver's seat sat vacant. Bradley backed his chair onto the platform and pushed the fob button. The ramp lifted him and his chair up to floor level, stopped, beeped, and then slid into the driver's position behind the wheel. The door panel followed and closed.

CHILDHOOD MEMORIES

Bradley stopped at Honey Farms convenience store on the way home to pick up some dog food. He bought four cans of beef with gravy and a box of Milk-Bones. He hadn't had a dog since he was a child, and he noticed the selection of animal foods had changed. Beef, chicken, turkey, and stew with vegetables were only a few of the choices stocked. He found himself thinking, *What happened to Kibbles?* A heaviness fell over him, a feeling he knew well but tried to evade. As he drove through Boston on his way to Revere, he thought back to when he was six years old and played ball with his dog Roscoe in his backyard.

Roscoe, a mutt who loved to play fetch, strutted a goofy and lovable personality. One day, Bradley pitched the ball to him. Roscoe jumped into the air, caught the ball, and fell back to the ground, and so did Bradley. Without warning, Bradley's legs collapsed from under him, and he flopped like an inflatable tube man when the air flow stops.

After Bradley spent months in the hospital, the doctors determined he had contracted an enterovirus, a one in a million poliovirus, that attacked his spinal cord and left him paralyzed in both legs.

His mother never left his side. His father received special leave from the Marine Corps to be with him. A year passed before the doctors pronounced his paralysis permanent.

Ongoing construction of the city of Everett's new casino parking area snapped Bradley out of his thoughts. Large cranes dotted the skyline, and heavy trucks moved concrete and gravel. The casino's business continued to grow since completion of the building two years before, and the need for parking increased.

Antonio's Italian Restaurant once occupied some of the land where the concrete structure rests. It had been one of Bradley's favorite local restaurants. He heard the offer made to the family by the casino proved too great for them to pass up.

With those thoughts circulating through Bradley's head, he almost forgot about Rusty. *What am I going to do with him?* He peeked at the passenger seat. Rusty sat upright and seemed happy. He looked straight ahead, as if what lay behind him didn't matter. *Ah, to have that gift,* thought Bradley.

In the late 1990s, the industrial park where Bradley lives became mostly abandoned. Manufacturing all but disappeared in the area, and the rundown buildings need substantial repair. Talk transpired of an out-of-town corporation wanting to renovate the old buildings into condominiums, but nothing resulted.

Bradley bought one of the smaller buildings that had originally served as a linen supply company. The company removed most of its equipment from the property before he purchased it but left an intact monorail system mostly set in the rafters of the building and previously used to move linens from station to station. Bradley removed the monorail when he had large fans and air conditioning installed. He kept the components in a storage unit out back. If he put any thought into it, he might realize that the influence of his grandfather on his father's side prompted him to keep the parts.

Doug Whitman Sr. made his living as an architect and routinely saved parts of old warehouses, libraries, schools, and other structures to repurpose in new and interesting ways. He turned a library card catalogue cabinet into a tasteful wine rack, the body of a piano into a noted bookshelf, and an old ladder into a stepped-up spice rack, all showcased in Bradley's home as the only noticeable personal features.

The art of repurposing eluded Bradley's father, Doug Jr. As a child, Bradley collected discarded items from neighbor's trash, store dumpsters, and yard sales. The castoffs took space in the Whitman's garage, a practice his father did not appreciate. But Bradley knew the refuse would come in handy one day. His crowning achievement occurred when, for his shop final in high school, he turned two old-fashioned top hats into hanging lamps.

Emerging from his thoughts, Bradley steered the truck onto the pock-marked parking area in front of his home. Topped with a galvanized, pitched metal roof, the building's tan metal walls stood twenty feet high. Five sizeable paned windows graced the upper half of sixty-foot-wide exterior walls, front and back. All in all, the building boasted three thousand square feet of open living space. A twelve-foot high and fifteen-foot wide, open front lean-to with a pitched roof connected to the right side of the building. He drove the truck into the enclosure and parked in front of his home's entry doorway.

His seatbelt still fastened, Bradley pushed the door button on the truck dashboard and waited for the sensor to acknowledge his task. He had learned the hard way, often working himself into a furor thinking himself trapped in the truck, that if the seatbelt became unbuckled while the chair sat on the platform, the door panel would not slide out.

Once on the ground he called for Rusty. The dog jumped out from the driver's side door and took his place next to Bradley.

Bradley unlocked his front door, motioned for Rusty to go inside, then followed him in. Mounted on the wall to his left, the alarm next to the coat rack beeped. Bradley punched in his five-digit code and tapped the off button.

The kitchen lay to his right. Custom counters, cabinets, and appliances lined the walls on both sides of the corner, his grandfather's stepladder spice rack displayed on the wall behind his stove. A round kitchen table, with no chairs, sat in front of the appliances.

Bradley retrieved a can opener and two bowls. He filled one bowl with the contents of a can of dog food and the other with water and set them on the floor to the right of the refrigerator.

Rusty didn't move.

"It's okay. Relax. Go eat."

Rusty devoured the food and drank half the water before returning to Bradley's side. Bradley reached out and stroked his back.

"Let's make you a bed."

Turning from the kitchen, Bradley rolled across the wood floor past his workout equipment. Designed by a paraplegic, the Equalizer 6000 sat next to sliding glass doors on the backside of the building, his bedroom and bathroom beyond that in the corner opposite the front door. His bathroom had the honor of possessing the only walls in his home. His office equipment, computer, monitors, file cabinets, and built-in desk filled the fourth corner of the open room. The meticulously organized piano bookshelf lined the wall between the office area and front door and held an impressive collection on varying subjects. Next to it stood the wine rack once used as a library card catalogue.

A leather couch and coffee table graced the floor in front of the bookshelves and faced a stone fireplace open on four sides in the center of the room. The stone chimney rose to ten feet before a black stovepipe took over and shot through the ceiling. Wood was stacked neatly on the couch side of the fireplace.

Bradley found a blanket in the cedar-lined hope chest at the end of his bed. It had once belonged to his mother's mother, Grandma Lilly. Bradley's grandparents had all passed away. Doug Sr. and Elsie Whitman and Thomas and Lilly Harding, the two couples combined, logged 118 years of marriage.

He centered the blanket on the floor amidst the couch, fireplace, and office area. Rusty wasted no time settling in as he fluffed up the bed with his paws. It wasn't long before he began to snore.

Bradley booted his desktop computer. Expecting to hear from his supervisor Derek, he checked his cell phone for messages. Nothing yet.

Before Derek Richards was his boss, he was his friend. Because of Derek, Bradley decided to go to work for the Federal Bureau of Investigation. When Bradley was twelve, his mother and father took him on a Caribbean cruise. While on vacation, they unintentionally became entangled in an FBI operation. That's when he met Derek.

His role in the operation earned Bradley an FBI commendation and the unshakable urge to become an FBI agent. He kept in touch with Derek over the years and with Derek's wife, Cate, whom he also met on the cruise. When Bradley graduated from Massachusetts Institute of Technology, the FBI had an analyst job waiting for him. The commendation he earned as a twelve-year-old hangs on the wall above his desktop.

The computer came to life, and Bradley searched for local dog officers and animal shelters. He called three telephone numbers and left his information and the dog's breed. He did not want to reveal Rusty's description, as he had heard stories of lost pets falsely claimed for devious reasons. He also called the police department closest to where he found the dog.

No one had reported a missing Doberman Pinscher.

His phone rang. It was Derek.

ONE DOWN

"Hey, Boss," Bradley answered.

"Don't you 'Hey, Boss' me, Bradley. What the hell were you thinking? How many times do we need to have this conversation? You're going to get yourself killed. And then I'll have to deal with the fallout—from my boss *and* your parents. I've made it a point to not piss off your father ever again, but you're going to do it for me, aren't you?" Derek unconsciously swiped the two previously broken fingers of his right hand over his previously broken nose.

"Look at me," Derek vented. "You've got me scolding you like you're still a twelve-year-old kid. You're a twenty-eight-year-old FBI agent, for chrissake. When are you going to stop this shit?"

"I'm sorry. I didn't think he would . . . "

"Stop right there. You didn't think. You didn't think? You're the smartest guy I know, Bradley. Don't try to pull that on me. You thought . . . you knew . . . and you went anyway. You are not a field agent. You are an analyst."

"Yes, Derek. I'm sorry. It won't happen again."

"You're right, Bradley. It won't. This is the last time we have this conversation. Do you understand what I'm telling you?"

"Yeah. Yes, Derek. I do."

There was a pause as neither hung up.

Derek took a deep breath. "You were right. He is our guy. We found the weapon in the dumpster. Preliminary results show his prints on it. Come see me in the morning. And Bradley. . . "

"Yeah."

"I'm glad you're okay."

He hung up.

Bradley didn't like disappointing Derek. And he knew Derek meant what he said. Derek might be his friend, but he also was one of the best FBI agents Bradley had ever known. Bradley had tread on thin ice and would have to keep his curious nature— and his ego—in check.

Good luck with that, he thought.

"Alexa, play some jazz," Bradley said to his wireless Echo device.

Rusty lifted his head and scanned the room. The sound of Louis Armstrong's trumpet bounced off the walls.

"Just talking to my imaginary friends, buddy. No worries. Go back to sleep."

Rusty rested his head on the blanket and closed his eyes.

There are only two places in this world where Bradley is at peace: sitting at his computer or reading a good book while stretched out on his couch. By habit, he plugged his chair's charging cord into one of the outlets at his desk and went to work.

One of few analysts able to work from home, Bradley went to the office an average of twice a week, sometimes more, sometimes less. There was nothing he couldn't do at his own desk that he could do in the office except sit in on meetings. He did most of that through an online meeting program unless the meeting was subject to security clearance. Then, he had to attend in person.

Other than the post office robbery/homicide they wrapped up that day, his research included home healthcare fraud, an international cyber security threat, and a low priority money laundering operation.

During the next couple of hours as the sun faded, Bradley finished his home healthcare research report and forwarded it to Agent Nick Gaston. He assumed Nick would still be busy with paperwork from the day's apprehension, but Bradley did his best to provide requested information quickly. He knew Nick would be pleased with his findings.

The clicking of Rusty's overgrown toenails on the wood floor interrupted Bradley's concentration as it signaled the dog's approach to Bradley's desk. Rusty looked at Bradley, then turned his head to the front door, then back to Bradley, obviously conveying nature's calling him to go outside.

Instead of the front door, Bradley led him to glass sliders that opened to a small, sparsely grassed backyard. Rusty took stock of the area. Grass extended only twenty feet out before dropping off to a steep decline that led to an abandoned sandpit about four times the size of a 1970s drive-in movie theatre.

Bradley watched as Rusty relieved himself, snooped around, and then returned to his blanket.

Bradley could tell Rusty needed rest. He began to understand Rusty had endured some rough days.

Tomorrow, he thought, *I will try to find out why.*

SANCTUARY

Bradley's morning routine was just that, routine. He woke at five, worked out in his home gym for forty-five minutes, showered, shaved, and dressed. Then to the kitchen for coffee and breakfast, usually fresh fruit and instant oatmeal. But on this morning, before he began his workout, he realized he would have to slightly alter his daily schedule.

He roused Rusty from his bunched-up blanket and guided him outside through the sliders. He watched the dog for only a moment before beginning his workout indoors. While executing his lateral presses, it occurred to him that possibly Rusty might not return, and the thought surprisingly saddened him.

He glanced out the glass doors but saw no sign of the Doberman. *I suppose it's not up to me*, he thought. Forty minutes later, as he finished his workout with lateral pulldowns, he noticed Rusty sitting outside the sliders, watching him. Bradley shorted his repetition count, moved from his seated position on the home gym into his wheelchair, and opened the door.

Rusty ran, slipping and sliding across the wood floor, over to the empty food bowl from the night before. Seeing no food, he glanced at Bradley with hopeful eyes.

Bradley couldn't help but grin.

Once fed and appropriately hydrated, Rusty seated himself next to Bradley at the computer desk. Three overhead monitors hung on the wall, where the one on the left displayed the current jazz selection playing through speakers, the middle scrolled stock exchange information, and the right, split into six squares, showed black and white security camera images of the exterior of his home.

Bradley clicked on the top right camera image, and it filled the screen. The live picture came from the camera on the back left of his building, the area outside his bedroom. A large portion of his tiny yard fell within the camera range. The outdoor cameras captured most of his home's surroundings with a couple of blind spots on two sides, but he thought the system adequate.

His curiosity got the better of him, so he reviewed the internal memory of the system and set the image to the point when he originally let Rusty outside. He watched as Rusty traced his path from the night before and relieved himself in the same two spots. *Creature of habit*, Bradley smiled.

Then Rusty disappeared over the ledge. Had the dog not been sitting by his side, Bradley would have worried. The drop-off from his property to the sandpit below was steep, very steep. It was one of the things that attracted Bradley to the property in the first place, because it would be nearly impossible for anyone to approach his home from behind.

Anything except, Rusty had taught him, an animal.

He continued to watch the footage and almost a minute later in the feed spotted Rusty walking away from the banking and into the portion of the sandpit where some of the homeless community had settled. Some lived in structures built with tarps, some built with boxes, and others with more elaborate construction of corrugated tin and wood. Several had campfires burning.

One of the more elaborate living spaces must have had either an inside firepit or a stove of sorts. Bradley noticed the tin structure had its own jury-rigged chimney protruding from the center of the roof. That's where Rusty headed first. He strutted to the opposite side of the tiny building and didn't reappear for several minutes. Then he went to visit more residents of the sandpit sanctuary, some for a short sniff, others for longer.

The footage warmed him. Bradley reached to his left and stroked the back of Rusty's head.

"Good boy," he said.

Bradley checked the time. 7:30. Time to go. He didn't like the idea of leaving Rusty alone. Not that he worried about what Rusty might do. But he didn't want him to feel abandoned.

"Alright, boy. I've got to go to the office. I'll be back as soon as I can. You relax and make yourself at home." Bradley knew he sounded ridiculous but couldn't help himself. From the moment he first looked into Rusty's eyes, he felt a connection, an understanding he just couldn't explain.

Rusty went to his blanket and lay down.

The drive from his home in Revere to the office in Chelsea could take anywhere from fifteen to thirty minutes, depending on traffic. Eighteen minutes after he left his home, Bradley pulled up to the gatehouse at 201 Maple Street, showed his FBI ID badge, and parked his truck outside the front door of the eight-story, window-ladened structure.

After chatting with Carl, one of the inside security officers, about his new baby, he took the elevator to the top floor.

"Hey, Bradley. You alone? Where's your muscle? Did you run out of Kibble?" Nick yelled from across the room.

All eyes—and snickers—focused on Bradley.

By now he was sure that the story, most likely embellished, of Rusty's rescue of Bradley had circulated throughout the building. For an agency that deals in secrets, there was no way to keep one from coworkers.

"Good one, Nick. Your wit is exceeded only by your tiny little brain," Bradley shot back in fun.

Desks for Nick Gaston, team leader; Mara Thompkins, the newest and youngest of the agents; and Jim Jansen with seven years of service sat by the windows on the far side of the Chelsea office. The top floor housed four other teams, each assigned its own investigations. Protocol required everyone to join the morning briefing unless a case prohibited it. Sometimes, agents got lucky and noticed overlaps between cases, but mostly meetings kept everyone in the loop in the event a case required their help.

Bradley rolled to Nick's desk.

"Did you get my report?" Bradley asked.

"I did. We got them by their assets." Nick grinned as he accentuated the word *ass* in assets.

"What's the plan?"

"Derek's going to include it in the briefing."

NEW ASSIGNMENTS

The briefing room, set with four long tables each with six chairs facing a white board on the front wall, filled quickly. Twenty FBI agents and analysts waited for Supervisory Special Agent Derek Richards to arrive. Bradley took his usual spot at the back of the room, where he felt most comfortable.

When Derek entered, the chatter stopped. His agents held him in high regard. Sixteen years before, he was instrumental in taking down two of the most notorious East Coast mob bosses, Benny White and Frankie Piscelli. It made him famous in the academy and the Boston bureau.

"Okay, wrap-up first. Congratulations to agents Gaston, Thompkins, Jansen, and Whitman on the Branson case. Looks like this one is tied up with a bow. We have confirmed that the prints on the murder weapon found in the alley off Elbow Street belong to Branson."

"Ruff, ruff, ruff," someone near the front of the room muttered.

"Enough!" Derek said. "Good work by everyone involved. Top priority today is executing search warrants for Berryman's Home Healthcare. The preliminary analyst report gave us enough to establish cause. The warrants are being issued as we speak. Gaston."

"Yeah, Boss?"

"Take Taylor's crew with you. I want this one all but in the bag before the day's over."

"You got it, Boss."

"Morrison, what's happening with the construction company money laundering case?"

"No movement yet. We're waiting on the analyst report."

Derek looked to Bradley.

"I'll have it by the end of the day, Boss," Bradley stated.

"Okay. Got some new case files to hand out." Derek held three manila folders. "Morrison. Jones. Carter. Pick them up on your way out. Any questions?"

No one spoke up.

"Okay, then. Good luck today. Be safe. Whitman, in my office."

"Ruff, ruff, ruff," the voice muttered again.

Bradley ignored the taunt and made his way to Derek's office. Hazel, his secretary, waved Bradley to go right in.

"Executive Assistant Director Davis got wind of your antics. As you might imagine, he doesn't like his analysts playing at being field agents. He wants you suspended. I talked him out of it—again. But this is the last time, Bradley."

"I hear you, Derek. I'm sorry I put you in that position. It was stupid. It won't happen again."

"How did you know?"

"Know what?"

"How did you know the knife would be in that alley?"

"It made sense. Branson's a local guy. He knows the area. He was running from Maverick Square toward Meridian and Chelsea Streets. There's no way he would head down Meridian past the courthouse and the A-7 East Boston PD.

"And there was heavy construction with police details at the corner of Maverick and Bremen," Bradley continued, "so he wouldn't go there either, which forced him down Chelsea Street. At the same time, there was a 911 call for medical assistance at 30 Chelsea on the corner of Chelsea and Emmons. Ambulance and police sat there.

"The logical route," Bradley went on, "would be Elbow Street, duck into the first alley on the left, drop the knife into the residential dumpster, remove the blood-stained jacket, and casually walk away, probably backtracking through the ambulance personnel."

"I didn't follow any of that" Derek replied with astonishment. "That's crazy."

"Not so much when you see it laid out. Sometimes it's just as important to know what's happening on the outskirts of your crime scene as it is at your crime scene. But I could have easily been wrong. That's why I wanted to check it out.

"I didn't account for the pressure Nick put on Branson during his interrogation to compel him to get rid of the evidence for good," Bradley admitted. "I should have, but I didn't. Either way, I should have waited for Gaston. I'm an idiot."

"Far from it. But you're reckless. And I don't ever want to have to make that call to your parents in New Hampshire."

That final statement stung more than the reckless comment. It reminded Bradley of the complexity of their relationship and Derek's difficult position.

"What happened to the dog?" Derek asked.

"He's with me. I'm going to try to find out who he belongs to and get him home."

"Okay. Moving on. Is this money laundering thing going to pan out?"

"There's something there, but it's not clear yet. I'll be sending the report to Morrison later today. I'll copy the email to you. My gut says to hold off. Whatever we get now may not be enough to stick."

"Let's sit on it. Send me the preliminary, but spend your time on the Berryman case. There will be a lot to go through. Grab a couple of junior analysts to help."

"Will do, Derek. Thanks."

It bothered Bradley when his analysis of the evidence provided did not make a good solid case. Field agents usually knew when they had little, and the agents counted on Bradley to figure things out and make it work. When it worked, it could make a field agent's career.

Nick Gaston reminded Bradley of Derek sixteen years before—smart, bold, and married to his work. No personal life to clutter his ambition. But Nick had lacked important traits that made Derek so good at his job. Derek listened to people and asked for help when he needed it. Once Bradley recognized Nick's potential, he made it his goal to instill those attributes in Nick. He slowly and discreetly succeeded. And as such, Nick's position in the unit had risen.

But Nick remained oblivious to Bradley's subtle refinement of his positive traits.

Bradley texted Gaston.

Text me when I can get into Berryman's office.

Ten minutes later, Gaston replied.

Plan on noon.

Bradley texted a thumbs up and headed to his desk. He had chosen office space in the corner of the room as far away from other agents as possible. Bradley liked it quiet and kept mostly to himself.

The computer equipment paled in comparison to his own at home, but it provided fine access to internal information.

He pulled up his exploratory report on the money laundering case, put finishing touches on it, and emailed it to Morrison and Derek Richards.

Until the Berryman information came in, he had nothing that required his attention, so he began making phone calls inquiring about lost or stolen Dobermans. No luck. Either the owner did not want the dog back or the owner had not or could not report the dog missing.

The fact that Rusty had no collar could mean that he somehow managed to slip out of it, possibly because someone or something forced him to. Bradley pulled up local 911 calls for the previous three days that involved the sudden death of a single person living alone. He concentrated on a two-mile radius around the Elbow Street alley. He got five hits, one of which, ironically, included 30 Chelsea Street.

He checked that case first. The report stated that police received a call requesting a wellness check on David Spencer, 74, a wheelchair-bound white male. The report identified his closest living relative as a daughter in North Carolina. Receiving no answer upon arrival, police broke into the home and found the elderly male slumped in his wheelchair in his kitchen. The coroner pronounced him dead at the scene. He had been there for at least three days.

Bradley dialed the phone number of the A-7 East Boston Police Station and asked to speak to the officer who performed the wellness check.

"This is Patterson," a female voice answered.

"Officer Patterson, this is Agent Bradley Whitman calling from Chelsea FBI headquarters. I'm calling about a wellness check you performed at 30 Chelsea Street yesterday on a David Spencer."

"Yes?"

"This may sound odd, but can you tell me if there were any signs of Mr. Spencer owning a dog?"

"Not odd at all, Agent Whitman. In fact, we found Mr. Spencer in his kitchen with a can of dog food on the floor beside him. But we could not find the dog. We think he was in the backyard tied up and somehow slipped his collar. Mr. Spencer had been deceased for multiple days before we found him."

"Were there any pictures of the dog? Do you know what breed?"

"Sure. He had a lot of pictures. The dog is an adult male Doberman Pinscher, black with kind of a rust color on his ears, nose, and legs. His name is Harley. Agent Whitman, did you find him? Is he alright?"

"Yes, Officer Patterson. We found him, and he is fine. Can you give me the phone number of Mr. Spencer's next of kin, please?"

"Of course. Let me find my file."

Officer Patterson gave Bradley Mr. Spencer's daughter's phone number. The daughter expressed her regrets but could not take responsibility for Harley. She asked that the local animal shelter make whatever arrangements necessary for the dog.

HEALTHCARE HATH NO FURY

The thirty-five-mile ride to Westford would take fifty minutes each way. After what he'd endured, Bradley felt concern about leaving Rusty (or Harley) alone for that length of time. He left the office, stopped at one of the big box pet store supply places, and bought a dog collar, retractable leash, therapeutic dog bed, and large rawhide bone. He stocked up on dog food and treats. He had no idea what he would do with the dog, but he reasoned wherever the dog ended up, he could supply those comforts for him.

When he reached home, he took the collar and leash from the bag and went inside. Rusty/Harley sat just inside the door as Bradley opened it. *He heard me coming. Smart dog.* Signaling an open door, the house alarm beeped until Bradley turned it off.

First, he put the collar on Rusty's thin neck, then the leash. The two went out together to the backyard. Once Rusty peed and pooped, Bradley brought him back inside.

"We're going to settle this once and for all," Bradley told him.

He held up his right hand and said, "Rusty."

Then he held up his left hand and said, "Harley."

With both hands held out in front on him, Bradley repeated the routine. Then he waited.

The dog lifted his right front paw and placed it on Bradley's right hand.

"Rusty it is," Bradley smiled.

Bradley retrieved a bottle of water and a bowl, latched the leash to Rusty's new collar, and said, "Let's go for a ride."

The trip took them just under an hour. Gaston met Bradley as he parked in the lot reserved for Berryman Home Healthcare Services clients. Bradley rolled down his window so they could talk.

"You brought the dog," Nick stated.

"I didn't want to leave him alone too long. Don't worry. He's not going to attack you, Nick. Not unless I tell him to," Bradley grinned.

"Give us about fifteen more minutes. We're packing shit up-computers and file cabinets. There won't be much left inside, but I know how you like to get your head inside a case."

"How soon before I get copies of the files?"

"I'm hoping the paper files are just duplicates of electronic files. Otherwise, I've only got two techs available for scanning. It might take a while."

"I can give you two juniors to help. Let me know where and when to send them." Bradley assumed they would occupy the larger of the headquarters copy rooms.

"Sounds good. I'll come get you when we're done."

The front of the business looked inviting. The grass had begun to turn the color of spring, but not yet quite as brilliant. Three white birch trees with black mulch at their base, the mulch in need of replenishment, gave the business a homey feel. Bradley reached for the bottled water and dish, lowered himself onto the pavement, and called for Rusty. The dog jumped from the truck and sat at Bradley's side while Bradley attached the leash to his collar. He loosely wrapped his end of the retractable leash around part of the lift mechanism of the truck, pulled fifteen feet of the lead from its casing, and locked it in place to enable Rusty either to stay outside on the grass or go inside on the driver's seat.

He felt good about his decision to bring the dog along.

He watched a constant stream of agents carrying boxes and hauling file cabinets on two-wheel dollies and loading them into FBI vans. The activity slowly subsided.

"All yours, Agent Whitman. Do your magic," Nick grinned.

Bradley turned to Rusty, who sprawled on the cool lawn, and said, "Stay."

Bradley traveled the handicap ramp through the front door into the reception area. He doubted there would be anything of use to him there but took a cursory look to satisfy his assumption. The primary office belonged to Mrs. Juliette Berryman, a widow of eight years according to the brochure. The agents did a thorough job of gathering business receipts and client files but left behind personal items.

On her desk, Juliette Berryman displayed a picture of herself and her deceased husband, the same photo used in the brochure. The happy couple wore Hawaiian flowered shirts and sunglasses and hats to protect themselves from the sun. Bradley stashed a brochure in his coat pocket. He found no other photos of her husband, family, pets, or vacations in the office.

He searched the desk drawers in case the agents left anything of interest behind. They usually did. In this case, they left a Maserati catalogue in the top right drawer.

Maps of New England covered the walls. Colored lines divided areas on each of the maps. A blue line surrounded much of Boston and its suburbs while a red line denoted mostly central Massachusetts cities and towns. In all, five separate colors grouped cities and towns together: blue, red, brown, green, and yellow. Using his cell phone, Bradley took photos of the maps. He guessed that the files would also be color coded by area. He wondered if the employees worked only within a single-colored area.

Having finished with the desk and the bookshelves, Bradley turned his attention to the table behind Mrs. Berryman's desk. A half-dead plant drooped onto the oak console table. Assorted seashells and colored rocks sat there as well. But to Bradley, the most fascinating thing it held was an old-fashioned abacus. A wooden frame stood on a base and included ten tiers of wooden beads. Each horizontal row had ten identical colored beads threaded on a small metal rod so the beads could move independently of each other, left to right or right to left. The color of each row from top to bottom: blue, red, brown, green, yellow, then repeated in that order. As a child, Bradley had a similar abacus. His friends called him a geek, dork, and nerd because he brought it to show-and-tell in the third grade. He found himself wondering where that abacus was.

Nick entered the room and found Bradley taking pictures with his cell phone.

"You about done?"

"Yeah. I'm done. I'm going to head back home. Send me the electronic files as soon as you can, will you? I think we have more here than meets the eye," said Bradley.

"Like what?"

"Don't know yet. Got a lot of work to do."

DEAD AHEAD

His brain went into overdrive on the trip back to Revere. He hadn't met Juliette Berryman, but he knew a lot about her. And he suspected there were few people who could say that.

Bradley directed his Chevy Silverado under the lean-to, reached for the bag he bought from the pet store earlier that day and lowered himself and his chair to the cement floor. Rusty followed him inside. Bradley returned to the truck to retrieve Rusty's new bed. *He will be much more comfortable tonight*, Bradley smiled.

Rusty sniffed the bed, pawed at it, and circled it five times before lying down. He wiggled his body and stretched his neck so his head lay on the floor. Bradley watched in amusement. He knew little about Dobermans, other than they are smart, loyal, and serious. Rusty, he thought, also seemed fun-loving and content. As many times as Bradley told himself he needed to find a home for Rusty, he felt in his heart Rusty was already home.

Bradley checked to see if Nick had forwarded any of the Berryman information. Finding nothing, he decided to do a general search to get a feel for the image Berryman Home Healthcare Services projected to its potential—and current—clients.

His search began at the Berryman website. Its muted tan background accentuated with brilliant blue, red, and gold accents suggested vibrancy emerging from despair. The site's pages filled with smiling elderly individuals interacting with happy people wearing colorful scrubs or white lab coats. Information about how to achieve such happiness, however, proved scarce.

Bradley clicked on the About tab. The picture of Juliette Berryman and her handsome late husband wearing Hawaiian-style, button-down shirts commanded the viewer's attention. Below the picture, a biography explains how Juliette lost her husband in 2010 to Alzheimer's disease, a heart-wrenching short story meant to give the reader compassion for the owner who perpetrated what could amount to as much as a hundred million fraudulent dollars.

The compilation of information Bradley analyzed in his previous report laid out enough evidence to arrest Mrs. Berryman. But he wanted more. After examining her office space and previously compiling evidence that unmasked her complete disregard for honesty and compassion, Bradley wanted to amass enough information to put the woman behind bars for the rest of her life. He considered her the lowest form of criminal, one who preys on the sick and vulnerable. *I'm going to enjoy this*, he thought as he logged into the Massachusetts marriage and death databases.

The database told him that Juliette Berryman, born Juliette Moss in January 1960 and raised in the central/western Massachusetts town of Erving, married Harold Berryman when she was eighteen. According to financial transactions associated with their Social Security numbers, they moved first to Chelmsford, then Acton, and then Lowell in the span of a short two years. One December evening in 1982 on a dark street in Lowell, an officer on routine patrol found Harold's body stabbed multiple times in the chest. Questioned in the murder, Juliette's alibi placed her in Erving visiting her mother at the time of his death. No arrest was made in the case, and Juliette never remarried. The handsome husband in the photograph bespoke a myth, as did the sympathetic story of losing him to Alzheimer's.

Two years later, using $150,000 of life insurance money received on the death of her husband of four years, Juliette established Berryman's Home Healthcare Services LLC with her mother, a registered nurse. The events took place thirty-seven years before. *Just how long has she been defrauding the system?* Bradley wondered.

The company became successful, adding employees and services throughout the years. Juliette's mother, Theresa, died in 1985 when she fell down the stairs of her new duplex in Westford only one year after she went into business with her daughter. The coroner labeled it an accident due to alcohol consumption. A two-month-old, million-dollar insurance policy paid double indemnity benefits for the accidental death to Theresa's beneficiary, Juliette Berryman.

All that information at the stroke of a keyboard and none of it ever accessed. But why would it be? Bradley considered. Simple enough. Nothing Juliette did required scrutiny. She acted as an administrator. She never professed to have a nursing license, she hired it done, and she had no criminal history on record.

Other than an original charge of overbilling for services not rendered, Bradley had nothing concrete although he felt confident he would find something. False advertisement is a crime largely unpunished. Faking marriage is hardly a federal offense. Her connection with three mysterious deaths, if you add her father's car accident due to a faulty brake line when she was seventeen, wouldn't move the case forward. Bradley would have to find thirty-seven years' worth of evidence in the files.

Daylight waned, and Rusty stirred. He hopped to his feet and ran to the sliders. Bradley let him out and moved to the kitchen to prepare Rusty's dinner. That's when Bradley realized he hadn't eaten since breakfast.

He loved to cook. His passion for food developed on a Caribbean vacation cruise he took with his parents when he was twelve. They had eaten in a variety of on-board and island restaurants, and he began learning soon after, cooking and baking with his mother and then teaching himself. He sometimes surprised her with dinner, usually an elaborate spread. He especially enjoyed cooking dinner when his father came home on leave from his US Marine post. His favorite meals to prepare include osso bucco, veal Marsala, and lasagna with homemade sauce, but he tried to keep such heavy dishes to a minimum. The current menu consisted of herbed chicken breast, roasted Brussels sprouts, and cheesy mashed cauliflower.

Cooking also provided Bradley with time to think. The process of combining ingredients with ideas appealed to him. He accomplished some of his best problem solving with a chef knife in his hand. He never cut corners or hurried the process. That would be akin to latching onto and pulling a newly sprouted parsley sprig to make it grow faster. Bradley enjoyed growing his own herbs.

Almost an hour had passed when he plated his dinner.

As Bradley worked in the kitchen, he periodically checked to see if Rusty had returned from his pre-dinner jaunt, but there had been no sign of him. He opened the slider and let out a sharp whistle, then followed up by calling the dog's name. Darkness prevented Bradley from viewing the sandpit below where he assumed Rusty had gone.

He whistled again and waited.

Five minutes passed before Rusty came bounding up the sandpit ledge. Even in the dark, Bradley sensed something off about the dog. As he opened the door to let Rusty inside, he noticed a piece of paper stuck on his collar. Rusty placed himself in front of Bradley and sat. Bradley unwrapped the paper from the collar. It was a canned soup label. Once Bradley removed the label, Rusty ran to his dinner bowl.

Bradley flipped over the cream of mushroom label. On the back, in black marker, it read: *Call 911. Dead body here.* It took Bradley a moment to process what he read.

Is this for real?

He decided not to take any chances. He dialed the local police precinct telephone number.

"Revere Police Department," a male voice answered.

"Yes. This is Agent Bradley Whitman with the Boston FBI. My address is 303 Industrial Drive in Revere. I don't know what to make of this, but my dog just came home with a note attached to his collar. It says, *Call 911. Dead body here.* I believe the *here* the note refers to is the sandpit behind my house."

"You said the note was attached to your dog's collar?" the voice asked.

"Yes."

"Please hold, sir."

"Okay." Bradley could hear mumbling.

"Agent Whitman, is it?"

"Yes, Bradley Whitman."

"This is Sergeant Doyle. Tell me about the note."

"It's on the back of a cream of mushroom soup label, and the words are written in heavy black marker. I found it wrapped multiple times around my dog's collar. There's no way it just got stuck there. Either someone is playing a practical joke, or this is the only way they knew how to get help."

"Okay. Stay put. We'll send a car over right away to check it out," Sergeant Doyle said.

"Could you let me know what you find, Sergeant?"

"You bet." He hung up.

ILLUMINATION

Rusty didn't seem fazed by the evening's events. He ate his food, drank his water, circled his bed, and lay down to watch Bradley stare out the slider doors.

After ten minutes, Bradley saw flashing lights below on the access road eighty yards away on the far side of the sandpit. He watched as two flashlights emerged from either side of a parked car. The flashlights split up, then, as one went toward the left side encampments, one toward the right. Curious, Bradley put on a lightweight jacket and wheeled himself out to his small patio to get a closer view. He tried to hear sound from below, but nearby traffic would not allow it.

The flashlights made their way closer to his side of the pit.

The flashlight on his left suddenly moved in a wide circle. The light to his right changed direction and moved toward the circling light.

They've got something, Bradley thought.

Bradley closed his eyes and tried to remember the view of the sandpit in daylight. *What is in that area?* He recalled a blue tarp draped over some sort of structure. He didn't recall seeing a campfire there the previous night.

One of the flashlights made its way back to the police vehicle. Another twenty minutes passed, and the sandpit lit up like Gillette Stadium during a Monday night football game. An ambulance arrived on scene but sat parked for fifty minutes before leaving without any lights flashing or siren sounding.

Bradley went back inside. The cold had slightly numbed his fingers. He imagined what the night would bring for the unhoused residents of the sandpit if any stuck around once the police arrived.

He guessed few did. He thought about getting into the truck and driving down there but knew it to be a bad idea. Besides, he fully expected a knock at his door.

He made sure to take a picture of the soup label note for his own purpose and wondered about the person who wrote it.

Within minutes, someone knocked on his door. Rusty sprang to his feet and placed himself next to Bradley.

Bradley opened the door to a man holding a Revere Police Department badge.

"Come in," Bradley said.

"I'm Sergeant Doyle. Are you Agent Whitman?"

"Yes, I'm Whitman. Come on in. Have a seat." He pointed to the couch.

Bradley retrieved the note from the kitchen table while Rusty placed himself between Doyle and Bradley.

"He friendly?" asked Doyle.

"Can't really say. I brought him home from a crime scene yesterday. His owner's dead."

Doyle raised an eyebrow.

"Natural causes. Nothing to do with the crime scene." He handed the label to Doyle. "That's what I found on his collar."

Doyle examined the note.

"So, you're an analyst for the FBI?"

"You checked on me."

"Wouldn't you?"

"Absolutely. Yes. I work out of Chelsea."

"What do you make of it?"

"Hard to say. Whoever wrote the note wanted to remain anonymous, but that's not surprising. I guess most everyone who lives down there wants to stay out of the limelight."

"What can you tell me about the people who live there?"

Bradley thought about it and realized how little attention he had paid to them. He felt ashamed.

"Nothing, I'm afraid. When I'm home, I spend most of my time sitting there." Bradley pointed to his office area. "The only reason we're here now is because of Rusty."

Rusty, hearing his name, sat upright at Bradley's side.

"He seems pretty attached to you considering you just got him yesterday."

"Yeah, I know. I don't think I found him as much as he picked me." Bradley smiled.

Sergeant Doyle glanced around uneasily then concentrated his gaze on Bradley.

"The medical examiner puts time of death this morning, between two and five."

"So, did this person die of natural cause or do you suspect foul play?"

Doyle hesitated before he spoke. Bradley recognized Doyle's reluctance to give away too much information.

"Nothing about her death is natural," Doyle somberly stated.

"A woman? Who is it? Do you have a name?"

"She didn't have any identification on her. Look, Agent Whitman . . ."

"Call me Bradley, Sergeant."

"Okay, Bradley. I can't give you any more information at this time. I'm sure you understand."

"Sergeant Doyle, I have security cameras out back. They're mainly focused on my backyard, but you can see some of the sandpit. If you'd like I can send you what I've got."

"I would appreciate it if you sent the camera footage to me. It might help." Doyle handed Bradley his business card.

"Of course. I'm not sure what, if anything, it will show, as it's so dark, but I'll start working on it as soon as you leave. Let me know if I can help in any other way."

When Doyle stood, Rusty stood. The three moved to the door.

"Thank you for your help, Agent . . . Bradley." Doyle stuck out his hand.

"Good luck, Sergeant."

Bradley understood his name would appear at the top of the suspect list. The circumstances called for it. He placed a phone call to Derek to fill him in.

He also knew once the police department realized there weren't any wheelchair tire marks, they could dismiss him as a suspect. That, of course, would happen after they verified that Bradley did need the wheelchair and was not perpetrating a fraud of some kind.

Fraud. His night had taken a completely unexpected turn. He had accomplished little on the Berryman investigation, and he still hadn't eaten his dinner.

The chicken would dry out and the Brussels sprouts would be soggy, but he placed his dinner in the microwave anyway. Rusty looked at Bradley as if he expected something for his troubles. Bradley remembered the rawhide bone he bought at the pet store, pulled it from the bag still sitting by the door, and gave it to him. Five circles around and a few fluffs later, Rusty and his bone sunk into the bed.

Bradley ate in front of his computer. He pulled up the security camera program and sought out the footage from one to six in the morning just to cover an adequate timeline. He copied the footage and emailed it to Sergeant Doyle. Then he replayed it at high speed on the middle monitor mounted above his desk, to see if anything stood out.

A light flickered. He hit pause. The time displayed on the recorder read 3:59. He hit rewind and played it back at normal speed. When the playback indicated 3:57 AM, he determined the flickering light he had seen came from headlights of an unidentifiable vehicle that appeared at the top of the access road. It parked and its headlights turned off. The camera then picked up a faint light in the same area, probably from the interior light when the vehicle door opened.

Then, nothing but darkness.

Almost two minutes passed on the recording before Bradley detected a small flash at the base of the access road. The unknown subject had turned in his direction and carried a small light. *The first mistake*, Bradley thought.

The light reached the area of the victim, but not before stopping for a brief moment three times along the way. *Second mistake.*

At 4:03 per the recording, the light disappeared.

Two minutes passed. A light flashed briefly near the tarped camp. Bradley imagined the suspect moving away from the scene quickly, retracing steps back to the vehicle. He never saw the light again.

At what the recording showed as 4:08, he saw a faint glow from inside the vehicle. The headlights shone almost immediately thereafter, and the vehicle pulled away.

Bradley had barely eaten half his chicken breast in the amount of time the killer apparently committed his—or her— crime. *The suspect is a professional*, he thought.

RESTRAINTS

Bradley pushed himself up to a seated position. He moved his legs so they hung off the side of the bed, then reached for his wheelchair waiting near the end of the mattress. He unplugged the charger cable and pulled it alongside the bed with the left side of the chair toward him. With wheels locked and the left armrest of the chair lowered, he moved his legs so his feet rested on the footrest. He set his right hand on the right chair armrest and steadied his left hand on the edge of the bed, then lifted and eased himself into the chair.

As Bradley adjusted his feet into position on the footrest, Rusty came to greet him.

"Good morning, buddy. You hungry?"

Rusty looked to the kitchen, then back to Bradley.

"Okay. Let's get you some breakfast."

Bradley emptied food into Rusty's bowl, which he set on the floor next to the water dish. He refilled the dish with fresh water, then rolled to the sliding doors.

Activity in the sandpit had decreased from the previous night. Two police cruisers, a white van, and a black unmarked SUV remained. Yellow tape cordoned off the crime scene. Bradley could see two detectives, he assumed, in plain clothes ducking in and out of the blue tarp. The van, he guessed, brought a forensic unit.

Bradley felt good knowing the Revere police took the evident homicide seriously. He knew of instances in different departments where crimes among the homeless fell low on the priority list.

Rusty finished his food and stood next to Bradley at the sliders. Bradley retrieved Rusty's retractable leash, pulled out the lead about fifteen feet, and locked it in place. He attached it to Rusty's collar, and the two moved outside.

Bradley wanted to prevent Rusty from descending into the sandpit.

Instead of staying outside with the dog, Bradley wound the handle end of the leash around a six-foot pipe sticking from the ground next to where he kept his gas grill. The pipe, one of two set close to the building and fifteen feet apart, remained from laundry service days.

I'm late for my workout, Bradley thought.

While transitioning from curls to presses, and woodchoppers to twists, Bradley kept an eye on Rusty. The dog sat himself as far toward the back edge of the yard as he could stretch the leash while he looked out over the sandpit.

His workout finished, Bradley called for Rusty. He didn't feel comfortable leaving him tied up outside while he showered.

Once dressed, Bradley snatched a banana for breakfast, booted his computer, chose jazz for background music, and opened his email. His text tone beeped. He noted the text came from Derek.

Just spoke with a Det Rome from the RPD. Told him you were a pain in the ass but not a murderer.

Positive Derek and Detective Rome had discussed much more, Bradley assumed the detective removed his name from the suspect list after the conversation.

Rusty lay at his feet as Bradley delved into the Berryman files Nick had uploaded to the FBI portal.

❧

Juliette Berryman employed twenty-four people, all women. That proved no surprise to Bradley as he had already discovered her hatred of men. Her father and husband aside, she had no male acquaintances, she never remarried, the only restroom in her office held a sign that read *Women's Room*, and the Maserati pamphlet displayed a sticker with the salesperson's name and contact information, *Marcia Stanton*.

Bradley did not think Juliette's feelings toward men stemmed from a sexual preference. He believed her hatred to be more visceral. Childhood records revealed no abuse, but her behavior suggested otherwise to Bradley.

Scouring her personal records and reading statements from neighbors in her hometown of Erving, Bradley found that Juliette had not had a good relationship with her father or her mother. Most of the neighbors still residing in the area suggested that Juliette married Harold to get away from home, and she never returned.

So, Bradley's theory suggested that Juliette nevertheless shared her healthcare scheme with her mother in exchange for obtaining an alibi in the death of her husband. She opened her business with the help of her mother's nursing status for credibility and licensing and then disposed of her mother as quickly as she could replace her.

Which means, Bradley thought, *it is quite possible that one of her first nursing employees must be a knowing and willing accomplice, as she would have needed someone to take her mother's place in order to retain the license.*

Bradley looked to see if the forwarded files included employee history and found a file titled *Employees*. He opened it and clicked on the name of current workers.

The employee file held information suitable for the Internal Revenue Service or anyone running a background check: name, address, phone number, Social Security number and, start date with the company. The file also recorded payroll figures and forms required by the state.

Bradley's concern involved how far back the records went. The Commonwealth of Massachusetts requires a business to keep payroll records for three years. He hoped she had kept them well beyond that.

She had not. Bradley created an Excel spreadsheet with current employee names. Next to each name, he entered the employee's start date and, if the employee no longer worked at the facility, the end date.

He found one employee, Sharon Stakes, age sixty-three from Lowell, Massachusetts, who worked for Juliette for thirty-six years, since 1985. A registered nurse, she had a reported income of $145,850 for each of the previous three years.

The next longest employee, Catherine Leeks, worked for Berryman Home Healthcare for twenty-eight years with a reported annual salary of $107,358.

Only two employees had worked for and then left the company in the previous three years. Bradley noted their names and dates of employment. Juliette Berryman did not have a high employee turnover rate—a rate, in fact, much lower than the national average.

Rusty suddenly jumped from Bradley's side and raced to the front door. Bradley switched his full attention to his surroundings. A car door closed, then another. He turned off the music and moved toward the door.

A knock sounded as Rusty stiffened his stance.

"Easy, boy. It's the good guys."

Bradley noticed Rusty relax slightly.

"Good morning, Sergeant Doyle. Come in."

"Good morning, Agent Whitman. This is Detective Rome." He motioned to a tall man of average build, short black hair, and hands that had surely wrapped themselves around a football at one time.

"Detective, it's nice to meet you." Bradley shook the massive hand.

"And you, Agent Whitman. We'd like to talk to you about the homicide if you have a moment."

"Of course. Call me Bradley. Can I get you anything? Coffee, water, juice?"

"No, thank you."

Bradley motioned them to the couch. Rusty stood at Bradley's side.

Bradley placed his hand on Rusty's back.

"Relax, boy."

Rusty sat.

"We are trying to track down the person who wrote that note, the one placed on your dog's collar. Is there anything you can tell us about that?" Detective Rome asked.

"I'm afraid not. I haven't had any contact with any of the residents of the pit. If they didn't build campfires on cold nights, I would almost forget they are there."

He paused. "That sounds awful, doesn't it?"

"I understand," Rome acknowledged. "The lab is dusting the note for prints. The author may be in the system. All the living quarters have understandably been abandoned, but we expect people to return in a few days once we leave the area. We were hoping you could keep an eye out, let us know if you see anything unusual or suspicious."

"Of course," Bradley said.

"We found the victim under her tarp. She was stabbed approximately twenty times, including three deep wounds to her face. The perpetrator is most likely right-handed. No physical evidence left behind. Just footprints. We didn't get much from your camera feed. Too dark. But the timeline coincides with the medical examiner's assessment. Unless we find a witness, our odds aren't good."

"Well, you've got a decent profile on the killer. That narrows the suspect list substantially," Bradley asserted.

"What profile?" Sergeant Doyle asked as he glanced at Detective Rome.

Detective Rome looked puzzled.

"Male, age twenty-five to thirty-five, a professional. You can check footprints and gait to figure approximate height. He's a sociopath, and he is smart, careful, and organized. He's also single, antisocial, and arrogant. He's an independent contractor." Bradley rattled off the information as if he were reading from a report.

Detective Rome's expression shifted from interest to skepticism.

"How do you figure?" he asked.

"The perpetrator chose the victim, killed the victim, and left the scene in eleven minutes. He didn't kill the first person he came upon; I'm guessing because there was some sort of barrier between him and the individual. He walked past three camps before he chose her."

"How do you know the victim wasn't targeted specifically?" Doyle asked.

"Because he stopped three times before reaching her. If she were targeted, he would have known where to find her."

"Maybe not," Doyle countered.

"Okay, but if he were looking for her specifically, he would have needed to spend more than a few seconds each time he stopped. He didn't look for a specific person to kill, he looked for the easiest person to kill. The path of least resistance. A professional. He drove in, walked the long access road, chose the victim, killed the victim, and walked back to his car in eleven minutes."

"How do you know he's a sociopath?" Rome asked.

"Well, I could be wrong about that. He could be a psychopath. You said the victim had stab wounds to her face. That shows total disregard for a human being. In the case of face wounds, statistics show that the attacker and victim usually have an intimate relationship. That is almost certainly not the case here. So that leaves sociopath or psychopath."

"An independent contractor?" Rome asked.

"He didn't linger. I assume he didn't take a souvenir either. He had a job to do, and he did it. Quickly, efficiently, and quietly. Again, I could be wrong but, in my experience, when a homicide is committed without cause or intimate connection, it's committed by an independent contractor."

"What about his age?" Doyle asked.

"That's a long way to walk in a short time. He's athletic, in good shape."

Doyle and Rome glanced at each other. Bradley saw the incredulity on their faces. He had gotten used to that. He had been receiving that look since childhood.

"Any theories on motive?" Detective Rome asked.

"No theory. But I've only watched the camera footage. I haven't listened or read any news. What can you tell me?"

"Nothing much. Your assessment is spot on. The suspect didn't take anything. And I think you're right about choosing the path of least resistance. The three makeshift structures he passed all had something that blocked the opening, a little like a door. As for motive, we have documented complaints from citizens unhappy with the homeless living there. We're checking those out. But there haven't been any problems associated with the camp. It's city owned property and the consensus has been to leave things be as long as it stays that way," Detective Rome said.

"I wish I could be of more help," said Bradley.

Detective Rome stood. Then so did Doyle and Rusty.

"You've been a big help, Bradley. Thank you for your time," Rome said.

"Any time I can be of assistance," Bradley replied.

Bradley followed them to the door, Rusty at his side.

"That's some dog you've got there," Rome remarked.

"Yes. Yes, he is." Bradley smiled as the two men left.

"Okay, Rusty. Let's get back to work. There's more to Juliette Berryman than meets the eye."

REAL ESTATE

The Berryman notes Bradley composed convinced him the home healthcare case would lead the FBI to more than just fraud and internal revenue charges. They might not be able to build a case for the murder of her husband, father, or mother, but in his gut, Bradley would not have been surprised to find more dead people connected to Juliette Berryman. And possibly Sharon Stakes.

He spent the next several hours compiling a report for Nick Gaston. He expected to include his theory as a separate document, as he usually did.

As he waded through BHHS employees and clients, midafternoon brought another knock on his door. Bradley and Rusty answered it together.

She stood five-feet, eight-inches tall with poorly dyed blonde hair and salon tan. She wore a designer knockoff dress. She showed a partial tattoo on her right shoulder, and an inked butterfly decorated her left ankle. The smile on her face disappeared when she saw the wheelchair.

"Oh," she said.

Then, gathering herself, she smiled again and held out her hand.

"My name is Shea. I'm with First Class Realty."

Bradley shook her hand.

"Can I talk to you for a minute?" she asked.

"Sure, come in," Bradley said.

She scanned the room in the manner of a robber casing a bank.

"What can I do for you?" Bradley asked.

He noted that Rusty remained alert. He did not relax at the sight of the woman.

"It's what I can do for you," came her flippant reply. "I have a client interested in purchasing this property, and he is willing to pay a very fair price for it."

"I'm sorry. It's not for sale."

"You haven't heard the offer yet," she said.

"Look, Shea, is it? I don't mean to be rude, but I'm not willing to sell my property for any amount. You're wasting your time."

"But . . ."

"Really. I appreciate you have a job to do, and I wish you well, but this . . . " he wiggled his finger back and forth from her to him, " . . . isn't going to happen."

"But it's a lot of money. The guy will pay you more than it's worth." *She is in the wrong business*, Bradley thought.

"Not interested. Thank you. Have a nice day." Bradley motioned her to leave.

In the time it takes to turn a key, Shea's painted smile stretched into a snarl.

"You're not even going to let me fucking finish?" she seethed.

"It's time for you to leave," Bradley insisted.

Rusty seemed to grow an inch. Without growling, barking, or sneering, he used every part of his body to intimidate Shea.

She turned and stormed out the door. Bradley watched to make sure she left the premises.

"Well, wasn't that interesting?" he said to Rusty. "Good boy. Good job."

Before Bradley jumped back into the world of Berryman Healthcare, he typed First Class Realty into the search bar on his computer. Of the eleven results, only one registered in Massachusetts. A single-page website displayed a beautiful home next to the ocean. The tagline *Live Life in First Class* in large print underlined the edge-to-edge photo. A telephone number appeared below the tagline with the urging to *Call Now* flashing in red.

"Wow. That's really bad," Bradley said out loud.

Rusty looked at Bradley and slanted his head.

"Not you, buddy. Not you. You're a good boy." He reached down and petted the dog. "Let's see if we can manage the rest of the day without an interruption."

He barely got the statement out when his text tone beeped. **Call me when you can.**

He had meant to call Derek after he spoke with the detective, but as per usual, he became engrossed in his work—never mind Shea's intrusion. He dialed Derek's number.

"Hey, Derek. What's up?" Bradley asked.

"How'd it go with Detective Rome?"

"Good. I don't think I'm a suspect anymore," he chuckled.

"No, you are definitely not. What did you tell him?"

"I just gave him a quick profile of the suspect."

"Ah. That's what did it."

"Did what?"

"I just got off the phone with him. He wanted to know if it would be alright with me if he contacted you about the case. I told him we would give him all the help he wants. Expect him to be in touch with you again."

"Sure. Okay. No problem."

"But, Bradley."

50

"Yeah."

"You help him from your desk. You understand what I'm saying?"

"I hear you."

"Cate wants you to come to dinner. When's a good day?"

"She's not going to invite one of her *friends* again, is she?"

Derek laughed. "Have you met my wife?"

"I'll let you know. Give her a hug for me."

"Will do."

Bradley vowed to spend the rest of the day working on the Berryman files. He had planned to have most of the current employee files reviewed and recorded by the end of the day, but the interruptions made that seem impossible unless he worked all night.

Out of the twenty-four people employed by the business, three worked in the office, thirteen held licensed practical nursing skills, and eight worked as registered nurses. Because registered nurses can administer medication, Bradley decided to begin with them. He added columns on his spreadsheet to include an employee's nursing degree, current salary, and hours logged.

The next time he looked at the time, it read 7:12. *Rusty must be hungry*, he thought. At some point during Bradley's inexorable research analysis, Rusty had moved from Bradley's side to his therapeutic bed. He didn't sleep. He just watched Bradley work.

Bradley prepared Rusty's food and, thinking it too late to cook, made himself a sandwich. He stacked logs in the fireplace, rolled a few pages from old newspapers that lay beside the woodpile, and used them to kindle the fire.

Before he returned to the kitchen table, he went to the backyard to survey activity in the sandpit. Darkness prohibited him a thorough examination, but he could see no evidence of police presence. He therefore felt comfortable letting Rusty roam free after dinner. Without a clear understanding of why it bothered him, the thought of keeping the dog tethered sat sour in his stomach. He opened the slider and turned on the backyard light. Rusty loped into the night.

Declaring his workday complete, Bradley picked up his sandwich and took a bottle of water from the refrigerator. He placed them on the end table next to the couch, then deftly removed himself from his chair and took his favorite spot in front of the fire. He sat and stared. His gaze became unfocused, and his brain gently touched flickering childhood memories of him and his mother sitting by the firepit in their backyard on a cool Saturday evening. They would talk about their week, their dreams, and how much they missed his father whose deployment oversees kept him away from his family much of Bradley's early years. Bradley's dream of following in his father's footsteps smoldered when Bradley could no longer take a step.

A slight jerk of his head confirmed that the last thought snapped him out of his remembrance.

He attended to his sandwich.

Bradley's friend Holly had sent him a new book, and he looked forward to a peaceful distraction. Holly owned a publishing company in Amherst, Massachusetts, and often sent Bradley some of her favorite titles. Lounging by the pool on the same cruise ship where he met Derek and Cate, Bradley and Holly had discovered their mutual love of books the second day they met. She was one of his closest friends. Although he met people easily and made friends quickly, Bradley remained reserved. Those he met on his vacation cruise sixteen years before counted among the inner circle Bradley trusted with his thoughts, his dreams, and his life. Closest among them were Derek and Cate. Cate's sister Sheila and Holly's father, Mike, also ranked among his dearest companions. They rarely saw each other, but when they did, years melted away, and they found themselves back cruising under a cloudless Caribbean sky.

Penned by a local author, *When Winter Ends* featured a tagline reading: *When a winter storm strands strangers in a New England hotel, it soon becomes obvious more than one of the lodgers are not who they profess to be.*

Sounds like fun, Bradley thought. He settled in with his sandwich, and after the events of the past two days, a much-needed sense of peace.

Dread replaced peace when, more than an hour later, he saw Rusty waiting at the glass sliding door. In his mouth he held a large bone.

THE SANDPIT

Bradley hoisted himself into his chair and made his way to the door. The closer he got, the lighter his dread. Having cooked many ribeye steaks, Bradley recognized the beef bone Rusty clenched. He opened the door, and the cheerful dog entered with his treat.

"Where in the world did you get that?" Bradley asked.

Rusty looked up at him with what looked like a wide grin. Then he trotted to his bed and gnawed on the bone.

Bradley turned off the outside light. He saw a campfire burning on the right side of the sandpit close to his backyard ledge. The smell of charred steak mixed with wood smoke wafted under his nose.

Hmm, interesting, he thought.

The next morning before Bradley opened the door for Rusty, he wrote a note on a piece of paper and, using a binder clip from his desk drawer, attached it to Rusty's collar. The note read: *Rusty thanks you for the bone!*

He didn't expect a response but hoped for one.

Bradley took a chance that whoever gave Rusty the bone also wrote the previous night's note. He wanted to talk to that person, but he didn't want to take the chance of scaring him or her off. Rusty, it seems, had already established a relationship with the individual.

His morning routine complete, Bradley looked out back for Rusty before settling in at his desk. He scanned the area of the campfire and saw no movement. He knew better than to worry about Rusty. *He is a survivor*, Bradley thought. He set himself in front of his desk, where he would spend the next two hours.

He emailed the employee analyses to Nick with his separate theory on Juliette Berryman. He still had an abundance of information to go through, but in his opinion, the bureau should arrest her at once and preferably oppose bail.

Neither of the decisions stood with him, however. And he knew neither would happen based soley on the report he just emailed.

When Rusty reappeared, Bradley let him in and removed the note attached to the dog's collar. The words, written in black marker on a torn page from a *Sports Illustrated* magazine said, **He earned it.**

Suddenly Rusty's ears perked, and he ran to the front door. Bradley didn't hear the car until it parked out front. He assumed it would be the detective. He was wrong.

"Hi, Mr. Whitman. Remember me? Shea?"

As if he could have forgotten.

"Yes, Shea. What can I do for you today?" Bradley politely asked.

"I came by to apologize to you. It's just . . . I was having such a crummy day," she explained.

"Sure. I understand. Thank you." Bradley tried to end the conversation and close the door as he had a more pressing issue on his mind.

"Could I come in and talk to you for a minute?" Shea asked.

"I'm really very busy," he replied.

"I only need a minute," she urged.

He knew it to be a mistake, but he found himself saying, "Sure."

He let her in but put his chair between her and the rest of his home. She froze when she noticed Rusty standing behind the door. Her eyes repeatedly shifted from Rusty to Bradley until Bradley told Rusty to relax.

"Um, I want to explain the situation to you," Shea began.

"The situation?" Bradley chuckled.

"Um, yes. You see, um, our client needs this lot and the surrounding properties for a business venture." She spoke slowly and deliberately, as if remembering a word-for-word presentation.

"But I already told you it's not for sale." Bradley remained calm.

Her shoulders slouched, forehead wrinkled, and head bowed, she said, "Um, yes, you did. But they told me to tell you, um, if you don't sell to them now, um, you will lose it to them later."

Bradley felt conflicted about how to respond. Should he show restraint and understanding toward the unfortunate, unknowing dupe? Or should he openly show his anger at the mere notion that someone would try to intimidate him into relinquishing his home?

He chose a middle ground.

"Shea, what you just said to me amounts to a threat, a threat that could get you in big trouble. I don't want you to get into trouble. So here is *your* situation. You can give me the name of your client or clients and tell me everything you know about them, or I will have Rusty guard you while I phone the police."

Shea stiffened and began to quiver. Her eyelids fluttered out of control, and an audible sound escaped from her ruby red lips.

"I . . . I . . ." Shea backed herself up to the door.

"Shea, relax. Just breathe. In. Out. In and out."

She followed his instructions.

"That's it," Bradley said. "Now, what can you tell me about your client?"

"N . . . Nothing," She blurted.

"Oh, come on, Shea. Sure, you can. A smart real estate person like you would be sure to get contact information. How do you get in touch with . . . wait. Is it a him or her?"

"Him," she stated before thinking.

"And how do you get in touch with him?" Bradley asked.

"Look, I gotta go." She turned around to open the door.

Bradley moved his chair to prevent the door from opening.

"Shea, did you do any prior research on the properties you are approaching for your client?"

Bradley knew the answer.

"No. I just have a list," she blurted, then winced, and then cursed under her breath.

Bradley's eyebrows drew together as he empathized. "I'll need the list, Shea."

Bradley took his FBI badge from his back pocket and showed it to Shea.

Shea slid down the door, hit the floor, and tucked her knees under her chin while muttering, "Oh, my God. Oh, my God. Oh, my God."

Rusty, who had sat motionless through the conversation, sat beside Shea and leaned into her. She put her arm around his body and leaned her head into his chest. Her breathing slowed, and her muscles relaxed. But she didn't move.

"Do you have that list with you, Shea?" Bradley asked.

She never lifted her head but jerked it up and down.

"Okay, good. You and I are going to move to the couch now. If you want Rusty to stay with you, that would be alright."

Another jerky head nod.

Together they moved to the couch. Bradley dialed Derek's direct line.

"Hey, Derek. I've got a small . . . " he paused, " . . . situation here."

Bradley quickly explained the series of events, beginning with Shea's visit the previous day.

"Do you really think there's anything to it?" Derek asked.

"I do. I can't explain why, but I do."

"Okay, I'll send someone right over."

"Thanks, Boss."

Shea sat hunched and shivering on the couch. Rusty sat at her feet. She had not made eye contact with Bradley since she entered the house. Shea was scared.

"Where's the list, Shea?"

"In th . . . the car."

"Okay, we can hold off on that for the moment."

Shea lifted her head and looked into Bradley's eyes.

"I can't go back. I can't go back to jail."

Bradley softened his voice and his posture. He had literally backed the poor girl into a corner and felt contrite.

"What were you in for?" he asked.

"Accomplice to breaking and entering. But I don't do that shit anymore. I don't hang out with those kind of people, and I don't do drugs, either. I'm clean. Maybe a few drinks now and then, but that's it." She spoke rapidly as if she had to get it all out before the opportunity slammed shut.

"How long have you been out?"

"Three months."

"How'd you get this job?"

"Through the prison work program. I got the real estate license while I was inside. They helped me get this job. I just started this week. They gave me a company car. Am I going to lose the car?"

"Let's not worry about that right now, okay? Listen, Shea, soon there will be an agent here. He will ask you a lot of questions. All you have to do is answer them honestly, and I promise you everything will be alright."

Shea nodded her head in response.

"Total honesty," Bradley reiterated.

Head bowed, Shea lifted her eyelids and glared at Bradley.

"A friggin' cop!" she exclaimed.

Bradley didn't have the heart to correct her.

Agent Philbin from the white-collar crime unit arrived. Bradley moved to his desk and continued with his work while Philbin questioned Shea in the living room. He kept one ear on the conversation. Rusty stayed with Shea.

"Okay, Miss Powers. You'll need to get me that list now," Bradley heard.

Shea Powers swayed on her feet. Agent Philbin held her by the arm, whether to steady her or to keep her from running, Bradley did not know. What he did know was that her fear was real. He sensed it, and so did Rusty. When the two returned to the living room, Bradley approached Philbin.

"I'd like to make a copy of that, Agent Philbin."

Philbin hesitated, then handed the two-page list to Bradley, who ran it through his copier.

Returning the list to Philbin, Bradley asked, "Are you through with Miss Powers?"

"For now," he answered, "but I will probably have some follow-up questions." He directed the latter toward Shea.

She nodded.

"I'm sure she'll be happy to help any way she can," Bradley grinned.

Glaring up from her bowed head, Shea flashed him a grimace.

Agent Philbin left.

"You did good, Shea. I believed every word you told Agent Philbin," Bradley said, staring her in the eyes. "But what is it that you left out? What are you holding back?"

Shea tilted her head back, and her dirty blonde hair dangled as she let out a heavy sigh. Wishing she could disappear, she placed both hands over her face.

"Nothing."

"Shea, even Rusty knows you're lying."

His head cocked, his eyes questioning, Rusty looked at Shea.

"Who the hell are you, dude? All I tried to do was make you some money, and you turned me into the feds. What is your problem?"

Bradley wondered if she forgot that he worked for the agency, too.

"I don't like anyone threatening me or trying to tell me what to do," Bradley replied honestly.

"Well, me either," Shea spit.

"Fair enough," Bradley said. "But what you're doing, how you're doing it, is illegal. You can't threaten people into selling their homes and businesses."

"I didn't threaten you. I just told you what the guy said, that's all."

Bradley laughed. He couldn't help but like the woman. She reminded him of himself at a much younger age, maybe thirteen or so. He had matured quicker than most.

"What are you laughing at?" Shea yelled as she pounded her fist on the couch cushion.

Rusty stood at attention.

"Easy, boy," Bradley said. "You really need to learn to control these outbursts, Shea. They're going to get you into trouble someday. Probably already have."

Frustration swept her face.

"So, what do you know that you didn't tell Agent Philbin?" Bradley asked.

Shea sat forward, rested her forearms on her knees, and hung her head. She surrendered a whispered sigh.

"I'm not the only one working the account. The real estate company started before they hired me. My boss accidentally gave me the list of properties they already got. There's a lot."

"Do you still have the list?" a wide-eyed Bradley asked.

"No. She took it back when she seen what she did."

"Can you remember any of the properties?"

"Don't know the addresses. But I don't have to. The map showed where they was . . . I mean, were."

Bradley smiled, mostly because of the information Shea supplied but partly because of her efforts to improve her grammar.

"If I pull up a map on the computer, will you be able to point out the area?"

"Yeah, I'm good with maps. Memory's good, too." She straightened up and held her head high.

"There's a stool over by the gym equipment. Bring it over to the desk. Sorry. I don't have a chair."

"What happened to you anyway? I mean, you know, why the chair?" she asked.

Bradley had heard the question many times, whether out loud or in people's thoughts. When asked outright, he answered it differently each time.

"Scuba accident. I got hit by a whale."

"Holy shit!" she screeched. "What the fuck are the odds of that?"

"About one in a million," Bradley stated with irony.

On his computer monitor, Bradley called up a map of Revere. He centered the sandpit in the middle of the screen.

"Can you show me where the properties are?" he asked.

"Give me the mouse," Shea said.

She zoomed in on the map and used a red marker tool from the program to draw a circle around the affected area. Then from memory, she marked off seventeen properties. She changed the marker tool to green and marked a few more. Lastly, she colored her remaining selections in yellow.

"Red are a done deal, green are in the works, and yellow are still up for grabs."

Bradley enjoyed the confident side of Shea's personality. He assumed she didn't get to display it too often.

A review of the map included his property along with other buildings along Industrial Drive. More selected properties included Park Street, Howland Avenue, and Jameson Street. The one common denominator, Bradley noted: each of the properties bordered the sandpit.

DATA

After trying to get Shea to commit to looking for a new job, Bradley succeeded only exacting her promise that she wouldn't tell anyone about her conversation with the FBI. He convinced her it was not in her best interest to do so.

Bradley gave her his cell phone number and told her to call him if she needed anything. Half the day had passed by the time Shea drove away.

Analysis of Berryman Home Healthcare had gotten nowhere. His secure FBI email account crammed with messages from Nick. Bradley downloaded the attached files. As for his suspicions of Juliette Berryman's possible involvement in the deaths of her father, mother, and husband, Nick emailed, *Sounds like a great thriller. You should write it someday.*

Bradley chuckled. He knew Nick would not take any of it seriously. But he also copied Derek on the email, and Derek knew not to dismiss Bradley's novel-like hunches.

Juliette kept excellent records. Every visit included the who, what, where, when, and why. But the *how long* most interested Bradley. His original report, the one that allowed for a search warrant, included a discrepancy in hours of service provided in conjunction with employee hours during one month. It just didn't add up. But he had yet to find another month's worth of records where service hours exceeded employee hours.

Juliette would need a reliable system to succeed in executing fraud of that size for this long without detection. And Bradley had a theory based on the presence of an abacus.

Each client's file folder included a color code, a blue, red, brown, or yellow dot. The abacus had the same colors plus green. Because he didn't have files in hand, Bradley made sure Nick had his people include each of the client's assigned color codes in the electronic file. After examining random files, Bradley saw that some clients had colored dots preceded by a black block. He had yet to connect that block to a theory.

Bradley created a program to review each file and categorize them all based on their color code. He then wrote a program to review each color-coded group of files and sort them into which day of the week the client received a visit. He allowed for multiple visits per week. Each program spewed a report, and each report resulted in Bradley's creating a new program.

Data to Bradley equals a rib bone to Rusty. As far back as Bradley could remember, he loved facts and numbers. Whereas most children struggle to remember the capital of each state, Bradley could recite the capital, its state flower, its main export, and its population. And if a state held the distinction of a highest point, lowest point, widest point, or narrowest point, Bradley would know that too.

While his computer programs sorted the Berryman data, Bradley downloaded the pictures of Juliette's office from his cell phone and used his three overhead monitors to display them. The colors of the outlined areas on the maps pinned to Juliette's office walls matched the colors of the abacus. The area outlined in blue included metropolitan Boston. Red encircled parts of both Middlesex and Worcester counties, and brown denoted Essex county. Parts of Norfolk, Bristol, and Plymouth counties showed in green, and Nantucket and Martha's Vineyard shared yellow.

Another of the photos centered on the abacus with its rainbow of beads, five top rows of colors repeating again on the bottom five rows. Something fresh caught Bradley's attention. He hit a few keystrokes, and the picture of the abacus appeared on his desktop monitor. He zoomed in on the abacus and saw halfway down the left side of the frame, between the fifth and sixth row of beads, someone had drawn a black box.

Bradley smiled.

Rusty woke. He had been napping on his bed since Shea left. He yawned and stretched, then jumped to his feet and ran to the water dish. He sniffed what remained of his beef bone, then as if something occurred to him, ran to the sliders. Dusk took hold of the fading daylight.

All day, Bradley had wrestled with an internal question. It wasn't until that moment that he made the decision to try. He wrote *Can we talk?* on a piece of paper and attached it to Rusty's collar with the same file clip he used for the last two correspondences.

Rusty trotted out the door and disappeared down the ledge.

It's been a full day, Bradley reflected. His latest programs would take overnight to compute because of the considerable number of records. He felt it a good stopping point for the day. He chose his favorite jazz channel from the online streaming program and summoned the earthy vocals of Norah Jones into the barren silence.

From his refrigerator, he pulled a fresh head of cauliflower and placed it on the lowered countertop near the fridge. Under the counter stood two sets of drawers, one on either end of the countertop with an opening in between. The opening allowed Bradley to pull up to the counter and comfortably prepare his dinner. The top right drawer held his knives. The bottom left larger drawer kept his cutting boards and some pots and pans.

He trimmed and cut the cauliflower into plum-sized florets and placed them in his countertop steamer. While the cauliflower cooked, he thinly sliced potatoes and soaked them in salted water to release excess starch.

He poured the cooked cauliflower into his blender with a quart of heavy cream, salt, pepper, garlic, and shredded cheddar cheese and pureed it until creamy. He set aside a cup of the sauce. He coated the bottom of a rectangular Pyrex dish with the creamy mixture, then alternately layered drained potatoes and sauce, finishing with the sauce and sprinkled grated parmesan cheese on top before placing it in the oven.

While the potatoes cooked, he removed the last of the herb-marinated chicken breast from the refrigerator, placed it in his heated cast-iron skillet with a light coating of olive oil, added sliced onions and mushrooms, and sautéed it on medium-low heat. When the chicken had cooked halfway, he removed it from the heat, added the two cups of retained cauliflower sauce, and put the skillet in the oven on the rack below the potatoes.

I did it again, Bradley contemplated. He found it nearly impossible to cook decent food for just one person. His freezer held proof of the overabundance of casseroles, stews, and roasts. He tried to donate boxes of leftovers to a local shelter, but city ordinances prevented them from accepting.

Bradley opened a bottle of Bogle Chardonnay and poured himself a glass. He built a small fire, noted he would need to restock his woodpile from the lean-to, and collected his book from the end table. Instead of moving onto the couch, he sat in his chair next to the fireplace with his wine and his book while dinner cooked in the oven.

Rusty returned by the time Bradley finished his dinner and washed his dishes. Bradley didn't care to use a dishwasher, even though he had one installed. It was rare for him to run it.

Once inside, Rusty sat at Bradley's feet. The clip held a fresh note. Bradley took the note off the collar and motioned Rusty to his dinner waiting for him along with fresh water. Rusty gladly complied.

I'll be sitting by my fire at 7 pm, the note read.

"Oh, okay then," Bradley murmured. Somewhat surprised, he had expected either more of a back and forth or an outright no.

He looked at the clock. He had half an hour. The drive would take him about five or more minutes, depending on the traffic lights. He had no direct way of getting down into the pit without driving around to the opposite side and using the access road.

"Being a dog has its advantages," Bradley said to Rusty. Bradley imagined Rusty agreed with him.

At ten minutes to seven, Bradley put on his coat, took a six-pack carrier with beer (two of the compartments empty) from his refrigerator, and loaded himself and Rusty into the truck.

The dark access road had a slight curve as it descended into the pit. Bradley drove slowly and cautiously since his headlights were all he had to show the way. He did not want to accidentally run over anyone's belongings. Further away than he expected, he saw flames in the distance. The sandpit looked smaller from his vantage point on the hill.

As he approached the camp with the roaring fire, he figured it easiest if his truck faced the fire as he drove in. He didn't think it prudent to try his chair on the sandy floor of the pit. His intention was to lower his truck ramp and sit in his chair on the platform to communicate with the individual from there. He parked in front of the fire.

The figure didn't move even as the truck lights shone on him. He sat rigid, his full torso extended, chest out, head high. He wore a deep brown t-shirt and light brown fatigue-style pants tucked inside boots bloused over the laces. He wore no jacket, and the fire seemed enough to keep him warm on the chilly evening. At ease with himself and his surroundings, he never looked Bradley's way.

Bradley turned off the headlights and pressed the button to operate the door. Only then did the man turn. Bradley lowered himself in his chair to the ground and remained on the platform.

The man called for Rusty. The dog jumped over Bradley into the sand and greeted the stranger as an old friend.

The man stood. "Hey, fella," the deep voice whispered as he stroked Rusty's head.

"His name is Rusty. But I guess I already told you that," Bradley stated.

"Yeah, you did."

"I'm Bradley Whitman. We live right up there." Bradley pointed to his place. He could see the lights through the sliding doors from there.

"You can call me Zayt," the man replied.

He stood strong and sturdy. *A man who takes care of his body*, Bradley surmised. He couldn't put an age to him.

"Military?" Bradley asked.

"Seals. Three tours," Zayt said without emotion.

"Want a beer?" Bradley asked.

"Sure," Zayt answered. Then he walked away and disappeared behind the shack.

Bradley heard thumping in the dark. Zayt reappeared with a half sheet of graffiti-covered plywood and laid it from the base of Bradley's platform to the campfire.

Bradley placed the beer on his lap and rolled over the plywood to bring him closer to the fire. He handed Zayt a bottle.

Resourceful, Bradley mused. "Thanks."

Zayt nodded.

As comfortable as a mint on a pillow, Rusty lay on the sand between them.

"Did you know her?" Bradley asked.

Zayt looked down at the beer he held in his hand.

"Yeah, I knew her."

"I'm sorry," Bradley said.

Zayt nodded again.

"Zayt. Is that a nickname?"

"Uh huh."

"Short for Vasily Zaitsev, the Russian sniper from World War II?"

Zayt looked Bradley in the eyes. Then from top to bottom he examined every part of Bradley's posture, demeanor, and expression.

"Yeah," Zayt answered, surprised Bradley had profiled him so quickly.

"You must have been good at your job," Bradley smiled.

Zayt did not respond.

"Listen, Zayt. I want to tell you something because I don't want you to think I'm blindsiding you."

He had Zayt's attention.

"I work for the Federal Bureau of Investigation. I'm an analyst. But that's not why I wanted to talk to you."

Zayt's eyebrows raised. He clearly had missed that when he sized Bradley up. But it didn't alter his original assessment of him.

"Someone killed a woman in my backyard and your front yard," Bradley continued. "I have no intention of letting the killer get away with it. I hoped you would tell me everything you can about her and the night she was murdered."

He leaned his body toward Zayt. Zayt took a swig of his beer.

"We called her Mamma Lise. She was a black woman in her late sixties, but she looked much older. She was a sweet lady. She could have been my grandmother, for all I know. She took care of the ones who couldn't take care of themselves."

He bowed his head.

"Anybody that you can think of who would want to hurt her? Has anyone been hassling her?"

"Not that I know of. But I'm not always around during the day."

"I realize you are a good distance from her camp, but did you hear or see anything that night?"

He slumped his shoulders and dropped his head.

"Not a sound," he whispered.

Bradley could tell Zayt blamed himself. If the case belonged to the FBI, then Bradley would not have spoken further.

"Don't beat yourself up, Zayt. This guy knew what he was doing."

"A pro?" Zayt sat tall.

"Don't know. But he was in and out quickly and quietly." Bradley allowed himself to go no farther. "What's her story?"

"She came from Dorchester. Her husband got sick, bills piled up, and when he died, she lost her house. No family. She was on the streets over ten years. Said she liked it that way."

"And you? You like it?" Bradley probed.

"Yeah," Zayt replied as he stared at the fire.

Bradley wrote his personal phone number on his business card and handed the card to Zayt.

"I'd appreciate it if you would contact me if you come up with any new information on Mamma Lise's murder. Maybe one of her neighbors heard something."

Zayt continued to stare into the fire as he took the card and nodded.

"If Rusty ever bothers you, let me know. I hate the idea of having to tie him up, though."

Rusty lifted his head and looked at Bradley, then at Zayt.

"No bother. I like dogs," he said.

They sat in silence, drank their beer, and stared into the fire.

GREEN

The morning escaped his notice as he buried himself in numbers. The Berryman analysis process proved as tedious as he expected. But Bradley knew Nick Gaston as an impatient man. In fact, it surprised him that Nick hadn't called him before.

"What's happening with the Berryman files? All I have so far is the employee report. I need more than that before I can start interrogating this bitch."

Bradley cringed at his crudeness. He knew Derek could not be in earshot or Nick would not have been so coarse.

"You can investigate theory, or you can investigate facts. Which would you prefer, Nick? Which would guarantee you success?"

Bradley had used the approach before on Nick. The first few times, Nick shot back with a derogatory remark. But as he learned the truth about the concept and also enjoyed the successes, he could do nothing but sigh.

"Alright, alright, smartass. When can I expect your next report?"

"I'm working on it as we speak. There's a lot more going on here than we first thought, Nick. This is big. This might be your next rung up the ladder. Just be patient. I'll send you some hard data soon.

"I suggest you lay off interrogating Juliette Berryman, Sharon Stakes, and the others who have worked there for more than ten years until we compile the right questions. Start with the low-level staff. Get corroboration on their schedules, pay, and client visits. That will give us a base to work with."

"Okay. But at least give me a crumb here, Bradley. When you say big, what are we talking?"

"Definitely over a hundred million."

"Holy shit."

Bradley could almost see Nick wetting his lips.

"Let me know if you need anything from me," Nick said.

"You bet. See you."

No one other than Derek could handle hot-headed, impulsive, and unyielding Nick the way Bradley could. But you couldn't question his dedication to duty. Bradley saw him going far in the bureau if he learned to tame his emotions. He hoped he could help Nick with that.

With client files sorted by color code, eight in all, Bradley saw a pattern emerge. At first Bradley assumed the color codes would connect to the maps. He thought all blue patients would live in blue-circled Boston and suburbs and red patients in red-marked Middlesex and Worcester county, and so on. But the theory proved wrong. That made him more intrigued as to what the green beads would indicate. But he set the thought aside.

On further inspection, the blue-designated clients shared a diabetes diagnosis. Those patients belonged to one of the largest color groups. Other underlining problems existed with the blue group, but all had prescriptions for insulin. Red clients receive visits a minimum of twice a week for physical therapy, occupational therapy, or speech therapy. Curiously, the brown-designated clients were all male and the yellow-designated clients consisted of patients who shared one of two doctors.

Bradley had gotten that far before Nick's phone call.

Several more hours passed before he determined the similarities in the black/blue, black/red, and black/yellow files. He ran into a data roadblock with the black/brown file, so he put it aside for further inspection. And, consistent with his previous findings, black/green was not represented by any client files.

As Bradley discovered consistencies, he included them in his report for Nick. Bradley noted the absence of information regarding black/brown coded patients but did not mention the absence of green coded groups. He had yet to mention his abacus supposition to Nick and doubted Nick had made any such connection on his own.

Rather than wait and take the risk of Nick doing something adversely impulsive, he uploaded the unfinished report to his secured FBI email account to Nick and copied it to Derek, as was his habit. In the same email, he asked Nick when he could expect the rest of Juliette Berryman and Berryman Home Healthcare Services' bank and tax records. Bradley had surmised there were additional masked accounts on her tax return. If he weren't able to connect cash to Berryman bank deposits, he wouldn't be able to prove a thing.

In his reply, Nick asserted his own eagerness in receiving the records and promised to pass them to Bradley as soon as he got them.

The absence of green overshadowed Bradley's productive morning. If he could not resolve the basis for excluding the use of the color in the client's files, the premise of the abacus became fruitless.

He was knee-deep in the black/brown files when his phone rang.

"Agent Whitman? This is Detective Rome. I wonder if I may

stop by and speak with you this afternoon around four?"

"Certainly, Detective. I'll be here," Bradley replied.

"Okay. See you in about forty-five minutes."

Rome arrived alone, holding a folder. Rusty, detecting no threat, didn't pay any attention to him.

"Come in. Sit down," Bradley said.

"Thanks for seeing me on short notice. I've got to tell you, you got into my head a little bit. Yesterday, when Doyle and I left, we were still skeptical about your profile. But we've got nothing in this case. And I don't anticipate we'll get anything if we continue our routine investigation. No one will talk to us and, as you know, the longer it takes, the less chance people remember the details. No one admitted to writing the note, and the only video we have is yours."

"Have you interviewed everyone who was in the pit that night?" Bradley asked.

"Everyone we could find. Most of them wouldn't talk to us."

Bradley decided to keep Zayt's name out of his discussion with Rome. He did not want to jeopardize the relationship he intended to cultivate.

"Before we go on, Detective, I want to clarify something."

Back straight, eyebrows furrowed, Detective Rome sat back on the couch.

"I believe I can get you information," Bradley said, "but I may not be able to get you any witnesses. If you are fine with that, then I may be of some help to you."

"So you're telling me I need to trust your information without knowing the source."

Bradley smiled.

"Yes."

"Do I have a choice?"

"Of course. But if I burn my bridges, no one will be able to cross them."

"Well played, Agent Whitman. What can you tell me?"

"Not much yet. The person who wrote the note is genuine." *Don't get crazy about this*, Bradley thought. "Hell . . . the man. A man wrote the note. He's intelligent and careful and very much a loner. He cared about her."

"He's a veteran, isn't he?"

Bradley did not respond to the question but said,

"He found her. She's known as Mamma Lise, and she's in her late sixties. She'd been on the streets for more than ten years after she lost her house in Dorchester because of her late husband's medical bills. She liked living in the pit. She took care of others around her. I don't know exactly how yet. She did not have any enemies, at least none that were apparent."

"Wow. Okay." Rome leaned forward and tossed the file onto the coffee table. "Her name was Elise Bowman, age sixty-seven. Her husband died twelve years ago of stomach cancer. The bank foreclosed on her house in Dorchester one year later."

Bradley felt pleased with himself.

Rome continued, "Before the insurance company could take possession of her property, she sold everything she had—their vacation house, two expensive cars, furniture, jewelry, and anything else worth selling. Seems they were well off before he got sick. The insurance agent estimated she garnered close to $250,000. The bank got her house, and the insurance company got what was left of the retirement and savings accounts, which wasn't much. She walked away with the cash, which the insurance company says belongs to them. An arrest warrant was issued, but they never found her."

It was Bradley's turn to sit back in his chair.

"Well, I'll be damned," Bradley almost smirked, but before it took hold, his face shifted to a frown. "Do you think the money had something to do with her death?"

"That is the question of the day," Detective Rome said as, hands behind his head, he leaned back on the couch.

Bradley sat quiet for a moment, then said, "You knew I would reach out to the note writer, didn't you?"

Rome smiled.

"And you knew I wouldn't tell you who the note writer is."

Rome said nothing.

"You intentionally played dumb when I gave you the profile on the killer," Bradley said to the detective.

"No, that was real." Rome leaned forward again and chuckled. "But I did have a nice long chat with Agent Richards, and he told me you would go off on your own. He also told me you would not be inclined to share your source with me. Says you are very protective of people, especially those who trust you."

"So, you want me to find out who knew about the money and where it might be, assuming the killer didn't walk away with it."

"That's right. We don't believe she would have kept it with her in the pit. Too many people around. And, had the police picked her up, it would be evidence against her."

"Who's to say there's any left? It's been ten years," Bradley observed.

"She would have to spend seventy dollars a day to use it up. A homeless woman spending that kind of money would stand out, don't you think? Besides, it stands to reason she would protect her future, having almost lost everything once."

"I suppose," Bradley considered.

"Have another conversation with the veteran. He may not be as honorable as you think."

Bradley trusted his own assessment of Zayt. But he couldn't rule out that Zayt may have known more than he was willing to tell. He decided to concoct a reason for another visit.

"Okay, I will. But don't be disappointed when you find he isn't your murderer," said Bradley.

"I appreciate your help, Agent Whitman. Homicide on the homeless is a difficult sell to the brass when results don't come quick."

"I understand, Detective. I'll do what I can."

After he left, Bradley admonished himself for what he considered allowing Detective Rome to dupe him. But Rome had had help from Derek who, Bradley was pretty sure, felt proud of himself for his part in the ruse.

Bradley threw some leftovers into the oven and returned to his desktop. Hoping that the next day he would have the rest of the financials to lock the case down, he set the Berryman case aside.

Killing time before dinner, Bradley decided to satisfy his curiosity about Shea Powers, her heavy real estate arm, and her map color coding. He did that kind of thing for fun. With Rusty lying by his side, he searched Massachusetts land records, beginning with the properties Shea had marked with red, meaning they had already sold.

As expected, each search revealed the same buyer. A business named Revere Industrial Properties, LLC. He dug deeper and found that the company owned only the properties in question. Formed eight years before, the limited liability company did not buy any acreage until five years later when it acquired the former Industrial Communications Company, ICC. Wireless products and cell phones had replaced interoffice wired phone systems and other wired communication devices, leaving ICC in the dust. The building sat empty for five years before Revere Industrial Properties picked it up at a bargain price.

According to the records, Revere Industrial Properties, LLC since purchased thirteen additional properties. But Shea had marked seventeen, so three of them would be in the final stage of acquisition.

She also marked four locations with green, which she described as *in progress*. The rest of the twelve addresses on the map, which Shea marked in yellow, remained on the company's wish list.

There's at least one on that list you won't get, Bradley scoffed to himself.

Bradley thought he would research the owner of Revere Industrial Properties, but the timer on his oven sounded. Before retrieving his dinner, he gave Rusty fresh water and his beef with gravy.

Bradley did not turn on any music. Questions buzzed his brain.

Why aren't there any green-coded clients in Berryman's files?

Is there really a stash of money that belongs to a homeless woman out there somewhere?

Is Shea mixed up in something that could send her back to prison?

How can I get Zayt here to ask him about the money?

Bradley reached for the cell phone in his chair pocket and began to text. A moment later, his text message alert sounded. Bradley looked at it and smiled.

Early in the investigation Bradley had assumed Juliette would have maintained hidden financial accounts. Intelligent fraud criminals do, of course. The key involves having various Social Security numbers to open the accounts. Without raising an eyebrow, Juliette had access to three such numbers plus her own. Bradley found that her dead father, mother, and husband had "opened" numerous accounts since their demise, and Nick found accounts for Sharon Stakes at the same banks.

It seems Bradley had guessed correctly. Sharon Stakes apparently turned out to be a bigger part of the business than simply a long-term employee.

In total, fifteen employees had worked at Berryman for more than ten years. Bradley sent Nick an additional list of employee names and asked him to check if any accounts existed using those names and Social Security information.

After dinner, Bradley checked his FBI email account. He found a message from Nick. The subject line read

Berryman bank accounts

He opened the email to find:

You were right. We searched for accounts in every name you gave me. We found 42 domestic and offshore accounts. See attached.

Forty-two accounts, Bradley thought. That was more than double what he expected.

The hour got late. Bradley wrote a quick note and attached it to Rusty's collar. He didn't know how Zayt would react, but he thought it worth a chance.

Do you know anyone who can help me stack wood tomorrow afternoon? My usual guy backed out last minute. The pay is decent.

The text Bradley had sent before dinner arranged for a delivery of wood in the morning. If he read Zayt correctly, Zayt would show up to help him. He might even refuse payment. If he did, Bradley would be ready.

While he waited for Rusty to return, Bradley began to write

a computer program to search for patterns in deposits and withdrawals of the known Berryman accounts. From experience he understood he would need to write many more programs to unearth the information he wanted and required.

Rusty returned home after only forty-five minutes. The note attached to his collar conveyed just one word, *Yes.*

CAYMAN ISLANDS, BERMUDA, AND BELIZE

Bradley and Rusty left home at 8:30 AM. Rusty had delivered a message to Zayt earlier that morning explaining that the wood would not get delivered until 2 PM.

Bradley wanted to be present when Nick Gaston interrogated the two Berryman employees who had worked less than three years under Juliette's employment. The first interviewee, Joanne Goyette, was scheduled for 9 AM.

Carl, the security guard, stood at his post inside the FBI foyer. A slight tilt of his head indicated his confusion at seeing the Doberman Pinscher alongside Bradley.

"Hey, Carl. This is Rusty," Bradley explained.

"Agent Whitman. Does Rusty have an FBI identification badge?"

"Not yet, Carl. But I have my hopes. He's visiting with me today. Let's call him my therapy dog, shall we?"

Carl smiled. "I assume you ran this by your supervisor?"

"Absolutely, Carl. I'd be crazy not to."

Carl handed Bradley a visitor tag, and Bradley attached it to Rusty's collar.

"I get dinged for this, and you'll owe me big time," Carl said.

Bradley smiled, and he and Rusty headed to the elevator.

Agent Morrison jumped at the sight of Rusty when the eighth floor elevator doors opened. "Jeez, Whitman. Who the hell is that?"

"Witness for the Branson case. Bringing him to interrogation now," Bradley said as they left Morrison behind.

Rusty stayed by Bradley's side. Questioning glances followed them. Mara was smiling when they reached her desk.

"You kept him, didn't you?" she asked.

"I can't get rid of him," Bradley replied as he reached and stroked Rusty's head.

"I knew deep down you were a softy, Agent Whitman."

"Which room is he in?"

"Interrogation Room B. He's got Goyette in there now."

"Thanks, Mara."

Bradley wheeled down the hall with Rusty by his side. As they passed Interrogation Room B, Bradley slowed his chair and evaluated the scene. Of the four walls, glass constituted only one. From the hall, Bradley could see Nick and Jim seated on one side of the rectangular table with Joanne Goyette seated on the other. He could not hear what they said, but he didn't need to hear Miss Goyette to know how she felt. She squirmed in her chair and picked at her bright red nail polish.

She glanced Bradley's way and held still, hoping the man and his dog would enter and save her.

Bradley and Rusty moved to the next doorway and entered a room with four solid walls. Derek stood inside. He acknowledged Bradley with a nod, then looked at Rusty. Derek closed his eyes and shook his head. Bradley could almost see the internal conversation playing out. No one spoke. They only listened.

The voices heard through the speakers came from Interrogation Room B. Without the presence of a two-way mirror in the room, Bradley relied on his listening skills to determine a suspect's emotional state. The cadence of an individual's speech, a slight stammer, or pause could speak volumes. Of course, each room came equipped with cameras to record interrogations, and time had proven that people felt less anxious with cameras than by the possibility of an unwanted voyeur on the opposite side of a mirrored window. From Interrogation Room B came the voices of Nick and Goyette.

NICK: And you left Berryman after only fifteen months. What made you leave?

GOYETTE: I decided to go back to nursing school. I enrolled at UMASS Amherst to complete my RN nursing requirements.

NICK: And did you?

GOYETTE: Yes.

NICK: Good for you. Congratulations.

GOYETTE: Thank you.

NICK: Are you employed as a nurse now?

GOYETTE: Yes. At Mass General.

NICK: Very good. What can you tell me about your position with Berryman Home Healthcare Services?

GOYETTE: I worked as an LPN and visited clients. Mostly I helped patients with physical therapy and general household activities.

NICK: Did you like the job?

GOYETTE: I guess it was okay. I liked the patients. There was a pause.

NICK: What about your coworkers? Did you get along with them?

GOYETTE: I really didn't see many of them. Only when I was paired with an RN. And that wasn't too often.

NICK: What about Juliette Berryman? Did you get along with her?

GOYETTE: I guess.

NICK: You guess? That doesn't sound very enthusiastic.

GOYETTE: She's a little uptight.

NICK: How so?

GOYETTE: Well, she's manic about paperwork. She was always checking my time reports and making me change something. Little things. She's very picky.

NICK: Can you remember any of the little things she made you change?

The room got quiet.

GOYETTE: Well, one day I visited one of my regular clients in Waltham. He's a diabetic, but I would go there once a week to monitor his vital signs. He had difficulty using his walker so I would get his insulin for him, but I couldn't give him his shot because I was only an LPN. He did it himself. But Juliette told me I had to put that I got his medication for him on the report. She was weird like that.

NICK: Anything else she was picky about?

GOYETTE: Well, this isn't picky, but it was odd. She would sometimes have me pick up therapeutic equipment from SEC and bring it to a client. But nobody ever told me to add new exercises to the regimen.

NICK: What's SEC?

GOYETTE: Styles Equipment Corporation. They are a medical supply company.

NICK: Where are they located?

GOYETTE: Chelmsford.

NICK: Do you know if the equipment ever got used?

GOYETTE: Not that I know of. But maybe.

NICK: Okay, let's move on to your work hours. How many hours a week on average did you work?

GOYETTE: I worked full time. Forty hours, no more, no less. Mrs. Berryman wouldn't pay overtime, but she made sure we worked the full forty hours.

In the side room, Bradley looked at Derek and shook his head side to side.

"Berryman's records show she worked overtime almost every week," Bradley said.

"We knew we would be able to get her on fraudulent service charges. It's the rest that I'm concerned about," Derek replied.

Nick continued to ask Joanne Goyette questions about her hours, general work conditions and how she filled out her paperwork. Then he got to the part that Bradley and Derek had shown up to hear.

NICK: Miss Goyette, when did you open the bank account in the Cayman Islands?

GOYETTE: Excuse me?

NICK: The account at Cayman Bank and Trust. When did you open that account?

GOYETTE: I don't have a bank account in the Cayman Islands. My bank is in Waltham.

Bradley noted the tone of her answer. She sounded genuinely confused.

NICK: Miss Goyette, is this your name, address, phone number, and Social Security number?

GOYETTE: Ah, yes. Except for the phone number. That's not my phone number.

NICK: So, when did you open this account?

The room went quiet, and Bradley could hear paper shuffling.

GOYETTE: I don't know what this is. I told you I don't have a bank account in the Cayman Islands. I don't even know where the Cayman Islands are.

NICK: C'mon, Miss Goyette. We know all about it. There's nothing you can do now but cooperate. We have your records.

GOYETTE: What records? I don't know what you're talking about. Oh, my God. What is going on?

Her shrill voice tremored.

NICK: Is this your signature?

GOYETTE: It . . . it looks . . . it looks like mine. But it's not. It can't be.

NICK: Miss Goyette, can you write down your email address? Any and all email addresses you use? And sign your name.

GOYETTE: I only have one email.

The silence lasted only a moment.

NICK: I'll be right back.

Seeing Rusty caused Nick to halt his entrance just long enough to be noticeable. Bradley smirked slightly.

"Dammit, Whitman. You should warn me when you bring your sister to work."

"I suppose it is too much to expect you to know the difference between a male and female," Bradley retorted.

"What do you think?" Derek ignored the banter and directed his question to Nick.

"I think she's telling the truth. The phone and emails don't match. But I think this guy knew that." Nick tilted his head toward Bradley.

"Suspected. I suspected that," Bradley said.

"So, what's happening here?" Derek asked Bradley.

"Juliette Berryman used the names and Social Security numbers of former and low-level current employees to open domestic and offshore accounts. Nick has found forty-two so far. She wouldn't use the names of the few employees that know about the fraud. It would be too dangerous to risk exposure."

"What about Sharon Stakes? She has multiple accounts in her name, including the Cayman Islands and Belize," Nick countered.

"I'd be willing to bet Juliette doesn't know about those. Stakes tried to hide her money, but she's not as smart as Juliette. That could be useful when it comes time to interrogate them," Bradley stated.

"See what else Miss Goyette can tell you, then send her on her way," Derek told Nick.

Nick returned to Interrogation Room B. Derek turned off the speakers.

"What's with the dog?"

"This is the dog from the Branson case. His owner is dead, natural causes. He's got nowhere to go. I call him Rusty."

Derek and Rusty exchanged a glance.

"I'm sure you two will be very happy together. Just make sure to take good care of him."

"I will," Bradley said.

"I was talking to the dog," Derek said as he walked out the door.

Bradley chuckled as he left the room. He glanced into the interrogation room and noticed that Joanne Goyette seemed more comfortable than the last time he heard her speak. Nick must have eased up on her. Sure that the second interrogation would proceed much as the first, Bradley decided not to hang around for it.

He made a pass by his desk to pick up his mail before he and Rusty made their way down the elevator to the lobby. Bradley dropped Rusty's visitor badge into the basket on Carl's desk, wished Carl's new baby well, and left headquarters.

He stopped at the local market on his way home to pick up a few items for dinner and, while there, a few treats for Rusty. If all went according to plan, he would have company for the nightly meal.

They got home to a pile of split wood dumped in the usual spot in the parking lot. Instead of pulling the truck under the lean-to, Bradley left it in the lot to make it easier to stack the wood under the cover of the lean-to later.

With the groceries put away and Rusty outside, Bradley played classic rock music through the speakers while he prepared dinner and dessert.

He also worked on his approach in questioning Zayt. He reasoned Zayt a guarded man and also quite perceptive. By the time he had the crust rolled for apple tart, Bradley decided he wasn't going to play any games with Zayt. He would mostly play it straight.

Bradley mixed sliced apples with sugar, cinnamon, nutmeg, salt, and a touch of fresh lemon juice and placed them in the crust. He folded excess crust over the apples toward the center of the pie plate, each fold overlapping the previous. After he brushed the crust with egg wash, he topped the apples with a few thin slices of butter, tossed the tart in the oven, and began to prepare vegetables.

He peeled root vegetables to the Lynyrd Skynyrd classic hit, *Sweet Home Alabama*. Once he had cut carrots, turnip, parsnip, and butternut squash into small cubes, he seasoned them with salt, pepper, garlic powder, onion powder, and fresh thyme. He tossed them with olive oil and laid them evenly on a baking pan. He would heat the leftover cauliflower creamed potatoes in the oven when he cooked the vegetables.

All he had left to prepare were the ribeye steaks. He reached for his own dry rub mix sitting in a jar in his cabinet, the recipe a secret he wouldn't even share with his mother, and coated the steaks, wrapped them, and stored them in the refrigerator until time to cook.

"Won't Get Fooled Again" by The Who rattled the speakers as Bradley made caramel sauce for the apple tart, a simple recipe that can go horribly wrong if not paid attention to. Bradley always paid attention.

He chose a protein shake for lunch and took it to his desk. His computer had worked nonstop overnight and into the morning compiling and organizing data from the bank files. It had finished while Bradley was at the office.

He had written the initial program to sort by date of deposit. Each deposit showed first the date, then time, amount, account number, bank name, and how funds were deposited. The next program translated account numbers to the account holder's name for easier analysis. While that ran, Bradley created another sort of deposits made in person, by wire transfer, or by automated clearing house, ACH transfer. The process of running both programs would take most of the day.

He had already removed the tart from the oven, and it cooled on the counter. He found himself with an hour and nothing to do. He wondered where Rusty had gone. The dog had been out since they arrived home. He wondered if Zayt would show or if he would send someone else. He wondered about Shea and if she quit that lousy job.

He reached for the map he had printed from his desktop, the one where Shea had marked properties in distinct colors. He smiled. *She's a smart woman. She just doesn't know it*, he thought.

He picked up his phone and dialed the number he had written on the map.

Hey, it's Shea. Talk to me after the beep.

Bradley hadn't prepared a message.

"Hi, Shea. This is Bradley Whitman. Remember me? I live at 303 Industrial Drive? I just wanted to check in with you to see how you are making out. Call me if you need anything."

He opened the sliders and looked down into the sandpit. There was no one in sight. But he could tell a lot of the residents had returned to their camps since the homicide, as items had moved or altered since then. He wished there were something he could do to help them since Mamma Lise no longer could.

He couldn't sit still. Bradley put on a light jacket and stacked some of the wood from the pile on his lap. He made three trips to stack logs by the central fireplace before Rusty ran through the open front door.

"Hey, buddy. Where've you been?"

Rusty led him back outside to the pile where Zayt waited.

"Hi, Zayt. I appreciate you coming by to help."

"No problem," Zayt replied, stone-faced.

"I've done this by myself before, and it's taken me two days to get it done. I stack it under the lean-to, on the right side over there," Bradley said as he stacked wood in his lap. "I have a wheelbarrow," he said, pointing to the side of the building, "but it doesn't do me much good."

Zayt retrieved the wheelbarrow and filled it with firewood. Bradley turned the music up loud so they could hear it while they worked. They didn't talk. Rusty lay in the sun and watched the two move back and forth from the pile to the stack.

A half hour into stacking, Zayt said, "You already had a good-sized stack of wood here. Why the delivery?"

Bradley had prepared for the question.

"The price is going up next week."

Zayt nodded, seemingly satisfied with the explanation.

Bad Company blasted through the open door as they continued to stack in silence. Bradley planned on saving any real conversation until dinner, assuming he could convince Zayt to join him. He knew he would need to ease into it. But then, Zayt spoke.

"You hear anything about Mamma Lise's murder?" Zayt surprised Bradley by asking.

"Yeah. Detective Rome stopped by yesterday. He had some interesting information. Kind of unbelievable, really," Bradley baited.

Zayt stopped adding wood to the pile and stared at Bradley.

"What kind of information?" Zayt asked.

"Well, I don't think it's the kind of thing the police want the public to know. Especially with the investigation ongoing."

"Look. She was my friend. I want to nail this asshole more than the police do. I'm not just some Joe Blow off the street. I know how to be discreet."

Bradley feigned processing the decision.

"Alright, but I'm not sure I believe it. It could be an excuse to brush the whole thing under the rug. They may be trying to keep me from pursuing this," he lied.

Zayt showed concern.

"What'd they say?"

"They think she was murdered for money," Bradley said.

"Money? What the fuck? She's a homeless woman," Zayt ranted. "I knew it. They don't give a rat's ass about her murder. To them she's just some animal living in a pit. Those sons of bitches don't give a damn . . ."

Rusty jumped to his feet and swiveled his head side to side.

"Whoa, whoa, Zayt. Calm down," Bradley interrupted. He could not tell if Zayt were sincere in his reaction or if he tried to evade the issue.

"It's okay, Rusty. Everything's okay," Bradley told the dog.

Rusty relaxed.

"They said she sold off some of her property before the insurance company could get hold of it and stashed cash away somewhere—apparently a lot of it," Bradley said.

"How much? What are they saying?"

"I don't know how much. They just said a lot. They think that's why she might have been killed—for the money." Bradley deflected from revealing that he knew the sum of money.

Zayt stood quiet as he brushed pieces of wood and bark from his arms. He hadn't looked at Bradley since the mention of money.

Rusty lay back down but kept his eyes open.

"You're right. They're just trying to get you to stop asking questions. They're not even going to try to catch this bastard."

Bradley suspected that, from his body language, Zayt knew more than he let on. But it wasn't the time to push. They stacked until after 4 PM whcn Zayt placed the final log on the pile.

"Want a beer?" Bradley asked.

"Sure. Why not?"

Zayt and Rusty followed Bradley inside. Bradley turned the music to a suitable level as Springsteen's 1975 hit *Born to Run* came over the speakers. He pulled two lagers from the refrigerator and handed one to Zayt.

"Nice place," Zayt said.

"Yeah, thanks. It's got everything I need. I spend most of my time over there," He pointed to the office area. "Grab that stool. Let's sit out back."

"Smells good in here," Zayt noticed.

"Yeah, well, I do my best thinking when I cook. Today I thought my way through a caramel-apple tart. Problem is, I can't eat all the food I cook. It's a waste. I've tried to donate to the local shelters, but they won't take it. Rules. Last week alone, I threw out a quart of chicken stew, a half pan of lasagna, and almost a full loaf of banana bread."

"Nobody will take it?"

"They can't. If they're caught, they'll get shut down."

"You sure it's not your cooking?"

Bradley raised his eyebrows. "Come over here. Take a look at this." Bradley rolled over to the counter and showed Zayt the apple tart sitting sufficiently cooled in its pan. Bradley took the opportunity to drizzle the homemade caramel over the top while Zayt watched.

"You a chef or something before the FBI?"

Bradley laughed. "No, I just appreciate decent food. Ever since I was a kid. Like I said, cooking helps me think, and I enjoy it. My problem is I can't cook for just one person. So a lot gets wasted."

"Well, don't throw it out, dude. If you got extra food, there are people out there who could use it." Zayt pointed in the direction of the sandpit. "Just let me know. I'll take care of it."

"That would be great, Zayt. A perfect solution."

Bradley moved to the sliders and rolled into the backyard. Zayt followed with the stool, and Rusty brought up the rear.

"Sorry I don't have a chair. I never really needed one. I suppose I should get a couple."

"This works." Zayt sat on the stool overlooking his sandpit. Rusty relaxed in between the two.

Bradley pulled some bills out of his pocket and held them out to Zayt.

"Here. Thanks for the help. I really appreciate it."

"No, man. keep your money. It was nothing. A good workout."

"Look, I planned to pay my regular guy anyway. It's the least I can do."

"Keep it," Zayt said.

Bradley showed reluctance when putting the money away. Then, as if getting the idea for the first time, he said, "Alright. Then join me for dinner. Once again, I prepared way too much food. I've got ribeye steaks marinating in my secret dry rub, roasted root vegetables, potatoes, and the tart. I eat at 6:30pm."

"Ah, I don't know."

"You have plans?"

"No. I just . . . I don't usually . . ."

"I get it. You like to be alone. Look around you. I'm the same way. But, I'm a damn good cook," Bradley declared with a smirk.

"Okay, I'll come back at 6:30."

They sat quietly as the sun began to fall behind the industrial buildings across the street behind them.

Then Bradley said, "Do you think it could be true?"

"What?" Zayt asked.

"About the money. Do you think it's possible?"

Zayt didn't answer.

As they both sat with their thoughts, John Lennon's "Imagine" wafted out the screen door and drifted into the pit below.

WHEN IT RAINS

At 6:25, Zayt returned with a fresh change of clothes and a six-pack of beer. Rusty heard Zayt walk to the door and waited there for Bradley to open it. Zayt didn't have to knock.

Surprised that the door had opened, Zayt looked around for a camera. "Ah." He pointed up.

"Nope. Rusty heard you."

"Could have used him in Afghanistan," Zayt said.

"He is smart. Smarter than me, I think."

"You get him as a puppy?"

Bradley grinned. "I got him four days ago."

Zayt's eyes widened. He shifted his glance from Bradley to Rusty and back.

"Seriously?"

"Yeah. I found him in an alley. He saved my life," Bradley affectionately glanced toward Rusty.

"It's like you two are inseparable. How can that be?"

They moved into the kitchen, the table set for two and furnished with a single new chair. Bradley described how he and Rusty became paired. He finished by saying that he thought Rusty got the short end of the stick. Zayt chuckled and formed a smile, the first Bradley had seen.

Bradley pulled two beers from Zayt's pack and put the rest in the refrigerator. He took out the steaks, gathered a set of tongs and a platter and went out through the sliders. Zayt and Rusty followed. Zayt saw a folding lawn chair on the deck with a price tag hanging from it but kept from making a comment.

With the steak on the grill, the two talked about the Boston Red Sox, Patriots, Bruins, and even the Revolution, New England's soccer team. Zayt loved hockey but did not enjoy soccer. Bradley countered that all sports had their own distinct qualities.

"I guess never getting to play any of them, I have a unique perspective on sports."

"Have you always been in a chair?"

Unconsciously, Bradley began to form the latest version of what put him in the wheelchair but then stopped himself. He told Zayt the truth.

"I was six years old playing catch with my dog in the backyard the first time my legs gave out. I spent months in the hospital before the doctors discovered I had contracted an enterovirus. It's a type of poliovirus that attacks the spinal cord. They say the odds are one in a million. Sometimes it's fatal. For me, it left both my legs paralyzed."

"Six. That must have been tough."

"Yeah. Well, we all have our crosses. What about you? Three tours?"

"I couldn't leave my guys behind. Just didn't feel right."

Bradley flipped the sizzling steaks.

"Are they all home now?"

"Depends on how you define home."

Bradley sensed a deep feeling of sorrow.

"Yeah, I guess that's true for a lot of people." He gazed down into the sandpit.

Bradley scooped the juicy steaks off the grill, placed them on the platter, handed it to Zayt, and shut the grill off. They moved inside.

"Just set that on the table. Could you put Rusty's dish on the floor over there, next to his water?" Bradley had planned and had the dog's food prepared already. But this time he added cooked rice to the canned food, one of the treats he picked up at the store for Rusty.

"No wonder he wants to stay with you," Zayt remarked.

Bradley laughed as he used an oversized glove to pull the hot dishes from the oven and set them on the table. He turned the oven off, placed the apple tart inside to warm, and shut the door.

"You like jazz?" he asked Zayt.

"I like all music."

Bradley found his favorite jazz station, and they sat down to eat.

"Jesus Christ, man. There's enough food here for my entire unit," Zayt exclaimed.

"I told you. I can't cook small portions of anything. And I'm getting tired of leftovers. This is the third time in three days I've eaten these potatoes."

"They're great. What kind of sauce is that?"

"Cauliflower."

"No shit."

Bradley laughed.

"No shit."

Bradley's phone rang. It was a local number he didn't recognize. He excused himself and answered.

"Hello?"

"Is this Agent Bradley Whitman?" the familiar voice asked.

"Yes."

"Agent Whitman, this is Sergeant Doyle from the Revere Police Department. We met the other day."

"Yes, Sergeant, I remember. What can I do for you?"

"I'm calling because we found your business card in the pocket of a female victim. A young woman, about five feet, seven inches, blonde hair, with a butterfly tattoo on her left ankle."

Bradley's heart thumped. He gripped the arm of his chair with his left hand and dropped his head.

"Sergeant, is she . . . is she . . ."

"She's alive, but she's in intensive care. The doctor put her in a medically induced coma. What can you tell me about her?"

"I just met her a couple days ago. Her name is Shea Powers. She's a real estate agent for First Class Realty. She came to me because her client wants to buy my property."

"Is that all you know about her?"

"No. I told her my property wasn't for sale, but she came back the next day and relayed a threat from her client. I called the bureau, and they investigated her. You can contact Agent Philbin at the Chelsea headquarters. He has the case."

Bradley paused before continuing. He pictured Shea's blonde hair bloody and matted.

"Sergeant, she's not a bad person. She's just had some bad breaks. What hospital is she in?"

"Massachusetts General. The doctor's name is Weaver. I'll call you if I have any more questions."

"Thank you, Sergeant."

Bradley had turned pale, and his left hand white-knuckled the arm of his chair.

"What happened?" Zayt asked.

"A woman I met the other day has been beaten up pretty bad. She's in a coma at Mass General. I'm sorry, but I'm going to have to leave. I can pack up the food for you."

Bradley had begun to gather his things to leave. He knew he had to get to the hospital and get there fast. He just hadn't reasoned why he felt so strongly about it.

"I'll go with you," he heard Zayt say.

"No. No, you don't have to do that," Bradley said.

"I'm going with you," Zayt said.

Bradley studied Zayt's eyes. Zayt had made up his mind, and there was no time or reason to try to change it. Bradley double checked to make sure the oven and stove were off before leaving. He decided to leave Rusty home. He didn't know how long it would take.

It took less than twenty minutes to get to the hospital and park the truck. Bradley knew the hospital well and headed straight for the intensive care unit. At the desk, he inquired about Shea. The nurse asked if he were family.

Bradley had learned of Shea's family status from Shea herself, confirmation of his previous profile.

"No. She doesn't have any family."

He showed the nurse his badge.

"Look, I'm not here to bother her. I just want to make sure she's okay and maybe talk to her doctor."

"Second door on the right. The doctor will be in shortly."

"Thank you."

Zayt followed Bradley down the corridor, and they waited outside the open door of Shea's room. Several people surrounded her, no curtain around her bed.

Bradley's pulse raced, and sweat formed on his upper lip. Both hands grasped his chair. When two nurses left the room,

Bradley got his first look at Shea. Dark crimson-stained white bandages wrapped around her head. The right side of her discolored and swollen face resembled an eggplant. A breathing tube hid her blueberry-colored chin and neck. She had bruises on both arms, but only the left had an IV line taped to it. Even though a white sheet covered her, Bradley knew the invading bruises reached further.

"Fucking bastards," Bradley muttered under his breath. The sound of hospital machines reverberated in the room, each echoing to him like the beat of a war drum.

"Hey, you alright?" Zayt looked at Bradley. "You're beet fuckin' red. Are you okay?"

Bradley relaxed his grip on the chair, closed his eyes, and took a few deep breaths.

"Yeah. I'm okay. I hope to God this isn't my fault," Bradley muttered.

"What do you mean? I assumed it was a mugging."

"Does that look like a mugging to you?" Bradley asked quietly.

Zayt took another look at the woman lying in the bed.

"No. It's overkill. Enough to warn you off but not enough to kill you," Zayt said.

Shea's doctor met them in the hallway.

"Are you her family?" she asked.

"Yes," Bradley answered, not wanting to waste any time explaining. "I'm Bradley, and this is Zayt. How is she? Is she going to be alright?"

"I'm Doctor Weaver. She's got severe swelling in her brain from a large contusion on the right side of her skull. We've put her in a medically induced coma to help her brain heal. She's got a broken nose, and her left eye has some damage, so I have a specialist coming to look at that, and multiple bruises to her body. No obvious signs of internal bleeding, but we will be doing more tests."

"How long will you keep her in the coma?" Bradley asked.

"There's no way of knowing. It depends on how her brain responds. We won't keep her under any longer than necessary. She's a tough young woman. We're going to help her every step of the way. Think positive."

"Thank you, doctor. Can I sit with her for a while?"

"Sure, but not too long."

"Okay. Thanks," Bradley almost whispered.

Bradley watched the doctor walk toward the nurse's desk. Sergeant Doyle got off the elevator in time to intercept her before she visited her next patient. They spoke for a moment, then Doyle noticed Bradley in the hallway and approached.

"I had a feeling you'd be here," Doyle said. He looked at Zayt and nodded his head.

"Sergeant Doyle, this is Zayt."

"Zayt? Interesting name. Nice to meet you."

They shook hands.

"Sergeant."

"Tell me what you've got," Bradley said.

"We got a call at 6:28 pm from an employee at the 7-Eleven convenience store on Park Street. He brought the trash out back to the dumpster and found her lying beside it. She wasn't beaten there, though. No signs of struggle or heavy blood stains in the area. We think she was dumped there so she would be found."

"What about their cameras? They must have picked something up," Bradley observed.

Doyle shook his head. "The outdoor cameras had been painted over, not sure when. They're not constantly monitored. Indoor cameras gave us nothing."

"Witnesses?"

"Still trying to track down all the customers that were in the store. We have a three-and-a-half-hour window of opportunity. That's a lot of customers."

"Dammit." Bradley slammed his hand down on his chair.

The nurses at the desk turned at the outburst.

"Easy, dude." Zayt put his hand on Bradley's shoulder.

"Sergeant, did you contact Agent Philbin?" Bradley asked.

"Yeah. I spoke with him a few minutes ago. He filled me in on the real estate investigation. He doubted it was related but said he wouldn't rule it out. He said he'll keep me informed."

"Goddammit. I should've just let her go. I shouldn't have made a big deal about it." Bradley slammed the arm of the chair again.

"Agent Whitman, this still could be a random mugging. You can't take responsibility for this. Even if it does have something to do with the real estate company, it's not your fault," Doyle said.

"Sergeant Doyle, this is no random mugging. Look at her." Bradley stared at Shea's beaten body.

"Yeah," Doyle could only think to say. Then, "I've got to get back to the station. I'll keep you posted on any leads."

"Thanks, Sergeant."

Doyle looked to Zayt, his soft expression conveyed empathy. Zayt silently nodded to Doyle as if to say, *I got this.* Doyle left.

Bradley rolled into Shea's room. Zayt followed. Bradley rested his hand on Shea's and bowed his head as if in prayer. But he didn't pray. He made a promise, a promise to Shea that he would find who had done this to her.

They sat quietly for the next five minutes before Bradley made a move to leave.

Zayt had resisted asking questions, but since Bradley seemed to have worked through his anger, he thought it time.

"You want to tell me what's going on here?" Zayt asked.

"I'll fill you in on the ride home," Bradley said as he made his way out of the intensive care unit.

When they got back to Bradley's place, they found Rusty waiting by the door, his stubbed tail wiggling back and forth so excitedly that he slipped and almost fell to the floor. Bradley nearly smiled.

Zayt went to Rusty and petted him while Bradley moved to a cabinet against the wall behind his couch, beneath his grandfather's bookshelves. He seized a bottle of Eagle Rare bourbon and brought it to the kitchen.

"Join me?" He held the bottle up so Zayt could see.

"You bet. I'll take it neat," Zayt said.

Bradley poured two fingers of bourbon into the glasses and brought them to the kitchen table. Their dinner still sat, hardly touched. Bradley thought how hard that must have been for Rusty not to eat any of the food from the table.

He and Zayt moved the dishes to the counter, neither one interested in eating cold steak and potatoes. Bradley did, however, retrieve the caramel-apple tart still in the oven, still slightly warm. He brought two dessert plates, two forks, and a knife to the table. Before settling in, he took the beef bone he had bought at the market earlier out of the refrigerator, unwrapped it, and gave it to Rusty.

"Yup, there's no getting rid of him now," Zayt joked and raised his glass.

Bradley raised his glass, looked at Rusty, and said, "That's okay by me."

"So, what do you think is going on?" Zayt asked.

"I don't know. This all happened so fast. I met the woman four days ago. She just started the job, and she isn't very good at it, but the client's company has been buying up property for three years, seventeen parcels so far."

Bradley's face went blank. He shifted his eyes to the ceiling. "That's a lot of willing property owners in only three years, don't you think?" He looked at Zayt.

Zayt took a sip of his bourbon and nodded his head in understanding.

"You're thinking there might be more incidents like this in the last three years. Maybe coercion?" Zayt speculated.

"It's certainly a possibility—that is, if this is all related. I'll call Doyle in the morning."

Bradley cut two large slices of the tart and placed one in front of Zayt.

"Damn, that's good," Zayt said around a mouthful.

After finishing dessert and draining the glass of bourbon, Zayt said, "I guess I should be going."

"I'll give you a ride." Bradley started to move.

"No need, really. It'll be quicker if I walk."

Bradley couldn't imagine how but knew better than to try to argue with the man.

"Wait. Take this with you." Bradley packed up his and Zayt's dinner and the rest of the leftover potatoes and handed the bag to Zayt.

Zayt stepped toward the door, then abruptly stopped. He turned to Bradley, serious and intense.

"It's true," he said.

"What's true?"

"About the money."

"Mamma Lise?"

"Yeah." Then Zayt turned and walked out the door.

Bradley hadn't been completely convinced, but Zayt confirmed Detective Rome's theory. And judging by his assertion, Bradley suspected that Zayt knew even more.

Bradley cleaned the kitchen as he contemplated the past five days and how quickly his life had become complicated. He moved to the office area.

The Berryman programs completed, Bradley thought he would begin analyzing them, but he just couldn't concentrate. His computer revealed it was almost ten o'clock. He thought about going to bed but found himself too unsettled. A lot of activity and revelations had occurred during the day, and he needed to take time to let them roost in his brain. He let Rusty out, then moved himself to the couch, put on some music, and leaned back.

But his time for rumination proved premature. The day had not finished with him yet.

Rousing Bradley from deep thought, Rusty pawed at the slider door. Confused and thinking maybe he had fallen asleep, Bradley looked at his watch, but it read a few minutes past ten. Rusty had been outside for only five or six minutes.

Bradley got himself back into his chair and let Rusty in. A note hung from his collar.

Call 911. We have another one.

Bradley placed his hand on his weighted chest and tried to rub the feeling away. He dialed the familiar Revere Police Department number.

"Revere Police Department."

"Can I speak to Detective Rome, please? This is Agent Bradley Whitman."

"I'm sorry, Agent. He isn't in the office tonight. Can I get you his voicemail?"

"No. How about Sergeant Doyle? Is he in?"

"Yes, sir. I'll connect you."

Bradley heard a couple of clicks.

"Sergeant Doyle," his voice gruff.

"Sergeant, this is Bradley Whitman. We've got another body in the sandpit."

"Holy mother of . . . ," he trailed off.

"I'm heading down there now. I'll meet you there." Bradley said.

"You're not there? How did you . . .?"

"Another note," Bradley said. He knew it would be impossible to shield Zayt any further, but he did not want to be the one to disclose the information.

Bradley and Rusty got into the truck and traveled the short distance to the access road. He planned on driving to Zayt's camp but saw the beam of a flashlight thirty feet from Zayt's shack. He headed toward the light.

Zayt stood outside a green tarp held up with sticks and splintered two-by-fours. Against the bottom edge of the tarp leaned a half sheet of graffiti-covered plywood.

From a distance, Bradley shone the truck headlights into the tent and saw a figure covered with dark blotches. Zayt came to Bradley's rolled down window.

"Same guy," Zayt said, his eyes like those of a wolf. A hunter determined to catch its prey.

"Face, too?" Bradley asked.

Zayt nodded.

They heard the sirens before they saw the flashing lights. First, two black and whites made their way to the horrid scene followed moments later by an unmarked SUV and then a sedan.

Sergeant Doyle exited the SUV and, seeing the sedan on its way, waited by his vehicle.

Detective Rome stepped out of the sedan and conferred with Doyle. Doyle pointed to Bradley's truck, where Zayt stood by the window. Rome approached the truck.

"Agent Whitman."

"Detective Rome, this is Zayt," Bradley said.

"Zayt. Is that your real name?" Rome asked.

"No, sir. Warrick Gaines."

Bradley raised an eyebrow.

"Did you find him, Mr. Gaines?"

"Yes, sir."

"Did you touch anything?"

"No, not tonight. Just flashed my light in his tent to check on him. Then I saw the mess and backed off. But I've been in there before," Zayt said.

"You wrote the note?"

"Yes, sir."

"You write the note the other night?"

"Yes, sir."

Rome grew stern. "Why didn't you come forward before now?"

Zayt looked at his feet, then lifted his head slowly and looked directly into the detective's eyes.

"Because I didn't think you would care."

It was Rome who broke eye contact.

"Do you know his name?" Rome asked.

"Gaffrey. Joe Gaffrey. He talked about an ex-wife in Somerville. He never mentioned her name."

"Why were you checking on him?"

"I check on all of them every night," he said, his voice monotone and quiet.

"Did you see anybody, anything unusual?"

"No, I wasn't here. I left around 6:15 and didn't get back until just before ten. That's when I found him. I didn't see anybody."

"Where were you?" Detective Rome asked.

Zayt looked at Bradley.

"He was with me. A woman got beaten, and we were at Mass General checking on her. Doyle can confirm it. He saw us there. Detective, if this is the same guy, then the murder-for-money theory doesn't work," Bradley said.

Rome's eyes glanced sideways at Bradley, surprised he had divulged the money motive with Zayt standing there.

Bradley shrugged his shoulders.

"Zayt already knows. You wanted me to ask him about her money, so I did," Bradley said as he glanced Zayt's way.

In return he received an intense, pointed stare.

Bradley felt the prick.

"Wait here," Rome said, then went to examine the crime scene.

"You lied to me," Zayt said, his voice low and angry as he glared at Bradley.

"I did. I'm sorry. I had to make sure you weren't involved. My instincts told me you weren't, but I had to make sure. This was the quickest way I could think of. I'm sorry."

Zayt walked away. Bradley watched him with a pit in his stomach, the same feeling he got every time he did something he was not proud of.

Bradley turned to Rusty sitting upright in the passenger seat and said, "I think I screwed this one up, buddy."

Rusty reached out his paw for Bradley to hold.

Rome returned with Doyle.

"Where's Mr. Gaines?" Rome asked.

"Over there in his shack." Bradley motioned to the back side of Zayt's camp. He smelled the beginnings of a campfire.

Detective Rome walked toward Zayt's shanty.

"What do you think is happening here?" Bradley asked Doyle.

"Well, it could be the beginnings of a serial killer. Easy prey, helpless, secluded. And he's got a signature, a gruesome signature. Three deep stab wounds to the face, just like the first victim. Or it could be a deeply disturbed individual who just doesn't like the fact that homeless people are living here."

"If this is a serial killer, these weren't his first murders." Bradley said.

"How can you be so sure?"

"You said the stab wounds were deep. If these were his first victims, the wounds would be more tentative. And most serial killers develop a signature over time, not with their initial victims."

"Hell of a night, huh?" Doyle said.

"Hell of a night," Bradley repeated.

When Detective Rome returned, he asked Bradley what he thought about Zayt.

"I think he's an honorable man. He cares about these people, deeply. He served three tours in Afghanistan because he couldn't bear to leave his buddies behind. And I feel like shit for lying to him."

"Well, at least we can rule out the money angle now," Rome said.

"Did you ask him about it?" Bradley asked.

"Yeah. He said he doesn't know where it is. But that's the insurance company's problem, not mine."

"Do you need me for anything else, Detective?"

"No. We're done here. But we will need your camera feed from tonight. Can you send it to me?"

"Sure."

Bradley drove slowly by Zayt, who sat staring into his campfire and never lifted his head to acknowledge Bradley.

Back home, Bradley could not stop thinking about him. He betrayed Zayt's confidence and, because of that, doubted he would see him again. But he decided he would try.

Although Bradley made friends easily, he didn't have many close ones. He considered Derek and Cate his closest along with the others from the cruise. But, other than Derek, he didn't see them much. He used his job as an excuse not to bond with people. But his reluctance to form personal connections ran deeper. His need for independence bordered on obsessive. Unless he orchestrated it, he vehemently disliked when people perceived him in need of help. Yet he had done just that to lure Zayt to his home.

Bradley's duplicity felt paradoxical.

He couldn't be sure if he had purposely exposed his lie to Zayt when he spoke of Detective Rome's suggestion that he talk to him about Mamma Lise's missing money. *Did I consciously sabotage what could have been a close friendship?*

He didn't like the thought. He looked at Rusty lying next to him on the floor. He already felt closer to the dog than to any of the colleagues he'd known for years. He would lay down his life for any one of them, but he wouldn't join them for a beer after a hard day's work.

His camera footage showed much the same images as the footage at the time of the previous murder. A vehicle up on the hill, a dark figure appearing then disappearing into the night. Bradley forwarded the images to Detective Rome.

Exhausted, he hooked Rusty to the leash, and they went outside. It was nearly midnight. Lights had been placed around the crime scene, and Zayt's fire still blazed as Bradley watched the coroner's wagon leave. Bradley could barely keep his eyes open. He just wanted to put the horrible day behind him.

BYE, BYE, BERRYMAN

Bradley welcomed the mundane work of matching Berryman's billings to bank deposits and bank deposits to travel dates, wire transfers, and ACH transfers. What better way to spend a Sunday morning? Besides, it distracted him from the fact that he had sent a note with Rusty that morning to Zayt, but when Rusty returned, the note was gone and nothing took its place. The note he wrote simply said, *Please let me explain.*

While analyzing the finances, Bradley found that Juliette Berryman deposited much more money than her fraudulent billing system accounted for. Millions more. However, Bradley could not find a source for the money. What made it more interesting is that the amount of excess money exactly matched the dollar amount of deposits made by wire transfers. Bradley separated those transactions from the rest.

Even without the wire transfers, Bradley knew they had enough evidence to put Juliette Berryman and her home healthcare cohort away for a very long time. The hard work done, Bradley wrote his report and an outline for wading through the information he had sorted and sent them to Nick. Then, even though it was Sunday, he picked up the phone and called Nick. He would want to hear what Bradley had to say.

"What's up, dogman?" Nick answered.

Bradley wasn't in the mood for banter.

"I just sent you the Berryman report and the sorted files. It's enough for conviction. But, I found something interesting."

"What?"

"There's millions of dollars, the origin unaccounted for. She made significant wire transfers to thirteen different Berryman bank accounts. The dollar amounts range from seven thousand to nine thousand and change. She kept them under the ten-thousand-dollar mandatory Internal Revenue Service reporting threshold and never deposited the same amount twice. I'm pretty sure she's running a money laundering scheme on top of her fraudulent activity."

"Holy hit-the-jackpot shit!" Nick yelled.

"I'm sending the files separate from the fraud case. I just wanted to give you a heads up."

"You're the best, man! When are you going to the office next?" Nick asked.

"I'm not sure, why?"

"I'm going to buy a big-ass bone for that dog of yours," he laughed.

Bradley managed a chuckle.

"Put your best foot forward on this one, Nick, and you might just get a promotion."

"Sounds good to me. And thanks, Bradley. Let's celebrate when this is over, huh?" Nick said.

"Yeah, you bet." Bradley knew he lied.

Bradley called Derek.

"Richards," Derek answered his phone.

"Hey, Derek. Sorry to bother you at home, but I thought you'd want to hear this."

Bradley ran through the information with Derek as he had with Nick.

"Any guesses where the money is coming from?" Derek asked.

"No. It wasn't even on my radar. But I can't think of anything other than money laundering that could produce that much cash. I think we should treat this as a separate case. No need to hold up the fraud investigation," Bradley suggested.

"I agree. I'll talk to Nick tomorrow and tell him we will tackle the possible laundering scheme separate from the fraud case."

"We had another murder last night. Another homeless person in the sandpit. Looks like the same perpetrator. He's got a signature. I'm going to run a database check to see if I can find any similar unsolved cases."

"Jesus," Bradley heard Derek sigh. Then, "Keep me posted."

"Have you talked to Agent Philbin?" Bradley asked.

"No, why?"

"That real estate woman, Shea Powers. She was assaulted. Bad enough that they put her in a coma. It looked like someone wanted to send a message." Bradley's voice tremored, then trailed off on the last part of his statement.

"Hey," Derek snapped.

"Yeah?"

"It's not your fault. None of this is your fault."

"Yeah."

After hanging up with Derek, Bradley logged into the database and started a search for victims of facial stab wounds. Such searches could take hours, sometimes days. The program would alert him by text when complete.

Bradley phoned the office main number and asked for Agent Philbin.

"I'm sorry, Agent Whitman. Agent Philbin isn't in the office today. Would you like his voicemail?" the voice said.

"Yes, thank you," Bradley replied.

After the recording, Bradley left his message: "*Agent Philbin, this is Agent Whitman. I'm calling to talk to you about the Powers case. I was wondering if you've made any progress on her assailant. Please call me as soon as you can at 555-2121.*"

It was midafternoon by the time Bradley felt he could speak with his parents without worrying them. His mother could always sense when something bothered him or if he held something back. The weekly Sunday phone calls usually served to relax him, center him, and remind him that work isn't all there is to life although Bradley always had trouble with the last part. His work defined him because he wanted it that way.

He touched the preprogrammed contact name on his phone.

"Hello, Bradley. We were wondering if you forgot us," his mother, Lynn, said. "I'll put you on speaker."

"Hey, Mom, Dad. How are you two doing this week?"

"Well, your mother has got me cleaning out the garage. I've got a pile for you to go through next time you can get here," his father, Doug, chuckled.

"Great, more junk. Just give whatever it is to the Salvation Army or somebody. I'm sure there's nothing I can't live without."

"But Bradley, your science awards from elementary school are in there with your top hat lights. And remember the stuffed dolphin you won for me when we took that cruise? That's there, too," Lynn said.

"I gave that to you, Mom. I don't want it," Bradley said.

"Oh. I just thought you might." His mom sounded disappointed.

"Alright, I'll go through the stuff next time I'm there."

"How about coming to dinner next Sunday?" she asked.

"Yeah, we can watch the ball game," Doug added.

"Maybe. I'll have to see what my schedule is like."

"What's the matter, Bradley? You sound tired," Lynn said.

"It's just been a busy week, Mom."

"Does it have anything to do with the murder behind your place?" Doug asked.

"What are the newspapers saying?" Bradley asked.

"Not much. Just that a homeless woman was killed at that location. They speculated it was another homeless person who killed her."

"Huh. Well, I haven't read the local news lately. I'm finishing a big case I've been working on the last month. You'll be reading about it in the papers in another week or so."

"Can't you give us a little hint? You know, a preview?" his dad asked.

"Derek would have my head. You know that, Dad."

"How is Derek? And Cate?" Lynn asked.

"Doing good. At least Derek is. I haven't seen Cate in a while. She keeps inviting me to dinner, but I'm afraid she's going to invite one of her single female friends to ambush me."

"What would be so bad about that?" Lynn asked.

"I already have a companion," Bradley teased.

Lynn's voice raised an octave. "Oh, really? Who is she?"

"He, Mom. His name is Rusty. And before you get too sentimental, I should mention that he's a dog. A Doberman Pinscher."

"You got a dog?" Doug asked.

"Well, he sort of found me. His owner passed away, and I found him in an alley. He's smart, fully trained, and he likes it here. So, I decided to keep him."

"Well, that's nice, sweetheart. I'm happy you have some company," Lynn said less than enthusiastically.

"What's the matter, Mom? You like dogs."

"Yes, but I always hoped your first roommate would be of the Homo sapiens variety. You know, someone you can have a conversation with," Lynn explained.

"Wait till you meet Rusty. He translates more useful information with one look in his eyes than most people speak in a day," Bradley laughed.

"Bring him with you next Sunday. Invite Derek and Cate if you want, too," his dad said.

"Maybe. We'll see. Listen, I've got to get back to work. I want to have this report ready for the morning," Bradley lied.

"Okay, son. Thanks for the call," Doug replied.

"I love you, Bradley. Please try to make it next Sunday," Lynn pleaded.

"Love you, too, Mom. Dad."

He hated lying to his parents, but he just wasn't in the mood to present a happy façade. He wasn't happy. He felt angry. Angry at the bastard killing homeless people and angry at the coward who beat a woman nearly to death. And guilty. Guilty knowing it could have been his fault that Shea lay in a coma at Mass General.

Watching a ball game did not sit on top of his priority list.

Rusty jumped to his feet, ran to the door, and stood. Bradley checked his front-door camera image, moved to the door, and waited for a knock. Three sharp wraps. The cameras revealed who stood on the other side.

Bradley took a deep breath and let it out slowly. He put a smile on his face and opened the door.

"Hey, Cate, Derek. What are you guys doing here?" Bradley had an inkling already.

Cate looked beautiful, as beautiful as the day he met her sixteen years before when he was a twelve-year-old boy. Her dazzling green eyes could shoot straight into your heart. Always fashionable but never pretentious, she turned heads wherever she went. And, as Bradley always said, she was even more beautiful on the inside than on the outside.

"Bradley!" She flung her arms around him and sat on his lap. "I've missed you so much." She kissed his cheek. "You wouldn't come to me, so I came to you," she explained.

Bradley looked at Derek, eyebrows raised. Derek, holding a bottle of wine, just stood and smiled.

Then Cate saw Rusty. She hopped off Bradley's lap and bent down to greet him. Rusty raised his paw to her.

"Oh, he's gorgeous. Derek told me about him. I think it's so great you are giving him a home."

"He didn't give me much choice," Bradley laughed.

Derek moved to the kitchen, went straight to the drawer with the corkscrew, and pulled the cork. Knowing just where to find them, he reached for three glasses and poured.

"She insisted that we come to meet him," Derek said.

In the background, Cate talked babytalk to Rusty. "Oh, youse a good boy. Pretty boy. Can you give me your paw? . . ."

"Right. I'm sure that's why you drove all the way out here," Bradley sarcastically said.

"All the way out here is only twenty-five minutes, Bradley. It's not like we live in Montana," said Derek.

"What are you doing here, Derek? Really."

"He told me you were having a tough week," Cate said. Bradley shot a glare at Derek. Seeing that, she continued. "He didn't tell me why. He just said it's been a hard week. It was my idea to come and visit. Besides, I really did want to meet Rusty."

"Well, Cate, I appreciate you wanting to console me or whatever this is, but I'm fine. I've had tough weeks before and survived."

Cate picked up two of the wine glasses and brought one to Bradley.

"Is that all you want to do, Bradley? Survive?"

Bradley took the wine, lowered his head, and softened his expression.

"Okay, Cate. You win," Bradley said.

"I usually do."

They clinked their glasses together.

Derek let out a sigh and relaxed his shoulders. He had been leery about the visit. He knew Bradley could be defensive when people tried to help him. But Cate was good at neutralizing him. She always had been.

"Hey, I just got off the phone with my folks. They wanted me to say hi."

"How are they? We really need to plan a night out," Cate said.

"Mom's got Dad cleaning the garage," Bradley laughed.

"Don't give Cate any ideas," Derek chuckled.

"Hey, you have an actual chair," Cate noticed the seat at the kitchen table.

"Yeah, Rusty likes to sit at the table for dinner," Bradley joked.

"You don't really," Cate said, flabbergasted.

Derek and Bradley laughed.

"Oh, Cate. I love how gullible you can be sometimes," Bradley said.

With the back of her hand, Cate lovingly hit Bradley on the arm. "Do you want to sit outside? It's a beautiful day," she declared.

"Ah, let me check." Bradley went out back to see if the police presence had cleared. Everything was gone except the police tape. Returning, Bradley said, "Yeah, let's sit out here. Derek, bring Rusty's chair."

He grinned.

Cate stuck her tongue out at Bradley, then laughed.

"I miss you so much. How can we live so close and not see each other for months?" She sat in the outdoor lawn chair.

"Come on, Rusty. Come on out," Bradley said, evading the question.

Rusty bounded out the door and down the embankment into the sandpit.

Derek sat in the new kitchen chair and inspected the pit below. He saw the tape and looked at Bradley who nodded inconspicuously and then turned attention back to the green tarped area. Cate never noticed.

"Where's Rusty going?" Cate asked.

"Oh, he's got friends down there." The heavy feeling that had diminished began to return. He looked down at his unsoiled sneakers.

Rusty headed directly to Zayt's shack. The three watched him go inside. A moment later, Zayt and Rusty appeared.

"Who's that?" Cate asked.

"His name is Zayt. He's a veteran of Afghanistan. Three tours."

Derek whistled. "Three?"

"Yeah."

"And that's where he lives?" Cate asked sadly.

"He says he likes it there."

Bradley did not want Cate to feel bad.

Derek sat quiet, but Bradley knew he had questions.

"How are Sheila and David?"

Bradley changed the subject.

"Oh, my sister's fine. David is producing a new movie. It's an adapted screenplay from one of the books Holly's publishing company recommended. Sheila said David thinks it's going to be a big box office hit."

"Wow, that's pretty cool."

"I keep telling Derek that we have to go to the movie premiere. You should come, too. We could have a cruise ship reunion in Hollywood."

Cate became animated.

"When will that be?"

"Oh, I don't know. They're just starting to shoot the film. It could take years," Cate said.

"Well, then. I'll clear my schedule," Bradley laughed.

"You are such a smartass, Bradley Whitman," she giggled.

They chatted as the wine bottle emptied. Bradley watched Zayt cut wood, converse with a few of the residents, and play with Rusty. Zayt never looked up toward his place.

"We should get going, Cate. I'm sure Bradley didn't plan for us to take up his entire afternoon," Derek said.

"I do have someplace I need to be," Bradley admitted.

"Okay, we'll go. But not before we pin down a time for dinner," Cate said.

"My parent's house next Sunday afternoon." Bradley surprised both Derek and Cate with the quick response.

"Really?" Cate asked.

"Really. I'll give Derek the details during the week," Bradley promised.

Cate gave Bradley a big hug and made him promise to hug Rusty for her. Derek and Bradley shook hands.

"You in the office tomorrow?" Derek asked.

"Yeah, I'll see you there," Bradley stated.

After they left, Bradley sighed. He found it exhausting to pretend everything was fine with his insides full of dread. Bradley had a lot of experience in the matter. Even as a child, not wanting them to worry any more than they already did, he tried to keep his spirits up in front of his parents. He did the same with his teachers, therapists, classmates, doctors, and bosses. He even did it with himself on occasion—a tricky, yet sometimes liberating experience. He likened the process to meditation, except instead of emptying his mind, he filled it with an alternate reality, one where he ran through a meadow or walked with a child on his shoulders.

Another sigh.

He whistled for Rusty and watched for a reaction. Rusty turned and ran toward the ledge and easily bounded to the top. Zayt ducked back into his shack.

"Let's go for a ride, buddy," Bradley said.

Bradley and Rusty got into the truck and headed to Massachusetts General Hospital. Once parked, Bradley rolled down the truck windows partway and left Rusty inside with a bowl of water. He did not expect to stay long.

Sundays in the hospital are mostly peaceful, with a reduced staff of doctors and others on call instead of on the premises. Of all the time Bradley spent in the hospital, he looked forward to Sundays most.

He signed in at the ICU nursing station and went directly to Shea's room. A nurse was checking her IV and vital statistics and made notes on the clipboard.

Noticing Bradley enter the room, she politely said, "Hello."

"Hello," Bradley returned. "How is she doing today?"

"Her vital signs are slightly improved today," she smiled as she whispered.

"That's good news," Bradley said softly.

The nurse nodded and left the room.

Bradley noticed Shea wore a clean head bandage and that the swelling in her face had gone down with a yellow hue around the edges.

Once again, heaviness invaded his chest, a feeling of utter helplessness, the same irrepressible feeling from his childhood that would send him into a deep depression for days. He closed his eyes and pictured a dolphin with him swimming alongside.

He steadied his breathing, in then out, in then out. He continued for several minutes. The heaviness subsided.

When he opened his eyes, he saw a woman standing in the doorway. She displayed flowing chestnut hair that dropped past her shoulders, silky brown skin with eyes the color of the waning sun, golden with shards of fiery umber, long thick lashes, and high cheekbones to complement her oval face. She wore dark-framed glasses and red lipstick and dressed casually. She looked familiar, but he couldn't recall why.

"I'm sorry. I only stopped in for a moment," he said, wondering if she were a distant relative.

"No. No. I'm sorry to interrupt. I just stopped in to check on her," the familiar voice said.

Bradley realized then that the woman was Dr. Weaver, Shea's doctor. He didn't recognize her without her work clothes and her hair up.

"Dr. Weaver. I'm sorry. I didn't recognize you. I'm Bradley. We met last night."

"Yes, I remember."

"Please, do what you need to. I'll wait in the hall."

"No need. I'm just going to check her chart."

Bradley moved to the hall anyway and waited.

She checked the chart and examined the IV and monitor, then met him in the hall.

"So, what do you think?" he asked.

"I think she is a strong-willed woman. She is showing promising signs, but we aren't out of the woods yet."

"I know you can't be sure, but how long does it usually take for swelling in the brain to reduce enough for you to take her out of the coma?"

"I'm sorry, Bradley. I can't give you a time frame. It would be tantamount to trying to guess the winning lottery numbers. Every brain trauma is different. She suffered a very deep contusion. We just need to be patient."

"I understand. Thank you."

"She is getting the best of care."

"Yes, I know. This is the best place for her. Are you done work for the day?" He wondered whether she was coming or going.

"I'm not working today. I just wanted to check on her."

"I really appreciate that," he smiled.

"Are you her boyfriend, brother?" She asked.

"Oh, no. I'm sorry. I lied last night. She doesn't have any family. I'm a friend," Bradley confessed.

"Well, I can see you care for her, so I'll pretend I didn't hear that."

"Thank you."

Dr. Weaver walked away. Bradley felt alone. Another of those feelings that, when it arose, he concealed from everyone around him.

TRAIN WRECK

Sometimes Bradley allowed himself to live on the dark side of the emotional spectrum but never for very long. He decided it was time to alter his disposition. Monday morning, feeling the need for a greater than normal endorphin surge, he performed a rigorous workout.

His murky morning took a turn. Whether it happened because of the positive energy he worked hard to emanate or because he conducted himself as a nuisance, he didn't know.

That morning he had sent Rusty outside with another note. This one read, **Don't be an ass. I fucked up. I'm sorry.** He wrote the note before his workout, which probably worked to his advantage.

Rusty returned with a message. **_YOU_ are the ass. I'm coming up.**

His hair hadn't dried from his shower when Rusty alerted him to Zayt's arrival.

"Hey," Bradley said.

"Hey," Zayt replied.

"Come on in. You want coffee? A protein shake?"

"You got juice?"

"Yeah. Orange or apple?"

"Orange."

Bradley brought Zayt a large glass of orange juice and set it on the kitchen table.

"Alright, let's hash this out," Bradley said. "I know I fucked up, and I won't make any excuses, but . . ."

Zayt raised an eyebrow.

"Look, I was just doing my job. Well, not my job, the job that Detective Rome asked me to do. I told him you had nothing to do with the murder. I knew that from the start. I should have been more up front with you. Again, I'm sorry."

Zayt drank his juice and then spoke directly. "I get it. I mean, you really pissed me off, but I get it. Let's forget about it. How's the girl?"

"I went to see her last night. They still have her in a coma, but her vitals are a little better. I ran into her doctor. I hadn't noticed that first night, but Dr. Weaver is hot."

"Hot? She's hot? You really are a tech weenie," Zayt winced.

"What's wrong with hot?"

"It's seventies white boy speak. Now, I'd say she's fine."

"Fine? That's black dude eighties," Bradley said. Zayt grew quiet.

Then neither could hold back laughter.

"I've been thinking. There's something strange about these killings." Zayt turned serious. "If this dude picks his victims randomly, why risk coming back to the same place?"

"RPD has a theory it could be a serial killer," Bradley told him. "I'm not buying it, but I'm checking the FBI database for similar modi operandi. They also said they've had complaints about the city allowing homeless to camp there. Could be one of them."

Bradley moved to his office, and Zayt followed. Bradley checked his email.

"The program must still be running." He logged on to a search engine and typed the words, *sandpit in Revere.*

Zayt retrieved the stool from the workout area and brought it to the desk. The first search result recounted the murder of

Mamma Lise, although it did not contain her name. Other topic headlines involved complaints to the city about use of the property, the history of the property, and a map of the area. But none of those interested Bradley as much as the one that began *City contemplating the sale of*.

Bradley clicked on the result. It brought him to the *Boston Herald* website and an article published two years before about a company named Eastern Entertainment Alliance. He and Zayt both read the article silently. Eastern Entertainment Alliance made a proposal to the town of Revere for purchase of the sandpit property in order to build a casino. It went on to say that the city council would review the proposal.

Bradley turned to Zayt.

"Have you heard anything about this?" Bradley asked.

Zayt shook his head.

Bradley typed *Casino project in Revere* into the search area of the *Boston Herald* website.

Pages of article headings surfaced, dating back four years. Bradley clicked on the most recent, published nearly four months earlier.

REVERE—Mayor Robert Reynolds, an outspoken proponent of the Revere Casino Project, has urged the city council to move forward with sale of the city-owned former Stansworth Sandpit Company property. The industrial property, located between Industrial Drive and Howland Street, has become a preferred location for the homeless to take refuge. Other proponents of the casino project include Governor Harold North, Construction Tycoon Webster Collins, and local television personality Linda Poule.

City Councilwoman Frances Bates has spoken publicly of her opposition to selling the property to Eastern Entertainment

Alliance. She argues that the use of the property serves better for the city's constituents than a for-profit corporation. She said, "I feel a casino would bring crime to the area and foster a gambling mentality which could prove devastating for some."

Other locals who oppose building a casino include Steven May, veteran's affairs director; the non-profit group Massachusetts Green to Lean; and Restaurant Association of Massachusetts, RAM.

The city council will make a recommendation about purchasing the sandpit to the mayor next month.

"I can't believe I haven't heard about this," Bradley stated, "although I don't read the papers or watch much local news. I guess I shouldn't be surprised."

"The article says the city council made their recommendation three months ago. So, what happened? Why isn't there an article about that?" Zayt asked.

Bradley searched the *Herald* website again, then the *Boston Globe* site, and those of other area newspapers. There hadn't been anything printed in the past four months.

Bradley picked up his phone and called Derek.

"Richards."

"Hey, Derek. You got a minute?"

"Sure, Bradley. What time should we be there?" Derek asked.

"What? Where?"

"Your parents'. Sunday."

"Oh. I don't know yet. Listen. Do you know anything about the Revere Casino Project?" Bradley asked.

"Yeah, of course. Pretty contentious issue."

"What's happening with it now? There's nothing in the news."

"Are you serious? Bradley, do you live with your head in that sandpit of yours?"

"I guess I do. What's going on?"

"A week before the city council prepared to make its recommendation, one of the councilwomen passed away. The city postponed the proposal until the city can hold a special election this spring. I guess they thought the issue too important to proceed without a full-board recommendation."

"Which councilwoman? Do you remember?"

"I don't remember her name."

"Bates? Councilwoman Bates?" Bradley closed his eyes as he spoke her name.

"Yeah, that's it. What's this about, Bradley?"

"How did she die?"

"Remember the MBTA subway derailment back in December? A bunch of people got hurt and five people died. She was one of the dead. What's going on? Why are you asking about this?"

"I'm not sure yet. I'll get back to you. Thanks, Derek."

Bradley hung up the phone and told Zayt what he had learned. The two sat quietly.

"Well, that would be a leap," Bradley said.

Zayt tilted his head to the right. "Just because it sounds crazy doesn't mean there's nothing to it."

"Alright. Let's hash this out," Bradley said.

"Really? Is that your go-to phrase? Hash it out?"

"What? Too white boy for you?"

"No. Too teenage boy for me."

Bradley just shook his head.

"We know Bates was going to vote no. She would only need two more votes to shoot it down. If she held the majority, it would be an uphill battle to push the project through, right?" Bradley speculated.

"Yeah," Zayt answered.

"Are we really contemplating that someone would cause a train accident, kill an untold number of people, and hurt a lot more to keep the city council from voting no on the casino project? Kill all those people to hide one murder?"

"Yeah," Zayt answered.

"And now that the project is on hold, they are murdering homeless people who live on the property to make the city think it's in the best interest to sell?"

Bradley let the scenario play out in his head.

"Yeah."

"Well, thanks for your input. You've been a big help," Bradley uttered.

Zayt had been listening, head down, hands folded in front of him. He lifted his head slightly. His eyes and eyebrows raised in unison.

"Don't forget the girl."

Bradley paused. "Shea."

He'd hoped he had been wrong about her. But no matter how he tried to dissuade himself, her beating kept circling back to him. Had her client found out she talked to the FBI? Or had she gotten beaten up because Bradley refused to sell?

Either way, Bradley concluded that he had caused it.

"So it was my fault," Bradley murmured.

"In the same way Mamma Lise and Joe were mine," Zayt sighed.

"Each one of these incidents, taken separately, is horrendous. You put them together, you have a psychopath with the perfect job."

They considered the weight of their conjecture. Both hoped they were wrong, but each feared the opposite.

"I've got a lot of research to do. You can stay if you want, but I warn you, once I go into a data dive, I don't come up for air until I've found a thread," Bradley said.

"Jesus, you're a strange dude."

"Like I haven't heard that before."

"Send me a note when you've got something."

Bradley had already jumped into his research and never acknowledged Zayt's leaving. Questions churned in his brain. He tried to sort them into a logical order.

Where to start?

Into the search bar he typed Eastern Entertainment Alliance. A link brought him to the company's colorful website with pictures of happy patrons in theatres, casinos, theme parks, and restaurants. A cheery jingle played in the background as he browsed the site. A list of venues allowed the user to find information for any single business including address, contact information, and services. For restaurants, menus of food offerings displayed as well as the chef's biography, manager's experience, and bar/lounge activities. Theatres boasted new Broadway and off-Broadway shows, including local and experimental theatre. EEA owned three casino/hotels: two in Las Vegas and one in New York. Bradley clicked on the *Coming Soon!* tab. The third listing on the page depicted a beautiful rendering of the intended Revere, Massachusetts, facility. Upper floor hotel rooms held virtual views of Boston Harbor. The interactive website allowed the user to walk virtually through the casino and hotel lobby.

"Wow!" Bradley exclaimed out loud. The site presented the casino as if it were a done deal. The projected opening date read October 2025.

He looked around for Zayt to relay the information, then recalled he had left. But that was okay. Bradley had a lot more diving to do.

For several hours Bradley swam through industries, corporations, enterprises, and limited liability companies that comprised Eastern Entertainment Alliance. Each of the businesses unveiled their own CEOs, CFOs, and COOs.

After four hours of research, Bradley still had no idea who owned Eastern Entertainment Alliance. He did know that someone—or group of people—had amassed an organization so grossly entangled and secretive that detection of improprieties could take years and, if detected, would give the offenders ample time to liquidate and disappear.

He called Derek.

"Hey, Derek. Are you available around three o'clock today?"

"Uh, let me check. Make it three-thirty?" Derek asked.

"Great. Could you call Detective Rome from RPD and see if he can join us? And Agent Philbin also? I would call them, but the invitation would mean more coming from you."

"I can do that. Just tell me what this is about."

"We might have a connection between the homeless murders and the beating of Shea Powers, the real estate agent."

"Does this have to do with what you called about earlier?" Derek asked.

"Yeah. I think so. We at least need to have the conversation to find out."

Bradley didn't want to commit too much to his speculation in case he turned out wrong.

CONNECT THE SHELLS

Rusty would need to go outside before they left for the office, so Bradley decided to update Zayt. **Heading to office to discuss connection. Fill you in tonight,** he wrote on a piece of notepaper.

Turn on your outside light when you get back, came the reply attached to Rusty's collar.

Bradley gathered his notes, and he and Rusty left for Chelsea.

Carl smiled when he saw Rusty. Without question he handed Bradley a visitor tag. Bradley rolled to the elevator, and they proceeded to the eighth floor. A little early for his meeting, he looked for Nick but saw only Mara at her desk.

"Hey, Mara. How's the case going?" Bradley asked.

"Moving along. I swear Juliette Berryman doesn't have a decent bone in her body. I guess I don't have to tell you."

"She is cruel. Especially to her male clients. She stole their medications, for chrissake, then sold them on the black market. This will be a good boost for you guys. It will look great on your record."

"I don't care about that," Mara said. "I'm just glad we may be able to nail her. Thanks to you."

"All I did was work the numbers. You guys still need to finish it. Speaking of that, where is Nick?"

"Oh, I thought that was why you were here. He's got Juliette in Interrogation Room A right now."

"Hey, can I leave Rusty with you? He won't be a bother."

"Sure. Hey. Rusty, come here, boy."

Rusty went to Mara.

"Stay here, Rusty," Bradley commanded.

Rusty lay on the floor beside Mara and watched Bradley head down the hall. Interrogation Room A was the first door on the left, the same design as Room B. Bradley could see Juliette Berryman on the left side of the table with a well-dressed woman seated beside her. Nick stood across from Juliette, and Jim sat beside him.

Bradley entered the third door on the left, the same room where he listened to Joanne Goyette's interrogation. Derek once again sat listening, this time to the conversation, coming from Room A. He nodded as Bradley entered.

". . . signed affidavits. They all say the same thing," Nick smiled.

"I have no knowledge of what my employees do with their own money, Agent Gaston." Juliette's smug reply oozed confidence.

"Even though you, as owner and chief operating officer of Berryman Home Healthcare, have access to their accounts?" Nick stated incredulously.

"My client does not admit to having access to the accounts of her employees," Juliette's counsel said.

Derek turned the speaker off as he addressed Bradley. "You positive we have enough on this . . . woman . . . to put her away?" His jaw tightened as he glared at the speaker box.

"Positive. She's smart, and she was careful. But once I found the thread in the tapestry, it all unraveled," Bradley smiled.

Derek chuckled. "You do have a way with words, Agent Whitman."

Bradley grinned.

They left Nick to his interrogation and went to Derek's office. His corner room had a view of Mystic River in the distance. Two walls of glass let light into the workspace. Behind his desk, Derek's wall displayed commendations, certificates, and pictures. A photograph of three people on a boat deck with a cargo ship in the distance stood out.

Bradley knew the photo well along with another that accompanied it. On the cruise where they all met, his friend Holly had unintentionally snapped the photo of three crime family employees involved in a high priority heist. Derek, a field agent at the time, stole Holly's camera to gain possession of the photo. The photo next to it, taken on the last day of the cruise, exhibited Bradley at age twelve surrounded by his family and cruise ship friends as he received a commendation from the then FBI executive assistant director.

"We have a few minutes before they show. You want to fill me in?" Derek asked.

Bradley dropped his head and rubbed the back of his neck.

"I don't like being this unsure about something, but it's nagging me. I might be stretching. I think the murders in the sandpit, the assault of the real estate woman, and . . . the death of Councilwoman Bates could be connected."

Derek's eyes widened. He could understand the murders and the assault could possibly relate, although he had no idea how. But the accidental death of a city councilwoman?

"Bradley, how can a train accident be connected to the beating of a woman found beside a dumpster?"

"I know. I know," Bradley said as someone knocked on the door.

"In," Derek called. "Agent Philbin, come in." Derek waved him to a chair.

Philbin and Bradley acknowledged each other with head bobs.

"I got your message this morning. Sorry I didn't get back to you right away. I got hung up," Philbin said to Bradley.

"I understand. No problem," Bradley replied.

Another knock brought Detective Rome into the room.

"Detective Rome, I presume?" Derek said. "I'm Derek Richards. Nice to finally meet you. This is Agent Mark Philbin, and you know Agent Whitman."

They all shook hands.

"Please, sit down."

"Go ahead, Bradley. The floor is yours," Derek directed.

"Okay. For Detective Rome's benefit, let me outline one of your current cases, Agent Philbin. You are working the case of a woman named Shea Powers because she approached me about selling my property on Industrial Drive. The company she works for, First Class Realty, has a client who wants it. When I emphatically refused to sell the property, Shea returned with what I would call a veiled threat from her client.

"That's where you came in, Agent. I called you, and you interviewed her. Two days later, Officer Doyle of the Revere Police Department found Shea Powers lying beaten almost to death next to a dumpster. Can you tell us what you have on the case so far?"

Detective Rome showed confusion. With a sideways tilt of his head, Bradley silently advised that the detective should be patient.

"Miss Powers is still in a medically induced coma and has yet to be interviewed," said Agent Philbin. "We didn't get anything from the cameras at the convenience store where they dumped her. Someone painted over them. The surrounding businesses didn't catch anything, either.

"So far interviews with the customers have proved useless," he continued. "The best we have is a dark SUV parked near the dumpster somewhere between 5 pm and 6 pm. The automatic lights on the back of the store are on a timer, but they don't come on until 7 pm, so it's pretty dark in the back corner around that time of night."

Philbin paused. "We've got nothing." He sighed and looked at his feet.

"Thank you, Mark."

"So, now for Agent Philbin's benefit," said Bradley, "Detective Rome is working the murders of two residents of the old sandpit behind my home, also in Revere—two homeless individuals, one female, one male, both viciously stabbed, including wounds to the face.

"Detective? Would you take it from here?" Bradley asked.

Still confused as to why, Detective Rome laid out the case as it stood.

"The two individuals suffered deep stab wounds from a right-handed perpetrator. Each had three wounds to the face in what looks like a triangle shape. The killer used a large, extremely sharp, blade. The cuts are clean and, as I said, deep. The first slash to the neck killed each of them. Both victims were found by the same person, a Mr. Warrick Gaines, also a resident of the sandpit. He has been ruled out as a suspect."

Rome glanced at Bradley.

"With Mr. Gaines's help," Rome began, "we have received cooperation from a few residents of the pit. One gentleman noticed a man in a hooded sweatshirt and dark pants walking from the scene toward the access road the night of the second murder. He couldn't say what time, but he did say the sun had gone down. We corroborated this with Agent Whitman's camera video. The subject walked back to his vehicle at ten after nine.

"Both murders happened quickly and efficiently," the detective continued, "and we believe both victims were chosen for ease of access. The killer may also know where the city cameras are set up, because we have not been able to match a vehicle to the area during either time frame. The assailant must have used back roads to get there. No prints, no physical evidence, just footprints. Our best guess is the prints were left by a man roughly six feet tall. Other than that, all we have is Agent Whitman's profile. We think he's right—this guy is a professional."

Rome glanced at the faces around the room.

Derek stood and walked to the window with the best view of the river. "Okay. So why are we here, Bradley?"

"Thank you, Detective." Bradley paused to gather his thoughts. "Shea Powers shared information with me about the realty company's client, the one who felt the need to threaten me."

Bradley pulled a sheet of paper from his pack and laid it on Derek's desk. They gathered around the map. He explained the meanings of the distinct colors: properties sold, properties under agreement, and properties yet to be acquired. Then he circled the center in the ring of properties, the large empty space in the middle of the paper. With his marker he wrote, *SANDPIT*.

"Four years ago, a company named Eastern Entertainment Alliance sent a proposal to the city of Revere to purchase the old Stansworth Sandpit property so Eastern Entertainment could build a casino and hotel. The proposal did not come without opposition. The mayor remains a proponent of the project. However, the leader of the opposition, Councilwoman Bates, died—killed in a subway accident a week before the city council planned to make its recommendation public."

Bradley looked at Rome and Philbin and saw pursed lips, raised eyebrows, and condescending smirks. Derek, however, held a neutral expression.

"Wait a minute. Are you saying you think the subway train derailment was not an accident?" Detective Rome's voice went high-pitched.

Bradley sighed. "I don't know. But I think it's something we need to explore. EEA had a lot at stake, and Councilwoman Bates stood in their way. Who investigated the train accident?"

"The National Transportation Safety Board investigates accidents on trains and subway lines. If I remember right, they determined the cause of the accident to be weather related. It happened in December. That's not too hard to imagine," Rome said.

"Yeah. Nobody would think to question it, would they?" Bradley said, thinking out loud.

"Hold on. A lot of people got hurt in that crash, but only a few died, right?" Philbin asked.

"Five. Five people died," Derek said.

"Well, how could anyone be sure she would be one of the victims?" Philbin asked.

Rome agreed, nodding his head vigorously.

"Was there an autopsy?" Bradley asked, then looked around the room.

Nobody answered. Bradley could see each of them working the scenario out silently in his own way. Rome's eyes darted back and forth, and Philbin began tapping his fingers on the arm of the chair.

"So, now that I've got your attention," Bradley cleared his throat, "would you like to hear about Eastern Entertainment Alliance?"

The three nodded their heads.

"I haven't had much time to work on it, but this is what I've got so far. EEA is a subsidiary of Billings Estate Industries, a real estate company. Billings is a subsidiary of Queen's Court Unlimited, a mobile home construction company owned by OC-CYX Industrial Corporation of Atlanta, owned by Mathematical Data Perception Enterprises, a software company registered in Minneapolis and owned by Kaishi & Jieshu Manufacturing, a Chinese company registered in Switzerland. Don't get too hung up on the names. Most of them are shell companies. If legitimate, why set up dummy companies?"

Bradley took a deep breath. Then he continued. "Noticeably, all the companies from EEA through Mathematical Data are registered in the United States. I had to dig deep to get the Switzerland connection. Now, I don't know anything about the process of obtaining a gaming license in Massachusetts, but I'm willing to bet it is easier to get one if your business is registered in the United States."

Rome and Philbin gaped at each other, then at Derek. Derek smiled.

"So, what do you do when you do have time to research?" Detective Rome asked.

Not realizing it a rhetorical question, Bradley began again. "There is another arm of OC-CYX Industrial Corporation, a medical equipment manufacturer, that I haven't explored yet. I believe they are one of the few businesses that functions as a real business. I plan . . ."

"Alright, Bradley. I think he gets it. So, let's hear it. What does everyone think about this?" Derek asked. He looked first to Rome.

"I think it's crazy. He's making huge leaps and suppositions based on no evidence. It's all conjecture." Rome sat back in his chair. "But . . . when I think about the homeless murders, the way they were committed, and why the killer chose those victims, I can't come up with a more plausible motive. I think it's worth looking into."

"Philbin?" Derek asked.

"Nuts! I think it's nuts. But my case is going nowhere. I'll bite. Tell me what you want me to do."

Bradley had thought he would feel relieved if he sold his theory to the group.

But he didn't feel relieved. He felt anxious. *What if I'm wrong?*

"Bradley?" Derek sat back down in his chair.

"Someone has got to talk to the investigator from NTSB. And we need to find out if there was an autopsy performed on Councilwoman Bates. If there was and it shows no signs of foul play, then we have nothing to go on. If there wasn't an autopsy, we might have to petition to get the body exhumed."

"This is a delicate situation here. We don't want to sound the alarm bell with Councilwoman Bates's family or anyone else. Philbin, find out who processed her body. Tell them you're doing a routine report on subway fatalities or something. Find out if anyone performed an autopsy," Derek said.

"I'll take the NTSB. I know one of the inspectors. She'll be discreet. I'll see if I can get a full copy of the report," Detective Rome said.

"Let's proceed with the cases as normal. We don't want anyone second guessing our motives. And if we do have grounds for charges, we'll need to have exhausted every other possibility." Derek flipped through his calendar. "Can we meet here again on Thursday, same time?"

Bradley, Rome, and Philbin checked their schedules and agreed to Thursday at 3:30 pm.

"Thank you, Detective Rome, for making the trip. We appreciate your help." Derek stood, came out from behind his desk, and shook his hand.

"Same here, Agent Richards. If anything, it will be an interesting exercise," Rome smiled.

Bradley hung back when Rome and Philbin left the room.

"Well, that went well," Derek grinned.

"Jesus, Derek. I hope I'm right about this. But part of me hopes I'm wrong, too." Bradley took a deep breath, turned his chair, and left the room.

"Me, too, Bradley. Me, too," Derek muttered as he rounded his desk and sat down in his chair.

DUTY

Bradley thanked Mara for looking after Rusty. He never got a chance to talk to Nick, as he was still interrogating Juliette in Room A. Bradley sensed that she seemed slightly uneasy when he rolled past the glass walls.

Before he left the parking lot, Bradley called his favorite brick-oven pizza place and ordered takeout. He planned to pick it up on the way home. A regular customer, Bradley got his order delivered to his truck. He tipped very well.

Once home, Bradley switched on the backyard light to signal Zayt to come up. He fed Rusty and, assuming he could convince Zayt to join him, set the table for two.

Ten minutes later, Zayt knocked on the door.

"I can't see any easy way up or down the embankment," Bradley said. "How do you get here so fast?"

"Stop looking for the easy way," Zayt said, "and you just might find the quickest."

"Food for thought," Bradley replied. "Speaking of food, I picked up a pizza on the way home. Help yourself."

"What? No Chateaubriand or berry torte tonight?"

Bradley chuckled as he brought a couple beers to the kitchen table. "Hey, I said I love to cook. I didn't say I live to cook. Besides, I had a busy day."

Bradley told Zayt what he had learned about the shell companies associated with Eastern Entertainment Alliance. He also described his meeting with Derek, Philbin, and Rome. He stopped short of exposing their next moves but did disclose that the three men were willing to investigate the matter further.

"Zayt, there's something you need to understand. I am first and foremost an FBI agent. My duty is to the bureau. Now that this could be a bureau case, there may be some things I won't be able to discuss. I won't violate FBI confidences or put my fellow agents in jeopardy. I'm telling you now because I don't want you to think that I don't trust you. It's just the way it is."

"Okay."

"That's it? Okay?"

"Yeah. I get it."

Bradley sat back, a surprised but relieved look on his face. "Okay."

They dug into the pizza.

"This doesn't mean I won't need your help you know," Bradley said matter-of-factly.

"You *are* going to get the accident report, right?"

Bradley didn't answer.

"And a toxicology report from the councilwoman's autopsy?"

Bradley closed his eyes.

"I get the feeling that keeping something from you will be like keeping a buzzard from roadkill."

Zayt grinned.

After dinner, Bradley called the hospital and checked on Shea. They would tell him only that her condition had not changed.

Bradley's demeanor shifted. His shoulders slumped as he stared at his empty plate. Rusty noticed the change, came to his side, and nudged Bradley's hand from the table. Without thought, Bradley petted Rusty's head in slow, even strokes. His eyes didn't move from his plate.

Zayt noticed, too.

"I had a buddy . . . in Afghanistan. Hell of a guy. Hell of a soldier, too. We were together for two-and-a-half tours. He joined the unit about two months before I got there, so he showed me the ropes—you know, how to take care of my feet; always have eye drops, lip balm, and sunscreen handy.

"He used to get these care packages from home and share them with me. His wife would create a . . . what do you call it? . . . theme on the inside of the box and decorate it with colored paper and stuff. She'd send ramen noodles and drink mixes, all kinds of things.

"After he wrote to her about me liking Charleston Chew candy bars, she would include a couple with every shipment." Zayt stopped and leaned forward, arms on the table, head bowed. "Halfway through our third tour, his military vehicle was blown up by a remotely detonated IED. Everyone in the vehicle died except him. He spent over a year in the hospital. He lost his right leg and a couple fingers and suffered severe burns over most of his body."

Bradley listened straight-backed and blank-faced without as much as a twitch. Zayt went on.

"I never saw him again. I had another three months to finish my tour. When I wrote to his wife, she told me he moved out of their house. She said he wished, every day, that he had died in the blast. That was a month ago."

"Where is he?" Bradley quietly asked.

Zayt stood, pushed his chair back, and headed for the door.

"I don't know."

The door closed behind him.

Minutes passed before Bradley moved, and when he did, he

felt an energy working against him as if grief and conscience swirled to form soundless hurricane force winds that inhibited forward motion. He could tell Zayt felt it, too. And something told him it was not Zayt's first storm, either.

He let Rusty out the back door. He hoped Rusty could give some comfort to Zayt, even if only for a little while.

He resolved it to be an early night. He tidied the kitchen and checked his text messages. One revealed that the search he initiated in the FBI database for unsolved victims with the same modus operandi as the sandpit murders had completed.

Bradley thought about waiting until morning, but he knew he wouldn't be able to sleep if he didn't check the results, so he logged into the database. The report printed out fifty-two unsolved cases with similar MO. Bradley quickly discarded all that involved stab wounds to the head but not specifically to the face. The murders devoid of an overkill quality were horrible and gruesome but likely not related to this case. He looked at the four victims with no neck wounds but face wounds, all of them brutal. One female victim was found stuffed in a closet after multiple weeks. He put those cases aside for later review. That left him with seven relevant victims.

He viewed the records, with photos, of the seven remaining victims. Five of the seven had almost identical wound patterns.

Bradley had found his man.

HIGH STAKES HITS

With thoughts of an early night behind him, Bradley studied the case files of the seven previous victims. Eight years before, three were killed in New York, two and a half years later two died in Florida, and three years after that, two in Maryland.

Bradley brought up the webpage for Eastern Entertainment Alliance. The Finger Lakes Hotel and Casino opened its doors three years after the Seneca Lake, New York killings. Two years after the New Smyrna Beach murders in Florida, the new and extravagant Cape Castle Yacht Club began mooring boats in its marina and serving diners in the marina's high-end restaurant. And the boardwalk in Ocean City, Maryland, would host the grand opening of the OC's Slots & Entertainment venue in four months.

Each victim either owned property acquired by one of the businesses, or the properties in question became the last thing they ever saw.

Bradley had no idea how long Rusty had been at the slider door, but when he noticed, the dog sat patiently for Bradley to let him in. He checked his watch. He had been at his computer for almost two hours.

He didn't want to stop his research, but he struggled to keep his eyes open. It would all be waiting for him in the morning, he decided. He shut down his computer and said goodnight to Rusty.

As tired as he felt, his brain did not want to give in. He found himself thinking of Zayt in his shack, surrounded by his ghosts.

How does he manage to live with it all? Bradley thought. *How much horror must he have seen? How many lives destroyed, living and dead?*

Then he thought about Mamma Lise, Joe Gaffrey, Councilwoman Bates, and Shea Powers. They were his war casualties. They were his ghosts.

He didn't know how long it took him to fall asleep, but when he woke, the clock read 4:59. His alarm would sound in one minute. Hoping not to wake Rusty, he turned it off. The Doberman looked so peaceful in his bed. As he watched the dog sleep, Bradley realized it had only been nine days since they met in the alley. It took only one day for Bradley to become attached to him, and he had a feeling Rusty felt the same.

With a smile on his face, Bradley maneuvered himself out of bed and into his chair. Rusty woke and came to him.

"Good morning, Rusty. You want to help me work out this morning?"

Bradley moved to the gym area and picked up a large rubber band. He dangled it in front of Rusty, baiting him to latch on to it. Rusty did not disappoint. Bradley tugged on the other end of the band, but Rusty would not let go. Bradley pulled harder, and still Rusty would not concede. With increasing strength, Bradley pulled on the band. Rusty's bared teeth would not open to unleash the elastic. His eyes showed will and determination as he began to slide on the wooden floor toward Bradley.

"Good boy. You are a strong one, aren't you?"

Rusty tried to keep his footing, but it proved too slippery. Bradley kept moving backwards as he held steady on the rubber band.

"Okay, Rusty. Leave it."

Rusty opened his mouth and the band snapped back to Bradley's hand.

"That a boy. Good boy, buddy. Come here."

Rusty took the two steps to Bradley.

"Up." Bradley slapped at his lap.

Rusty looked at Bradley's lap and tilted his head.

"It's okay, boy. Up," Bradley said again.

Rusty gingerly placed his left front paw on Bradley's right thigh and lifting himself up as he placed his right paw on Bradley's left thigh, his hind feet still on the floor. Bradley wrapped his arms around Rusty's neck and hugged him. Rusty licked Bradley's face.

Rusty had filled out in the last week. He looked healthy at approximately ninety-five pounds, but Bradley did not feel an ounce of it.

He roughhoused with Rusty a little more before opening the slider to let him outside. As he watched him scamper down the banking, he wondered what he had ever done without him.

Unsure where his cheerful mood came from, Bradley took advantage of it and performed a hearty workout. He got dressed after lingering in the shower, then plated Rusty's breakfast.

The two had fallen easily into a routine, and he knew Rusty would crest the hill shortly. When he did, Bradley sat at the kitchen table with his coffee, juice, and instant maple-flavored oatmeal while Rusty devoured beef with gravy and cooked rice.

Seated at his desk, Bradley brought up the files of the seven victims found through the FBI search. He created a spreadsheet including the victim's name, age, gender, home address, where and when the victim died, and how long before the ensuing business opened its doors—or projected opening. He added Mamma Lise and Joe Gaffrey's information to the list.

And then there were Shea Powers and Councilwoman Bates. Although he could connect each of them to the property buyout attempt, no physical evidence tied them to the equation. Bradley felt the attack on Shea more a threat to unwilling property owners or maybe to Bradley himself than a necessity in the judgment of EEA. And, if proven, the councilwoman's murder a week before the recommendation announcement would raise too many flags. Hence, the train accident.

If Bradley were to have the authority to issue search warrants, he would approve them right then. But, really, he had nothing but coincidental speculation. And he wouldn't know who or what to search if he had any evidence.

He gathered his research about Eastern Entertainment's corporate chain of owners. No crossovers existed in chief executive officers, chief financial officers, or chief operating officers across the corporations. Next, he would delve into the shareholder information for each of the corporations and members of each of the limited liability companies. He hoped to find similarities there.

In his element, Bradley did what he did best. The sun set, yet he had never left his desk. When he realized how late it had gotten, he felt bad that he had ignored Rusty all day. He fed him a few treats before he let him outside. As always, not until he left his desk did Bradley feel tired. He had been at it for almost thirteen hours and felt still no closer to identifying the person who orchestrated the murders.

Tomorrow I'll dig deeper, he thought.

As long and tedious a day as he had had, he wanted to extricate himself from his self-proclaimed hive and get some fresh air. Having not seen Shea for two days, he wanted to check on her. He preferred going into the hospital later in the day when most of the doctors had gone. To him, daytime in a hospital coincided with what he imagined as the interior of a budding hornet's nest: constant activity with each individual heading to a specific location, crossing paths with others doing the same, creating a dull flapping sound like an electric fan. At night, he imagined the sound reduced to the quiet whisper of a breeze through an open window.

When Rusty returned, Bradley packed him into the truck, and they took the short ride to Mass General. It wasn't until he parked that a thought occurred to him. If he put Rusty through the service dog program, he would be able to bring him into the hospital or almost any other building with him. He could even arrange for Rusty to serve as a therapy dog for children in the hospital. How he would have loved that as a child! *I'll have to give it some thought*, he said to himself as he made his way to the intensive care unit.

As Bradley got off the elevator and headed to the nurses' station, he spotted a flock gathered at the doorway to Shea's room. Bypassing the desk, he raced down the hall and stopped by the side of Sergeant Doyle.

"Sergeant. Is everything alright? Is she okay?" he asked nervously.

"Agent Whitman, what are you doing here?"

"Is she alright?" Bradley demanded.

"She's fine. They called me when she woke. Apparently, she's healed enough for them to bring her out of the coma," Doyle explained. "I asked them to call me when she came out of it."

"Well, why the hell didn't you call me?"

"Jesus, I just got here."

Put off by Bradley's demeanor, Doyle stepped back.

Bradley shook his head.

"Sorry, I . . . I didn't mean to snap at you. I saw all the people and thought the worst."

"They haven't let me in to see her yet," Doyle said, seeming to accept Bradley's apology. "I guess it took her a while to come around after they stopped giving her whatever they gave her to knock her out. The doctor said she has no idea whether Miss Powers will have memory of what happened to her."

"The doctor is in there with her now?" Bradley asked.

"Yeah. She even kicked these guys out." He pointed to the four nurses standing next to him who watched the activity in the room with curiosity.

Bradley tried to see past the pack of hospital personnel but could not. His heart pounded. He needed to see for himself that Shea was okay.

"Alright, everyone back to work. She needs her rest," came a soft voice behind the pack.

The staff slowly moved from the doorway, and Bradley could see Shea. IV still flowed into her arm, and a tube provided oxygen into her nostrils, but the ventilator tube had been removed. Her bruised face displayed the colors of a dark sunset.

Dr. Weaver joined Sergeant Doyle and Bradley in the hallway. An intern stayed with Shea.

"Hello, Sergeant Doyle, Bradley. Shall we go sit down?" Dr. Weaver moved to a bench a few yards down the hall. The two sat while Bradley moved his chair to face them. She turned to face Doyle.

"Sergeant, I don't think it is in Miss Powers's best interest to talk to you tonight. I'm sorry about getting you down here. The staff should not have called you without consulting me first. She is in a very fragile state, unsure of her surroundings, and she is scared."

"Doctor, I understand the situation. I just need to ask her one question. I need to find out if she knows who did this to her. I don't need details tonight. I just need to know if she saw her attacker. I need to know if there's a chance we will catch this guy," Sergeant Doyle sounded sincere.

"Doyle, maybe you should wait until tomorrow," Bradley said. "I'm guessing she's pretty confused right now. Give her time to clear her head. Twelve hours isn't going to make a difference." He didn't want Shea to feel any more stress than she already did.

Doyle threw his hands in the air, stood, and said, "Alright, Agent Whitman." He turned to Dr. Weaver. "I'll come back first thing tomorrow to get a statement from her."

"Thank you, Sergeant." She responded.

Doyle left.

Doctor Weaver angled her head and peered at Bradley.

"Agent Whitman?"

Bradley bowed his head slightly. "Guilty. Federal Bureau of Investigation, out of Chelsea."

"Why didn't you mention you were with the FBI?"

"Because I wasn't here in that capacity. And I'm still not."

"In what capacity are you here, then, if you don't mind me asking?"

"Shea is an acquaintance. I'm just checking to make sure she is okay, that's all."

"An acquaintance?" Dr. Weaver drew her eyebrows together and wrinkled her nose.

"Well, what do you call someone you just met? She's not a friend, she's not a stranger, and she's not a very good realtor," Bradley chuckled.

"Ah, so she's a professional acquaintance," Dr. Weaver said.

"I don't think that came out the way you meant it to, Dr. Weaver," Bradley laughed.

The doctor blushed, then laughed. "It definitely did not."

She reached out her hand to shake. "Laney. My name is Laney."

"It's a pleasure, Laney," Bradley smiled.

"I'm sorry the nurses brought you here prematurely."

"Oh, no. They didn't call me. I just stopped to check in on her."

"Oh. Well, she is doing much better. But she still has a long recovery ahead of her. We haven't been able to find any family members."

"She told me she doesn't have any family," Bradley said.

"That's unfortunate. A trauma like this is tough enough. It will be much more difficult for her if she's alone," Laney said.

"She won't be alone," Bradley stated. He had intended to help Shea any way he could, but at that moment he committed himself to her full recovery. Whether she liked it or not.

Laney smiled, not sure of what to make of Bradley's statement. "I'd best get back in there."

She stood. "Goodnight, Agent Whitman."

"Goodnight, Dr. Weaver."

THE FIX

Bradley shut the alarm clock off and lay in bed. He didn't have too many days when he just did not want to get out of bed, and when he did, it usually came with a feeling of hollowness. But this morning started differently.

Comfortable and content with his thoughts, Bradley felt he could stay daydreaming in bed for hours. He could only surmise that his nighttime dreams had something to do with his relaxed state.

From what he could remember, his dream had him flying above the clouds. Through periodic breaks in the iridescent vapors, he could see down below. He saw his mother pushing him, a boy, on a backyard swing. He then flew over the ocean and saw a ship and, as he swooped down to take a closer look, he heard his father: "Be careful son. Hold on tight." With those words, Bradley tightened his grip on someone's hand. He looked to his right, and there flying beside him he saw Dr. Laney Weaver. That's when the alarm rang. And that's when Bradley cursed.

He reflected on which part of the dream he enjoyed more, the flying or the flying with Laney Weaver. It made him smile.

Probably wondering why Bradley had not made the move to his chair, Rusty sauntered over to the bed. He rested his head on the side of the bed and stared at Bradley.

"Yeah, I know, buddy. I know I've got to get up sometime. Alright, let's do this day."

Expertly, Bradley hoisted himself into his chair.

"Do you ever dream that you're flying, buddy? I hope for your sake you do because it's awesome."

Bradley waited until eight o'clock before he made a couple phone calls, one of them to Nick Gaston. He wanted to hear how Juliette's interrogation went.

"Gaston."

"Hey, Nick. You got a minute?"

"Sure, Whitman. What's up?"

"How'd it go with Juliette Berryman yesterday?"

"Jesus, this woman makes Cersei Lannister look like Mary Poppins for chrissake."

"What the hell does that mean?"

Nick paused, unsure what Bradley meant. "What do you mean, what does it mean?"

"Who the hell is that?" Bradley asked.

"Which one? Lannister or Poppins?"

"Jesus, Nick. Just tell me how the interview went," Bradley snipped.

"Okay, Okay. We didn't get anything out of her, but I think she's beginning to feel the pressure. I wouldn't be surprised if her lawyer bails on her before this is over. She denies opening the overseas accounts, but we knew she would. I think she'll try to dump this on her partner, Sharon Stakes."

"Did you slip in a reference to money laundering, like we talked about?" Bradley asked.

"Holy shit. You would've thought she was inches away from a chainsaw to her privates," Gaston exclaimed.

Bradley recoiled at Nick's allusion.

"So, you're saying she was scared?" Bradley asked.

"Scared shitless," Nick replied.

"That's good news. Thanks, Nick. Oh, and Nick?"

"Yeah?"

"Whatever video games you play at night? You may want to stop." Bradley hung up the phone.

He called Derek.

"Yeah!" Derek barked.

"It's Bradley. What's the matter?"

"Nothing. What do you want?"

"Derek, what's wrong?"

Derek paused, then let out a frustrated sigh.

"Philbin fucked up. I just got off the phone with the Bates family's lawyer. They want to know why the FBI is investigating Frances Bates's death and what we know that we're not telling them. This is exactly what we didn't want."

"Dammit. Alright, we can fix this. Did Philbin let any of our theory slip? Did he talk to anyone?" Bradley asked.

"He says no. He said the coroner must have contacted the family after he left. Apparently, Philbin didn't sell the routine train accident story very well."

"Let me talk to the family," Bradley said.

"What? No."

"Derek, we need to stop this before it becomes a story. I can talk to the husband and explain without completely explaining. Call the lawyer and set it up for this morning."

Bradley knew it had to happen quickly.

"Bradley, I don't think . . ."

"It's the only way, Derek. Stop for a minute and think about it."

The phone grew quiet as Bradley contemplated his next argument.

"Alright. But you'll need to be especially careful what you say."

"Well, then, we should send Nick," Bradley kidded.

He heard Derek's slight chuckle on the other end of the phone and felt much better about the call.

"I'll set it up and email you the time and place," Derek said. "What were you calling me about?"

"Just an update. We'll catch up after I talk with Mr. Bates."

"Okay. Good luck," Derek said and hung up.

Bradley started to sort through the information from the case. He felt he could make a compelling argument for asking questions about the handling of the bodies after the accident. But first, he had to call Agent Philbin.

"Mark, what exactly did you tell the coroner?" Bradley asked Philbin.

"I told him we were doing a routine report on train accidents to see if victims' bodies are processed any differently than after a car accident or other form of unnatural death," Philbin answered.

Exasperated, Bradley dropped his head, his hand dangling in midair with the phone. Then he spoke back into the phone, "Let me guess. He got defensive, right?"

"Yeah. Right off the bat he says the FBI is accusing him of cutting corners, not doing his job. I told him that wasn't the case, we just wanted to make sure he didn't miss anything."

Oh, boy, Bradley thought.

"Okay, Mark, thanks. I'll see you Thursday." Bradley hung up. *Wow.*

He had never worked directly with Mark Philbin. It made him appreciate Nick Gaston a whole lot more, even with his crude comments.

His text alert sounded.

9:30AM, 84 State Street #13, Maloney & Bryant Law Offices

Great. Downtown Boston on a Wednesday morning. He figured he better leave soon.

Before leaving the dog home alone, Bradley made sure Rusty had everything he needed. He didn't like the idea of leaving him behind, but he liked the idea of him alone in the truck for any length of time less.

He took route US-1 South to I-93, considering it the quickest route for that time of morning. Once off the highway, his path took him past one of his favorite Boston structures, the Custom House. As he drove by, Bradley reflected on the Greek temple design. He remembered, among several facts he recalled about the building, that a Quincy quarry provided the granite and that the neoclassical edifice sported twelve columns, each twenty-nine feet high and supporting a skylight dome. When increased shipping required expansion of the building, the famous 496-foot clock tower resulted, making it the tallest building in New England until the Prudential Center rose in the 1960s nearly a half century later. *It stands as an iconic landmark,* Bradley thought. *It's strength and beauty defy time.*

He parked the truck in the nearby 75 State Street Garage. A twelve-story brick and concrete structure housed Maloney & Bryant Law Offices. Bradley scanned the directory and found Suite #13 on the seventh floor.

A reception desk sat straight ahead as the elevator doors opened. A young man looked up as Bradley neared.

"May I help you?" He smiled.

"I have a 9:30 appointment. My name is Bradley Whitman." Bradley decided it best not to announce himself as *Agent.*

"Of course, Mr. Whitman. I'll let them know you are here," said the pleasant young man, who then pressed an intercom button and spoke. "Mr. Bradley Whitman is here to see you."

Bradley heard a female voice. "Send him in, please."

The receptionist stood up, showed him to the appropriate office door, and opened it. The spacious area with large windows had a perfect view of the Custom House clock tower. Dark rich wood-paneled walls and lush carpeting gave the room an elegant yet comfortable feel. Behind the glass-topped desk stood a woman in a grey business suit. Bradley guessed her age at somewhere in the late fifties. Looking ten years her senior, a tall, balding man stood beside her.

Sitting in a chair in front of the desk sat Haynesworth Bates. Bradley recognized him from the research he had done. Bates stood as Bradley entered the room.

"Agent Whitman, thank you for coming. My name is Amanda Maloney. This is Todd Bryant and Haynesworth Bates." She pointed to each as she introduced him.

Bradley placed his chair in front of the desk about four feet to the left of Bates.

"Well, thank you all for seeing me. I appreciate you making the time in your schedule," Bradley said.

"Yes, well, as you can imagine," Maloney said, "Mr. Bates is somewhat confused as to why the FBI is asking questions about his wife's tragic death."

"Yes, Agent Whitman, I am. Imagine my surprise when Dr. Reynolds called me to say an agent questioned him regarding the accident. And the agent accused him of misconduct." Bates raised his voice slightly at the last notion.

"Mr. Bates, I truly apologize for the misinformation. Agent Philbin did not mean to question anyone's ethics or abilities.

Although after speaking with Philbin directly, I completely understand Dr. Reynolds's reaction. Please allow me to explain," Bradley said with the most sincerity he could muster.

"Please do," Haynesworth Bates responded.

"Agent Philbin was sent to Dr. Reynolds office to ask one question. His instructions were to be discreet. We, the FBI, wanted to know if any autopsies were performed on any of the victims of the December train derailment. According to Agent Philbin, he asked about your wife first. Unfortunately, he asked the question in such a manner that he profoundly insulted the doctor, and the conversation never got back on track."

"Why did you want to know about autopsies?" Bates asked.

As if put in an uncomfortable position, Bradley cleared his throat.

"This is a delicate matter, Mr. Bates. I'm afraid I cannot tell you everything you may want to know, but I will tell you everything I can."

Bradley paused for effect. "Two weeks ago, we almost lost another train. You won't find the information in the newspapers or on local television. The media has not had access to the story. In fact, the passengers on board don't really know what happened."

Another pause.

"The operator on that train noticed a slight increase in speed just when it should have begun to slow down due to an upcoming track change. Luckily, the operator, whose only job is to open and close the train doors, broke protocol and walked to the front car to talk to the driver after not receiving a reply over their communication system. He found the driver incapacitated and slumped over the control panel, which propelled the train. The operator took control of the situation and averted a derailment."

"What's that got to do with my wife's accident? The NTSB determined that weather caused the derailment," Bates said.

"Yes, I'm getting to that," Bradley replied. "First, we don't know that they are connected. That's the point. But, if there is a possibility, we need to find out. After the investigation into the cause of the driver losing consciousness, doctors found traces of . . . let me just say, a substance that did not belong in his system. Enough to knock him out but not kill him. The substance only registered in his system for a short period of time."

Bradley stopped as if in deep thought. Then he continued slowly.

"I'm sorry. I can't say more about that except to say that the way the substance was delivered leads us to believe it must have also reached the passengers closest to the conductor. However, by the time the doctors realized that, it was too late to check the passengers' systems. The substance had already worked its way out."

"Look, Agent Whitman. This is all very interesting and unsettling, but I still don't understand the connection," Bates said.

"Have you read the NTSB report on your wife's train accident, Mr. Bates?" Bradley asked.

"Yes, I did. They said the train derailed due to ice buildup on the tracks," he answered.

"I'm sorry, sir. No. They said the *probable* cause would be ice buildup on the tracks. Your wife, sir. She was sitting in the front car with the rest of the victims?"

Bates's jaw dropped, and his face turned pale. He could say nothing.

"Please, Mr. Bates. Understand that I am not saying that this is what happened to your wife's train. This is exactly why we tried to quietly ascertain the information. We don't have any indication that this is the case. But it is our responsibility to investigate the possibility."

Some color returned to Bates's face, but his mouth still gaped, and he could not speak.

"Agent Whitman, what good would autopsies do if the substance leaves the body that quickly?" Todd Bryant asked.

"According to the experts, once human organs cease to operate, the substance has no way of leaving the body. If a person dies with the substance in the system, the remnants remain in the system. That's why we wanted the autopsy reports—to see if anything unusual had been documented."

Bradley felt confident he had accomplished his goal. They seemed to believe every word he said.

"So, I'm sorry to be so bold. Was there an autopsy performed on your wife?" Bradley asked.

"No," Bates said in a soft voice. "I thought it to be unnecessary." A tear streamed down his face.

Bradley felt a sharp stab of remorse. He hated to put the man through the charade. And, if his instincts were correct, Bradley knew it would only get worse for Bates.

"I'm so sorry for your loss, Mr. Bates, and for putting you through this." Bradley meant it.

"Agent Whitman, what if it wasn't an accident?" Bates asked. "What if it was because of this substance?"

"Again, sir, it's a very small possibility that that is the case. But if it were, the only way to find out would be to . . . examine the bodies." Bradley looked into Bates's eyes and saw the weight of his statement.

"I'm sorry, but there is one other thing I must ask of you," Bradley continued. "The information I just revealed is extremely sensitive. If any of what I've told you gets out, it could do damage to our investigation and potentially alert the person or persons responsible, if anyone is responsible. So, we must ask that you not speak of this to anyone. Let it stay here, in this office, with us."

"I understand completely," Bates said.

"Absolutely," said Amanda Maloney.

"Of course," Todd Bryant said.

Bradley handed each of them his card.

"Please, if you have any questions, feel free to contact me directly. I'll let you get back to work."

Bradley left the room.

Once in the elevator, he took a deep breath and blew it out with puffed up cheeks. He felt good about his accomplishment, but he didn't feel good about himself, sometimes a hazard of the job.

While waiting to cross the street to get back to his truck, his phone rang. *Sgt Doyle* came up on caller ID.

"Good morning, Sergeant Doyle," Bradley spoke into his phone.

"Agent Whitman, I'm calling to tell you I will be questioning Miss Powers in her hospital room shortly. I would hate for you to feel left out, as you most certainly did last night," came Doyle's sarcastic remark.

"Well, thank you, Doyle. I do feel the love. I'm on State Street. I can be there in twenty minutes or so, accounting for traffic."

"Right."

Doyle hung up.

The day never really goes as planned, Bradley thought. Instead of heading to the office in Chelsea, he headed to Mass General. He hoped not only to speak with Shea but maybe to Laney Weaver as well. The thought made him smile.

MEMORIES

Bradley spotted Doyle in line for coffee in the hospital lobby.

"Order me an orange juice, would you?"

Bradley pulled up beside him and thrust a five-dollar bill toward him.

"My treat," Doyle said.

"Doyle, go easy on her. Don't push her, okay? She's had a tough time."

"What do you take me for, Whitman? You think I'm heartless?" Doyle asked, clearly offended.

"Not heartless. Maybe a little brash." Bradley smiled up at him.

"Well, we all can't be Don Juans like you, Whitman."

"I'm going to be in the room with you," Bradley said.

Doyle thought about that for a moment before he replied.

"Okay, but I do all the talking."

Bradley shrugged his shoulders.

A nurse came from behind the counter when they got off the elevator.

"Sergeant Doyle?" she asked.

"Yes, I'm Doyle," he replied.

Confidently, the nurse said, "Dr. Weaver has instructed me to keep an eye on Miss Power's vital signs while you question her. If she shows signs of stress at any time during your visit, I will ask you to leave immediately. Also, per doctor's instructions, you may have only ten minutes with her. She is still very weak and in need of rest."

Doyle grimaced at Bradley, then at the nurse.

"Does everyone think I am the bad guy here?"

"I think you are a powder puff, Sergeant," Bradley grinned.

Doyle mumbled under his breath as he walked to Shea's room.

When he saw her eyes closed and her breathing steady, Bradley considered asking him to leave her alone. But he knew Doyle had to speak to her.

Doyle knocked on the frame of the open door. Shea's eyes flew open. Startled and unsure of her surroundings, she looked left, then right, then toward the door.

"Miss Powers, my name is Sergeant Donovan Doyle. I'm with the Revere Police Department. I'd like to ask you a few questions."

He entered the room.

As if she wanted to crawl and hide, Shea tried to inch back in her bed. Uncertainty splashed across her face. Bradley moved into the room behind Doyle, and she saw him. A flicker of recognition softened her expression.

"Mr. Whitman," Shea almost whispered, her rough voice still healing from the ventilator. "How's Rusty?"

"He's doing well, Shea. He wanted to come see you, but . . ." he shrugged at her surroundings.

She smiled a small but welcome smile.

"Shea, Sergeant Doyle has some important questions he needs to ask you. Is that alright?" Bradley used his quiet voice.

Shea looked at Doyle, then Bradley, then Doyle again.

"Okay."

"Miss Powers," Doyle spoke loudly and brusquely, then cleared his throat and proceeded with a softer tone, "what do you remember about the day you were attacked?"

Shea closed her eyes. "I don't like to think about it."

"I'm sorry, Miss Powers, but if we are going to catch this person, we are going to need your help."

Shea began to breathe more quickly, shallow breaths filled with fear. Bradley moved to her bedside and put his hand on top of hers. Her breathing slowly grew deep and rhythmic.

"I had a meeting with my boss in the afternoon, around three. It sucked. They took the company car away from me, and she yelled at me a lot. She said if I didn't close more deals soon, she would fire me. I didn't know what to do. So, I decided to go see you."

She pointed to Bradley.

Bradley flinched. Shea felt it as his hand lay on hers.

"You said you could help me find a new job. I was walking down Industrial Drive when this guy pulled up in a black SUV. He asked if I knew where 303 Industrial Drive was."

Bradley's upper body tensed. He removed his hand from Shea's so she would not feel his reaction.

"I told him that's where I was headed. He said he would give me a ride if I showed him."

She stopped, closed her eyes again, then continued.

"When we got to your place, I told him to stop. But he didn't. He just looked at it and drove by."

Shea began to quiver, and tears streamed down her face.

"He pulled . . . behind the abandoned tool and die building . . . at the end of the road. When I tried to get out of the car, . . . I couldn't . . . . My door was locked."

Her breathing quickened again, faster and harder to control. A beep on her monitor sounded in rapid succession. The nurse ran into the room and told them to leave.

"But we aren't . . ." Doyle started to say.

"Now," she demanded.

Another nurse entered the room and escorted them into the hall.

Bradley watched from a distance as they tried to calm Shea. Her body shook uncontrollably, and he could hear her struggling to breathe.

"Dammit," Doyle exclaimed.

Bradley did not bother himself with Doyle's unhappiness. His concern fell only to Shea. But Bradley had misread Doyle's emotion. His reaction didn't stem from the interruption of the interview. It came from a sense of suspicion and betrayal.

"What's going on here, Whitman? Why would her attacker ask about your home address? Is that why you didn't want me to question her last night? What the fuck is going on?"

His voice began to rise.

"Whoa, whoa, Sergeant. Calm down."

Bradley moved down the hall toward the sitting area.

"Where the hell are you going?" Doyle asked.

Bradley stopped by the bench and held up his hands, palms facing Doyle. "Jesus, Doyle. We're in a hospital. Quiet down."

Bradley saw Dr. Weaver get off the elevator and walk quickly to Shea's room. Glad to know she was with Shea, he focused his attention on Doyle.

"I didn't know any of this," Bradley stated. "But . . . look, I can't . . . . Take a deep breath, then call Detective Rome. It's not up to me. It's not my place."

"What does Rome have to do with this?"

"Just call him."

Confounded, Doyle walked to the end of the hall and pulled his phone from his jacket pocket.

Bradley took the opportunity to call Derek.

"What happened? I've been waiting for your call," Derek said.

"Shea Powers is awake. Doyle called me and said he would be interviewing her this morning, so I came straight to the hospital after the lawyer's office. There's a lot happening right now, Derek."

"Start with the lawyers' office and Bates."

"I don't think we will have any trouble with them. They seemed satisfied when I left. I've even opened a path to possible exhumation if it comes to that."

"How the hell did you manage that?"

"Look, can I stop by when I'm done here? I'll go over everything step by step with you. Right now, I'm trying to diffuse Sergeant Doyle. He thinks I've been lying to him all this time."

"Why would he think that?"

"Because Shea just told us her attacker used my information to get her into his vehicle."

"How the hell?" Derek stopped.

"I don't know, Derek. We had to cut the questioning short because she started shaking and hyperventilating. I don't know if we'll get any more out of her today. I'm not sure we should try," Bradley said.

"What about Doyle?"

"I told him to check in with Rome. If he wants to fill him in, then I'm not going to stop him. Doyle would be a good one for our team. I wouldn't be surprised if you got a call from Rome any minute now."

"Ah," Derek said.

"What?"

"I've got a call coming in now. Come see me as soon as your done there."

Derek hung up.

Bradley looked down the hall at Doyle, who looked befuddled and irritated. And there Bradley sat, the cause of both.

Dr. Weaver appeared from Shea's room. She approached the bench and took a seat.

"How is she?" Bradley asked.

"She's upset, but her breathing is better. I just gave her a sedative."

"Good," Bradley said. "Thank you."

"This means you are done speaking with her this morning."

"Yes, I understand that."

"Agent Whitman."

"Bradley. Please call me Bradley."

"Okay, Bradley. She may never be able to talk about this. She's in an extremely vulnerable position. It's likely she will resist trusting anyone, especially a man."

"But, doctor, she already made the tough decision to come to me for help once. I may be able to convince her to accept my help again. Besides, as far as trusting men, my chair is a natural pacifier."

"Well, Bradley," she smiled, "your chair may well be a pacifier, but your charm is disarming." Doctor Weaver stood and walked away.

Stunned, Bradley did not move. Positive he looked like a fool sitting with his mouth agape and unable to speak, he watched Laney Weaver until the elevator doors closed. He felt as if he were soaring.

"What the hell are you staring at?"

Doyle brought Bradley down from the clouds.

"Huh? Oh. Dr. Weaver said she gave Shea a sedative, so we can't go back in to talk to her. What did Rome say?"

"Nothing yet. He had to make a call. I can't do anything else here, so I'm going to head back to the precinct and talk to him now," Doyle said. "You know who he called, don't you?"

Bradley glanced at Doyle. "Call me when you're done."

Doyle left.

Bradley moved to Shea's doorway but did not go in. He watched her sleep. He tried to keep her peaceful state in the forefront, but his mind kept projecting her as she stepped into the SUV with a psychopath and the subsequent beating that took place.

His heartbeat quickened and a scowl formed on his face.

"Are you alright?" a nurse asked him.

He hadn't heard the man approach. "Huh?"

"Are you alright?" he repeated.

Bradley took control of his emotions. "Yes, thank you. I'm fine."

He headed to the elevator.

When Bradley entered the lobby of FBI headquarters, Carl seemed disappointed that Rusty wasn't with him.

"Where's Agent Rusty?" Carl quipped.

"I had a lot of running around to do this morning, places I couldn't take him."

"Ah, too bad. He lightens the mood around here," Carl smiled.

"That he does."

Nick spotted Bradley getting off the elevator and called him to his desk.

"Hey, Nick. What's up?"

"What's happening with the other part of the Berryman case. You said there could be money-laundering charges coming," Nick said.

"Yeah, I've been busy with something else. I haven't got back to that yet. Didn't Derek talk to you about making that a separate case?"

"Yeah, but I really want to nail this bi . . ." Nick scanned the room, ". . . woman."

Someone must have warned him about his language, Bradley thought.

"We'll get her, Nick. I just need more time. Maybe I can work on it a little today. I'll do my best. How's it going, otherwise?"

"She's squirming. I'm sure her lawyer has advised her to plea bargain, but I think she's too arrogant. People like her always think they are smarter than the rest of us."

"She did get away with it for close to thirty years, and who knows how much money she made. I'd say she's smarter than the average criminal."

"True. But we only got the case five months ago," Nick asserted.

"Only" because a multi-million-dollar computer spit out an anomaly in the Massachusetts Department of Revenue Employer wage reporting system. Dumb luck, Bradley thought.

"It must be nice to be so humble, Nick," Bradley laughed as he headed to Derek's office.

Hazel announced Bradley's arrival over the intercom.

"Send him in, please."

Derek sat, pen in hand, behind his desk, a three-inch stack of folders piled to his left and a two-inch stack to his right. He had the bogged-down look of a fly caught in the sap of a pine tree.

"It's about time." He tossed his pen down on the desk and stood. He threw his head back, stretched his shoulders, and arched his back. "Goddam paperwork." He took a seat next to Bradley in front of the desk.

"What happened?" he asked.

"Which do you want first? Lawyers or hospital?"

"Lawyers."

Bradley gave a detailed account of his visit with Bates and his attorneys. When Bradley finished, Derek sat back in his chair and smirked.

"Genius. That was genius. And they bought it? Everything?" Derek asked.

"Yes. So much so that I feel like a heel. Haynesworth Bates doesn't deserve to be lied to."

"Well, Bradley, if your theory holds true, you will have exposed her murder and an opportunity for justice to be served," Derek rationalized.

"Yes, but how will that be any better for her family, emotionally, I mean?"

They contemplated the situation.

"Unfortunately, that's not for us to determine," Derek said. "What about the hospital?"

"Jesus, Derek. The bastard used me. I don't know how he got wind of us talking to Shea, but he must have. She was coming to see me when he nabbed her. He stopped and asked directions to 303 Industrial Drive. She got in the car willingly. He drove her past my place and took her to the end of the cul-de-sac behind the old tool and die company. That's where he beat her."

"Did she get a good look at him?"

"We didn't get that far. She had some kind of anxiety attack, shaking and struggling to breathe. The doctor had to give her a sedative." His voice grew soft and concerned.

"Okay. So, we work the case. I wish I could give you Nick for this, but he's tied up with Berryman. How about Mara? Nick and Jim can stay on Berryman."

Bradley didn't have to think about it. He knew he would need all the help he could get, and at her young age, Mara Thompkins was smart, levelheaded, and unwavering.

"Okay, I could use the help," Bradley answered.

Derek moved to his desk and pressed the intercom. "Mrs. Hadley, could you please ask Agent Thompkins to come in here?"

"Yes, sir," his secretary replied.

While they waited for Thompkins to arrive, they discussed their course of action.

Hazel's voice came over the intercom. "Agent Thompkins to see you, sir."

"Please send her in, Mrs. Hadley," Derek replied.

"Why do you still call her Mrs. Hadley? Every other person in this building calls her Hazel," asked Bradley.

"I've known Mrs. . . . . Hazel, since I joined the bureau right out of college at age twenty-two."

Mara Thompkins entered the room. and Derek waived her to a chair.

"I called her Mrs. Hadley then and I will until the day she, or I, retire."

Bradley laughed. "She'll outlast us all."

Derek started. "Mara, I know you are working the Berryman case, but we need you for something else. You are going to work with Bradley on a sensitive and confidential case. I'll explain to Nick and Jim, but if they ask you any questions, just tell them to come see me. Take the rest of the day to turn your work over to them."

"It will only take me an hour or so to get them up to date with my reports," Mara enthusiastically stated.

"Bradley? How do you want to proceed?" Derek asked.

"Well, I could still be wrong about this, but I think it's best we do this outside this building. Keep the curiosity to a minimum. We'll work from my home office. Mara, can you meet me there in two hours?" Bradley asked.

"Absolutely. Where do you live?" She asked.

Derek laughed as he provided an answer. "A cozy little neighborhood. Quite industrial."

Bradley rolled his eyes.

"I'll text you the address."

TEAMWORK

Rusty waited at the door. His butt wagged uncontrollably when Bradley entered.

"Hey, buddy. I'm sorry I was gone so long. You want to go out?"

Rusty raced to the slider and bounded outside. Bradley wondered how Zayt was doing. He decided to send him a message later.

He gathered his notes and put them in order. He didn't know how much Mara knew about the sandpit murders, and he hadn't watched the news to know what they reported, which he chastised himself for. It doesn't happen often, but sometimes you can pick up nuggets of information on the newscasts, seemingly unrelated to a case, that prove beneficial. He turned on his computer and streamed the local news channels on one of his overhead monitors. The young brunette anchor spoke of the Hasbro company's promise to neutralize the gender of Mr. and Mrs. Potato Head. *No nuggets here*, he thought. He turned off the news.

Not sure if Rusty had tuned him in to new arrivals or if it was just luck, Bradley heard Mara's car as she parked. He watched her on camera as she looked hesitant. He moved to the front door to let her in.

"Wow. Now I get it. Industrial," she said.

"Yeah, well, Derek isn't very imaginative."

"This is amazing," she exclaimed as she scanned the large open room. She found herself drawn to the central fireplace.

"How beautiful it must be to sit here and read." Then she studied his office and, careful not to linger, scanned the bedroom area, his workout equipment, and then the kitchen.

"I guess I don't have to give you a tour. Except to say that the bathroom is over in that corner." He pointed to a door beside the bedroom.

"Where's Rusty?" she asked, concerned.

"Oh, he's out. Probably down in the sandpit visiting friends." Bradley showed Mara the view out back. "So, I'm no host. Help yourself to anything you need. There's a coffee machine over there and drinks in the refrigerator."

"I'm good. Let's get to it."

Bradley had moved the kitchen chair next to his desk. "I cleared a space there for you. Did you bring your laptop?"

"Yes."

She pulled it out of her bag and set it up on the cleared desktop.

"The plug is under the desktop."

Bradley pointed. Then, to charge the battery, he plugged his chair into the same outlet.

"How much do you know about the deaths of the two homeless victims here in Revere?" he asked.

Mara showed surprise. She had wondered what kind of case could be so confidential that they chose to work it away from the main office.

"Not much," she said. "Just that they were found in a sandpit." Her eyes widened. She involuntarily looked toward the sliders. "Is that . . . ?"

"Yes."

Bradley told her everything he knew about the two murders. He told her about Zayt and how he found the bodies and sent the notes with Rusty. He presented her with the profile of the suspect and stressed that the case belongs to the Revere Police Department, investigated by Sergeant Doyle and Detective Rome.

"Okay. Then why are we here?" she asked.

"There's more. A lot more."

Bradley told her about Shea Powers, how they met, how she relayed what Bradley discerned as a threat, and how they found her beaten. "That case also belongs to the Revere Police Department, Sergeant Doyle particularly," Bradley said.

Mara still looked confused.

"Bear with me," Bradley said. "Remember the train derailment back in December, the one where five people died?"

She nodded.

"One of the victims in that crash was a councilwoman by the name of Frances Bates. At the time of her death, Mrs. Bates and the rest of the council were deliberating the application for a new casino project here in Revere. Here. Right here." He emphasized his point by using his forefinger to tap his desktop.

He watched as Mara analyzed the information he presented. He'd hoped he wouldn't have to spell it out. Her eyes darted back and forth as if looking at the writing on a chalkboard.

"You think they're all connected," she said with a thin smile. "But I thought the train derailment was an accident?"

"The investigator listed probable cause as weather related. You know what probable cause means in a report like that?"

"Yes. It means they had no conclusive evidence, so they determined the most likely reason a train would derail in December—weather," she said.

Bradley nodded. He spent the next hour filling in details and answering her questions. He told her about his morning ruse at the lawyer's office and listed everyone aware of the hypothesis—Derek, Detective Rome, Agent Philbin, and, possibly, Sergeant Doyle. He left Zayt out.

Bradley also did not mention that Agent Philbin's approach caused him to have to talk with Haynesworth Bates. He told her only that the coroner became suspicious of Philbin's questions and spoke to Mr. Bates.

Neither one had heard or noticed a car park out front. When the doorbell rang, Bradley looked at his camera monitor and saw Sergeant Doyle at his door.

"It's open," he yelled. "Come in."

Heavy footed and highly agitated, Sergeant Doyle entered. He slammed the door behind him. "Why the hell didn't you . . ."

Then he noticed Bradley was not alone.

"Oh, sorry. I didn't know you had company," Doyle said.

Bradley laughed. He loved Doyle's high-spirited nature.

"Ah, Sergeant. Come in. Meet Agent Thompkins."

"Mara, this is Sergeant . . . Doyle. What is your first name, Sergeant?" Bradley asked, realizing he didn't know.

"Donovan. Sergeant Donovan Doyle."

He and Mara shook hands.

"Yes, a good Italian name," Bradley joked.

Doyle glared.

"You should have told me what was going on, Whitman."

Doyle peeked at Mara.

"It's okay, Sergeant. She knows," Bradley said.

"Of course. Everybody knew except me," he bellowed.

"If it makes you feel better, Sergeant, I just found out a few minutes ago," Mara stated.

Doyle took a deep breath, let it out, and sighed.

"You let me go in that room with my pants down. How am I supposed to do my job if I don't have all the facts?" Doyle asked.

Bradley and Mara chuckled.

"Look, Doyle, I'm sorry, but it wasn't up to me. How much did he tell you?"

A perplexed expression splashed on Doyle's round face. "How much is there to tell?"

"Doyle, what did he tell you?" Bradley grew weary of the coddling.

"He said you think the sandpit murders, Shea Powers's beating, and the train accident are connected somehow. Something to do with the proposed casino."

"That's right. The train incident killed Councilwoman Bates. She led the opposition to the casino project. The council had scheduled their recommendation announcement for the following week. I think the council meant to reject the proposal, so someone created a supposed accident to get rid of their staunchest adversary."

"Who created the accident?" Mara asked.

"That's the problem. We don't have any idea. Eastern Entertainment Alliance, the company who proposed the casino, is part of an endless weave of shell companies, dummy corporations, and legitimate businesses. I haven't unraveled it yet. The only lead we have is we think the same person is responsible for the two murders and the Shea Powers beating, but we don't have any physical evidence or witness. I'm also running on the assumption that the train derailment may have been caused by the same entity."

Bradley told Doyle what he found out about the murders in New York, Florida, and Maryland and how they coincided with the building of EEA businesses.

"This sounds like a mob-run business," Doyle said.

"Could be. But I don't want to assume that."

"So where do we start?" Mara asked.

"As close to the beginning as we can get."

"Alright. I'll make a cup of coffee and review all this information. You want one?" Mara offered.

"No, thanks. Doyle? Coffee?" Bradley asked.

"No, thanks. Tell me about the cases in those other states."

Bradley told him everything he had found out. When he finished, Doyle said, "I'll call the local PDs and see what they can tell me."

"I was hoping you'd do that," Bradley smiled. "Nice to have you on board, Doyle."

"What about Shea Powers?"

"I'll talk to her when the doctor says it's okay. I think she'll be more comfortable with me, no offense," Bradley said.

"Huh, no offense." Doyle clearly felt a little slighted.

"She was coming to see me for help, Doyle. And she got beat up for it." Bradley tried to hide his anger.

"No offense taken," Doyle capitulated.

Rusty stood at the door. A note dangled from his collar. Bradley let him in and read the note.

I'm coming up.

"Zayt is on his way. Be careful how much you say. This guy is smart. He's on our side, but I'm not sure how much we can share with him."

"I'm heading out anyway. I'll get started on my calls," Doyle said.

Bradley gave him a copy of his notes about the stabbings, and Doyle left. Mara buried herself in Bradley's research, and Bradley delved back into the world of hidden ownership.

Rusty ran to the door.

Before Zayt knocked, Bradley yelled, "Door's open."

"That's a little eerie, dude," Zayt said, before he saw another presence in the room.

"Psychic." Bradley pointed to his head.

"Right, and I'm the ghost of Christmas past."

Bradley pulled himself away from his desk to shake Zayt's hand.

"Where have you been?" Bradley asked him.

"Busy" was all he said.

"Zayt, I want you to meet Agent Mara Thompkins. Mara, this is Zayt."

"The name's Warrick, Warrick Gaines, but you can call me Zayt." He smiled and reached for her hand. Bradley raised an eyebrow.

"It's nice to meet you, Zayt." She stood and shook his hand. The handshake lingered just a bit longer than one would expect.

"So, Bradley. What can you tell me, and what can't you tell me?" Zayt asked.

"Smartass. Let's sit outside and leave Mara to her work. Come on, Rusty," Bradley called.

Rusty didn't move. He had set himself down next to Mara and seemed perfectly comfortable.

"Well, that's a first," Bradley said as they went out the door. Once outside he stopped and soberly glanced at Zayt. "She was coming to see me."

"Who? Shea?" Zayt asked.

"Yeah. We talked to her this morning. She told me she was walking over to see me when a guy in a black SUV asked her directions for 303 Industrial Drive. That's my address. She got into the truck. He took her past the house to the cul-de-sac and beat the shit out of her. Because of me."

Zayt shook his head. "Not because of you. Because someone told him to. Because there's some entitled asshole out there who thinks he—or she—is better than the rest of us. It's not a new story, dude."

Zayt paused. Then, "So, what are you going to do about it?"

"I'll dig deeper than the sandpit if I need to," Bradley said defiantly. "This bastard has got to show up at some point."

"I've been talking to some of the locals. It seems there's been a rash of thefts, vandalism, and assaults in the immediate area in the last two years. Enough so some have sold their homes and businesses. Apparently, whoever is buying will pay above market value. They're seen as saviors to the folks being harassed."

"I'll have Doyle look into it," Bradley said.

Bradley filled Zayt in on the murders in the other states. He also told him that there had been no autopsy on Councilwoman Bates. He didn't mention the mess that Philbin had made.

"We'll need to be vigilant about the sandpit. They'll keep killing until they get what they want," Bradley said.

"I'll cover that. I'll do what I do. You do what you do. Dig."

"Alright," Bradley agreed.

"What else did Shea have to say?"

"Other than that her boss threatened to fire her? Nothing. We had to stop questioning her. She's not strong enough yet."

"What did the hot doc have to say?" Zayt asked.

Bradley grinned. "That Shea's not strong enough yet."

Zayt raised an eyebrow.

"Hey, I've got some thinking to do. Come back later for dinner." Bradley looked at his watch. "About 6:30."

"Last time that didn't work out so well."

"I'll have you back to the pit by 8:30. He never strikes before 9."

Bradley watched Zayt walk along the top edge of the pit until a building obscured his view. He went inside to think—and cook.

In his refrigerator sat a two-pound package of steak tips that he wanted to use, so he decided on beef bourguignon for dinner. He turned his oven to 450 degrees. Into his red oval Dutch oven, Bradley placed half-inch squares of thick-cut bacon. He allowed them to sizzle while he patted the steak tips dry and tossed them with seasoned white flour. He covered the bottom of the pot with olive oil, brought it up to temperature, and added the steak tips to sear. He cut carrots and onion into large chunks.

Mara looked in his direction, and he tapped his temple with his forefinger to gesture he was thinking. Once the meat had browned, he removed it, added the vegetables, garlic, thyme, and bay leaf, and cooked them slightly. After draining excess fat, he returned the steak to the pot and added a dribble of Merlot wine to let it simmer a few minutes. He then added a mixture of hearty beef broth and tomato paste barely to cover the contents of the pot.

"I don't know what you are making, but it smells wonderful." Mara said.

"Good. I hope you can stay for dinner, because there is enough for an army here."

"I could be talked into it. My frozen dinner can wait," she laughed.

He placed the covered Dutch oven on the middle rack and turned the heat down to 325 degrees. He knew what came next.

Smells would permeate his house, and he would be famished by the time it was ready to eat in three hours.

He moved to his desk to make some notes, then back to the kitchen to peel potatoes. He peeled five pounds before he realized what he had done. So deep in thought, he forgot he only meant to peel half the bag. He set the potatoes in cold water to cook later.

He went back to his desk and began his investigative project. He had charted his course while cooking. Things had moved so quickly that Bradley forgot he had to abandon his research of Revere Industrial Properties, LLC to finish work on the Berryman report. He decided he needed to determine if there were any connection between Eastern Entertainment Alliance and Revere Industrial Properties. So far, he had not found one.

He recalled OC-CYX Industrial Corporation as owning several businesses he hadn't yet explored. That's where he would begin.

He determined OC-CYX was a burgeoning medical equipment company based in Atlanta with a net worth of 104.6 million dollars. Bradley made note of the corporate officers and moved on. Not only did OC-CYX own the Billings Estate and the Eastern Entertainment businesses Bradley had already uncovered, but the corporation also owned King's Court Unlimited, and a separate but identically structured mobile-home construction business known as Queen's Court. Bradley noted the names on both King's and Queen's Court organizational charts, then continued.

He discovered that King's Court owned Revere Industrial Prop.

"Bingo," Bradley said out loud.

Mara looked up. "Did you find something useful?"

"I found a connection between Eastern Entertainment and Revere Industrial Properties, LLC, the real estate company buying all the land. It's no smoking gun or anything, but we'll need to connect the two if this is going anywhere. The problem is, the LLC is registered in Delaware where they don't require businesses to list ownership publicly. And, of course, they opted not to."

"There must be a way to find out who owns it," Mara said.

"We'll have to go through Delaware state channels. Who knows how long that will take? But at least it's something. How are you making out over there?"

"I've gone through most of your notes. I'm not sure how you put all this together, but once you see it, it's hard to ignore, isn't it?"

"Yeah. I mean, I could still be way off base, but every little piece seems to corroborate the theory."

Bradley studied Revere Industrial Properties but could only find financial information. The thirty-two-million-dollar limited liability company also owned a business named KIC Laundry Services.

"Mara? KIC Laundry Services. Where have you heard that before?" Bradley sat as still as a statue.

"KIC? I just went through those files in the Berryman case. What do you need to know?" she asked.

"Everything."

Wide-eyed and mystified, Bradley turned to Mara.

"What is it?"

"Revere Industrial Properties owns KIC Laundry. Who is listed as the CEO or president?"

"It doesn't list the name. The business is registered in . . . Delaware. Well, that's one heck of a coincidence." Mara started to laugh but then grew serious. "Isn't it?"

"Maybe. Maybe it is. Berryman? Could she possibly be connected to . . . do you have those files on your laptop?"

"Yes." Mara typed into her computer. "Sending them to you now. Berryman Health Homecare spent a lot of money with them. They must have been one of KIC's biggest accounts."

Bradley opened the file as soon as it arrived in his email. Mara had been thorough in her approach to organizing the information, and Bradley appreciated her instincts.

He scanned the statements. Everything seemed normal. RIP billed Berryman, who paid the bill within thirty days. As Mara said, the bills appeared abnormally high. Unless Juliette's company did the laundry for all her clients, he didn't see how she could spend so much for the service.

"Is Nick interrogating Juliette again tomorrow?" Bradley asked.

"Yes."

"We've got a lot of work to do. I'm going to send you a list of wire transactions that Berryman made into thirteen different bank accounts. I want you to see if the deposits match the billing statements."

"Okay, but why would her deposits match a bill she received?"

"I found money in Juliette's offshore banks that I couldn't account for. I speculated that she may have been laundering money for someone but couldn't find a connection. If I'm right, we just stumbled into the connection."

"But why leave a paper trail?"

"The money looks clean if it is received as payment for services. Let me explain. An entity, let's say RIP, hands Juliette Berryman cash received from an illegal activity to transfer via wire to one of her accounts. The cash amounts are always under the ten-thousand-dollar mandatory reporting threshold, and they are never the same exact amount. Banks must report repeating deposits of the same amount. She wires the money, then RIP bills for fake services, and she uses the laundered funds to pay the fake bill, probably minus a percentage fee."

"So the only way they get caught is if someone, let's say you, scrutinizes every transaction the company makes and finds unaccounted for cash?" Mara questioned.

Bradley grinned. "And dumb luck."

Bradley dialed Nick's cell phone number.

"What's with breaking my unit apart, Whitman?" Nick said as he answered.

"I thought Mara deserved a break. Babysitting can be so exhausting," Bradley replied.

"What do you want?" Nick sounded tired.

"I'm going to send you a list of questions to ask Juliette Berryman tomorrow. I think we may have found the money laundering angle. But I only want to bait her, you know, see how she reacts."

"Yeah, alright," Nick responded.

Something wasn't right. Bradley could sense it. He moved his chair to the kitchen area and fabricated busy work.

"Hey, Nick, what's wrong?" He spoke softly, not wanting inadvertently to share something Nick wouldn't want known.

"What? Nothing's wrong."

"Yes, something is. What is it?"

Nick didn't speak for a few seconds, then said, "I'm just tired and frustrated. This case is draining. You won't believe some of the shit she put her clients through."

Bradley had a thought.

"Hey, why don't you come over for a beer. I made a huge dinner. Mara is staying, and my friend Zayt will be here. We could use a fourth. We eat at 6:30, so come any time before that. Then we can talk about how we are going to put Berryman away for life."

"I don't know."

"What are your options? A frozen dinner in front of the television? If you don't want to stay for dinner, you don't have to. Just come by, and we'll have a beer, and I can tell you my plan for Berryman."

"Okay. I'll stop after work. First I have a shit ton of paperwork to do now that Mara isn't here."

"Yeah, sorry about that."

Bradley did feel a little bad about taking her away from the team.

They hung up. Bradley couldn't remember a time when Nick was off his game. He always presented a confident, energetic, and cocky demeanor. He knew something bothered Nick.

Bradley and Mara spent the next ninety minutes putting together a list of questions for Nick and matching wire transfers to KIC Laundry Service payouts.

"It looks like Juliette Berryman gets a solid fee of twelve percent for money laundering. The total amount wired to these thirteen accounts over the years could be close to fifty million dollars. That's another six million dollars in her pocket just for moving money from one place to another." Mara's tone grew higher and higher as she grasped the enormity of the transactions.

"Are you thinking of changing professions?" Bradley laughed.

"I wouldn't know what to do with all that money. Why would anyone need that much?" She wondered.

"It's not the money. It's the game. I mean, yeah, she spends her money. She planned on getting a new Maserati, she's got multiple estates all over the country and a private jet with a pilot. But she could pay for those with the interest she makes on her bank accounts. She's all about the game. She wants to prove that she is smarter than everyone else, especially men. That's why Nick is the best person to take her down. It's her worst nightmare."

Mara laughed. "It would sure annoy the heck out of me."

"Well, he's the guy to do it. He's one of the best. And he's a good guy. He's just a little rough around the edges sometimes." Bradley grinned.

"No, I know. I love working with him. I just wish he would give me a little more responsibility, that's all."

"We've all been in your shoes before, even Nick. Be patient." Bradley smiled.

FIND A WEAKNESS

"That smells amazing. It's been torture smelling it for the last two hours," Mara said. "Where did you learn to cook? Your mother?"

"A little from her, but I mostly taught myself," Bradley said as he added portabello mushrooms to his beef bourguignon and placed the pot back in the oven. He drained and mashed potatoes, added butter, cream, sour cream, roasted garlic, salt, and pepper.

"Do you prefer beer or wine? I have both," Bradley said.

"Either is good. I'll have whatever you're having."

Mara had set the table as Bradley finished preparing dinner. Around the table sat the kitchen chair, the stool, and the outdoor lawn chair. Bradley poured two glasses of Merlot, and they sat back in their chairs.

Rusty ran to the door. By the dog's reaction, Bradley knew Zayt stood on the other side.

"Come on in, Zayt," he yelled.

Zayt opened the door and looked at Rusty. "One of these days, buddy, I'm going to come in covert. You'll never hear me coming."

"My money is on Rusty," Bradley said.

"Mine too," laughed Mara.

"Wine or beer?" Bradley asked.

Zayt took a deep breath, filled his nostrils with the aroma of beef, and said, "I'll have some wine."

Bradley poured him a glass.

Zayt sat on the stool next to Mara. "How did your research go?"

"I'd say we had a productive day. But then the allure of dinner distracted me, and I couldn't concentrate anymore."

Mara smiled.

"He's a man of hidden talents," Zayt said.

"I'm beginning to notice that."

Bradley rolled his eyes.

Rusty ran to the door.

"Thank you, Nick," Bradley said, glad for the interruption as he went to the door to let Nick in.

"Who's Nick?" Zayt asked Mara.

"Another agent. He's kind of my boss."

Nick came through the door and stopped when he saw Rusty.

"He's not going to chew me like he did Branson, is he?"

"I don't know. Are you going to sneak up on me with a gun?" Bradley asked.

"Depends. What's for dinner?"

Bradley laughed.

Bradley could tell Nick put on a good face, but he could also tell his colleague felt tired and drawn.

"Beer or wine, Nick?"

"Beer."

Bradley brought a beer and a glass and set them on the table in front of the lawn chair.

"Sorry about the furniture. I don't entertain much."

"Hey, Mara. How's the new guy?" Nick nodded toward Bradley.

"He's keeping me busy."

"Nick, this is my friend Zayt. Zayt, this is Agent Nick Gaston." The two shook hands.

"Are you all working the same case?" asked Zayt.

"We are in the final stages of a big fraud case," Bradley quickly answered.

The quick response signaled to Zayt and Mara not to mention the murder case. Bradley pulled the beef bourguignon from the oven and placed it on a trivet in the center of the table. He piled mashed potatoes in a large bowl and put them on the table with a basket of warm rolls.

"Dig in. Just be careful of the hot pot," Bradley said.

"Bradley, this looks delicious. You said you taught yourself to cook?" Mara asked.

"Yeah. It relaxes me."

Dinner conversation revolved around food.

"What's your favorite food?" Zayt asked Mara.

"That's easy. Any kind of seafood. How about you?"

"Ribeye steak. I could eat one every day. What's your go-to dessert?"

Bradley noticed Zayt and Mara seemed to enjoy each other's company. He also noticed Nick had a sneer on his face that increased in potency with every question. He could swear he saw Nick clench his teeth at one point. It delighted Bradley. Up until then, he had thought Nick incapable of thinking of anyone but himself. But the observation proved that Nick did have other feelings, even if he never acted on them.

Bradley decided to test his theory by pulling Nick away and leaving Mara and Zayt in private conversation.

He followed through after dinner. Bradley said, "Hey, Nick. I want to go over the information we uncovered today. Let's move to my office and leave these two to their food fetishes. Get yourself another beer from the refrigerator and meet me at the desk."

"You two help yourselves to whatever you want," he advised Mara and Zayt.

Bradley watched as Nick slowly got out of the chair and walked to the refrigerator, looking back twice in five steps. He got himself a beer and walked to the desk. He looked back at Mara and Zayt, who laughed over something one of them said.

"You'll need your chair, Nick," Bradley smiled.

"Huh? Oh, yeah."

Nick went back to the table and took hold of the lawn chair. He lingered while Mara told Zayt a story from her college days. Mara stopped and stared at Nick.

"Do you need something, Nick?" she asked.

"Ah, no. Just the chair," he said as he hauled it away.

Bradley couldn't help but chuckle as Nick found himself knocked off his game. Bradley wondered if Mara knew Nick had feelings for her.

It took several minutes for Bradley to regain Nick's full attention. Once he did, Nick became a little more upbeat and grounded. His cocky attitude returned.

"So, we're not going to play the money laundering card yet? You just want me to ask her about actual laundry?" Nick asked.

"That's right. Mix the question in with other service questions. And don't ask her right away. Wait until you've been talking for a while. Ask if Berryman's services include cooking, cleaning, laundry, et cetera. Is laundry done on site or sent out? Give her time to respond between each."

"Okay, but what's the point?" Nick asked.

"The point is, she pays an enormous amount of money to KIC Laundry Services, but it has nothing to do with her actual business."

Bradley picked up the report and handed it to Nick.

"I think if you can catch her in casual questioning, you will get the real answer, which is that they don't provide laundry service to their clients. We will have her on record and nailed."

"So, you want to go through the back door."

"Yes, exactly. What time is she coming in?" Bradley asked.

"Nine-thirty. Her lawyer has court at one o'clock, so we'll finish up at noon. When are we going to take this witch into physical custody?"

"The grand jury has the case. As soon as we have the indictment, I imagine we'll bring her in. But that starts the clock ticking. We'll only have seventy days to go to trial. Ducks in a row, Nick."

"The goddam fucking ducks are killing me," Nick exclaimed.

"Hey, what's up with you?"

"Forget it. Nothing."

"No, I won't forget it. It's obvious something is wrong. You're never this impatient when it comes to getting things right."

"It's nothing. Not important."

"Nick, I'm not letting you out of here until you tell me what's been eating you. I could tell there was something wrong just being on the phone with you. Don't you think Derek is going to notice something? Maybe I can help," Bradley said.

Nick cleared his throat. "I just found out yesterday that my uncle, my mother's brother, was one of her clients. He died three months ago. Complications from diabetes."

Bradley swallowed hard, closed his eyes, and cursed under his breath.

"Nick, I'm sorry. How did you find out?"

"I was reading your report on the black-market drug angle. You included a list of names of the affected clients. His name is on it," Nick said. "This whole thing got personal for me, Bradley. My mother is heartbroken about her brother. What am I going to tell her when all this comes out?"

"Nick, I'm sorry about your uncle."

"Yeah."

Nick sat sullen.

"Here's what you'll be able to tell your mother. You tell her you put this monster behind bars forever so she won't be able to hurt anyone's brother, ever again."

Bradley patted Nick's shoulder.

"Okay, so we talk about laundry tomorrow," Nick said confidently.

Laughter flowed from the other side of the building. Nick only glanced, then looked back at Bradley's report.

Not long after, Zayt announced he had to leave.

"Hey, take Rusty with you. He's got to go out," Bradley said.

"Come on, boy. Time to go out."

Zayt thanked Bradley for dinner, said goodbye to Mara and Nick, and went out the back door.

"I have to go, too," Mara said. "It's been a long day."

"Yeah, it has."

Nick perked up.

"I'll walk out with you."

"Thank you for dinner, Bradley. It was the best meal I've had in years. I'll see you in the morning," Mara said.

"You're welcome, Mara. I'll have coffee ready at eight," Bradley said.

Mara smiled. "I really like my new office."

Nick grimaced.

"We'll be in the office tomorrow afternoon, Nick. Maybe you can fill us in on how the interview with Juliette went," Bradley said.

"Yeah, if I'm not too busy," Nick snipped.

Bradley had seen Mara clearing the dishes and put them in the dishwasher. He decided it wasn't a bad idea to use the machine. He searched for his dishwasher liquid stored under the kitchen sink and found it way in back due to lack of use.

Instead of returning to work, Bradley picked up his book and read while he waited for Rusty to return. It had been a series of busy days and late nights. When Rusty came home, they each settled themselves into bed.

Bradley could not anticipate just how harrowing his next few days would be.

ON THE ATTACK

Dressed in gym shorts and t-shirt, Bradley let Rusty outside before beginning his morning workout. Bradley loved that time of day. The sun would not rise for another ninety minutes, and Rusty had his own morning routine. Bradley could concentrate solely on his workout.

Partway through his exercises, Bradley heard someone yell. He couldn't make out what the voice said, as it seemed to be under distress. He reached for his towel and wiped the sweat from his face. Again, but closer, he heard a deep voice bellow. It seemed to come from behind his house.

Bradley rolled his chair to the sliders and switched the outside light on. That's when he saw him. It was Zayt, and he was running toward the backyard. He held something, something large. Bradley opened the door. As Zayt got closer, Bradley could see what he cradled. It was Rusty.

Bradley's throat constricted, and he found it hard to breath. He gripped his chair and swallowed hard.

He backed his chair away from the door so Zayt could enter and saw thick white foam drip from Rusty's mouth. His eyes looked dazed, and he breathed rapidly.

"What the hell happened?" Bradley barely managed to ask.

Zayt replied in short, breathless segments.

"I don't know. I was out for my morning run, and I saw him at the base of the ledge. He wobbled and swayed as if he were drunk. Then foam started coming from his mouth. I think he ate something he shouldn't have. I found him next to a pile of food."

Not likely to panic in emergency situations, Bradley nonetheless found himself feeling uncertain and nauseated.

"Call the vet," Zayt directed, snapping Bradley from his stupor.

Bradley reached for his phone and found a contact number for the local veterinarian. The recording announced a phone number for emergency services and instructed the caller to dial it if it were after hours. He did.

"Family Pet Services. How can I help you?" a woman's voice answered.

"I think my dog ate something poisonous. He's foaming at the mouth. and he's wobbling like he's drunk. His eyes are kind of glazed over, too." Bradley spoke rapidly. "What do I do? I don't know what to do?"

"Do you know what he ingested?"

"No. It was something he ate outside."

"When did this happen, and how much does your dog weigh?"

"It couldn't have been more than twenty minutes ago, and he weighs about, ah, I don't know, maybe ninety pounds. He's a Doberman."

"Has he vomited, or is he having difficulty breathing or having seizures?"

"No vomit or seizures. He's breathing fast, though."

"Sir, do you have hydrogen peroxide in your house?"

"Hydrogen peroxide? Yes, I think. I'm pretty sure."

"Put three tablespoons into a syringe or a turkey baster if you don't have a syringe and give it to him orally. Be careful not to let him inhale it. Just squirt it into his mouth so he will swallow it. Once he's done it, come back to the phone."

Given a task, Bradley sprang into action.

"Hold this."

Bradley handed the phone to Zayt.

Zayt put Rusty on the floor.

"It's alright, boy. You're going to be okay," Zayt soothed. He tenderly swiped his shaking hand along Rusty's neck. He heard Bradley banging things around in the bathroom.

Bradley came out of the room with a bottle of hydrogen peroxide and a large plastic syringe. Mentally measuring three tablespoons, he poured the liquid into the syringe.

"Hold his head up," he told Zayt.

Zayt lifted Rusty's head and helped Bradley open the dog's mouth. Bradley pushed the plunger on the syringe, and the liquid flowed into Rusty's mouth. Bradley closed the dog's mouth to make sure he swallowed it. He rubbed Rusty's throat, remembering that's what they did with his childhood dog to make him swallow his medicine.

Rusty swallowed.

Bradley took the phone back from Zayt.

"Okay. Are you still there?" he asked.

"Yes, I'm here," the voice said.

"I gave him the hydrogen peroxide. What now?"

"The peroxide should induce vomiting, but you should get him here as soon as you can. If possible, see if you can find out what he ate," she said. "Do you know where we are located?"

Her words jumbled in his head. *Break it down, Bradley*, he told himself. *One thing at a time. Vomit—I'll get towels. Poison food—I'll send Zayt. Location? Got it.*

"Zayt, can you get some of whatever he ate? Take his bowl."

Zayt took the bowl and ran out the door.

"Yes, I know where you are," he told the woman "I'll be there in twenty minutes."

Bradley hung up the phone.

He looked at Rusty and thought how scared he must be.

"You're okay, boy. We're going to get you to the doctor right now. Stay with me."

Rusty started to gag. He tried to stand but couldn't. His legs twitched, and his eyes rolled back.

"Stay with me, boy."

Bradley got Rusty's bed and threw it in the back seat of his truck. He used his remote to start the engine.

"Okay, buddy," he said as he rolled back inside. "You got this. You're going to be okay."

Bradley wished he could believe his own words, but he just didn't know. He reached for a stack of kitchen towels and put them by his side in the chair.

Rusty began to make a hoarse coughing sound. Bradley rushed back to him and reached down to hold his head up as much as he could. Rusty violently vomited, coating Bradley's sneakers with phlegm and bits of some unidentifiable meat.

"Good boy, good boy. That's what we want. Stay with me. You got this."

Bradley knew he could not get Rusty into the truck. He would have to wait for Zayt. He took water from the refrigerator and an empty bowl from the cabinet. He didn't know what else to do. He sat with Rusty and leaned over in his chair so he could lift the dog's head each time Rusty vomited.

Helpless. He felt helpless sitting there waiting for Zayt. *I should just stand up, pick Rusty off the floor, and carry him to the truck right now*, Bradley thought. But he knew if he tried, Zayt would be picking them both off the floor.

The helpless feeling soon fed his anger, anger at his limitations, anger at whatever caused Rusty to be sick, and most deeply, anger at himself.

Zayt came through the slider, closed and locked it. Out of breath, he said, "Here. This is it. This is what he ate."

Bradley put the bowl in his lap and headed for the front door.

Zayt picked Rusty up and brought him to the truck.

"Back seat," Bradley said. "I have his bed back there."

Zayt placed Rusty on his bed and climbed into the backseat with him as Bradley elevated himself into the driver's position.

"Hang on, boy. This won't take long," Bradley said.

The emergency services veterinary office was only three miles away. Disregarding the speed limit, Bradley raced down the streets. If no other vehicle approached from the side, he ignored red lights. He reached the vet's office in less than four minutes.

The doctor stood in a side doorway off the parking lot and instructed Zayt to bring Rusty into the examination room. Bradley made his way up the ramp to the front door and found it locked. He pounded the door in desperation. A young woman opened the door and showed him to the exam room. The doctor hovered over Rusty.

"Do you know what he ingested?" she asked.

"This. We think it was this. Zayt found him next to it." Bradley handed the bowl to the veterinary technician. She promptly took it to a room in back.

"Has he vomited?" the veterinarian asked.

"Yes. Three times. The second two were less, but the first time was a good one," Bradley said, looking at his shoes.

After taking blood samples, the doctor immediately inserted an intravenous line into Rusty's front leg.

The veterinary technician returned to the room with a large plastic syringe.

"I'm going to inject activated charcoal into his system. This will help absorb any remaining poison in his stomach."

She proceeded to do so.

"Is he going to be alright?" Bradley asked nervously.

"We don't know what he got into. You got him here quickly. That's the most important thing. We'll do everything we can for him."

Rusty lay on the exam table facing Bradley. His eyes gazed into Bradley's, and Bradley felt his pain.

"You got this, buddy. You can do this."

Bradley stroked his head.

"I'm sorry but I'm going to have to ask you to go into the waiting room. I have a few more procedures to take care of. I'll be out as soon as I'm done," the doctor said.

The technician waited for them at the front desk in the waiting room. "Excuse me, sir. I'll need some information from you. Could you fill out these forms please?"

Bradley quickly browsed the forms. He didn't know the answer to most of the simple questions, such as: How old is he and who is his doctor?

Bradley filled out the paperwork as best he could. Then, seething, he turned to Zayt. His distress had morphed back to anger.

"Did you see what was in that bowl?" Bradley asked Zayt.

Zayt nodded.

"He deliberately poisoned him. He knew Rusty's routine and put a pile of poisoned ground meat where he knew he would get it." Bradley's nostril flared and his eyes filled with rage. "Did you hear anything? See anything?"

"Nothing. This guy is a shadow. He's quick, he's quiet, and he is bold."

"He's made this personal right from the start, and I didn't see it." Bradley slammed his fist to his chair. "How could I be so blind? First the sandpit murders in my backyard. Then Shea. Now Rusty."

"Come on. What are you? Clairvoyant? How could you know?" Zayt said. "What possible reason would there be for you to suspect that?"

Bradley thought about it. What possible reason *would* he have to suspect that?

"You're right. Why would I? I didn't find out about the casino project until a week after Mamma Lise was murdered. And Shea first came to my house that same week, before I knew anything about it. This can't be about the casino."

He looked at Zayt.

"So, what were you working on that would piss this guy off?" Zayt asked.

"Juliette Berryman," Bradley said. The realization startled him. His thought process reviewed everything that had happened in the past ten days and especially the past couple of days.

Bradley found his phone in his chair pocket.

"You know it's only six o'clock in the morning, right?" Zayt pointed out.

Bradley dialed the phone.

"Yeah?" Derek answered.

"It's Bradley. You need to get a police detail on Juliette Berryman right away."

"What? Why?"

"No time to explain. Dammit, I hope I'm not too late," Bradley barked.

"Okay, I'll get someone over there."

Derek hung up.

Bradley commenced his version of pacing. He ducked his head down and placed his hands on his knees, then threw his head back and placed his hands on the arms of his chair. He did this over and over until the doctor came out.

"He's resting. We got his heart rate down to a more manageable level. I'll send the meat to the lab today. I probably won't get results until later this afternoon, maybe tomorrow. Rusty will have to stay with us at least a couple of days. We'll monitor his heart rate and keep him hydrated and as comfortable as possible. There's nothing more you can do here. Go home, and I will call when I have more information," she said.

"Can I come by later and check on him?" Bradley asked.

"Of course," she smiled.

"Thank you, doctor. I'm sorry, I never got your name."

"Dr. Hebert. Paula Hebert."

"Thank you, Dr. Hebert."

They left through the front door and down the ramp.

Zayt got into the passenger seat.

"So, who did you call?" he asked.

"My boss. I have a bad feeling this has something to do with the fraud case I worked on or, I should say, I'm working on. I found a connection yesterday between the suspect in that case and the corporate structure of the casino project."

"Yesterday. If you found it yesterday, why would he have targeted you a week and a half ago?" Zayt asked.

"To distract me, pull me off the case. And it worked. He bought time," Bradley hissed.

"You think he's going after her now, too? To shut her up?"

"He's already shown he will kill for a lot less reason."

He started the truck, and they drove the short distance to his house in silence. The sun peeked over the sandpit, and an orange glow filled the eastern sky. Bradley didn't notice it.

The stench hit them as soon as they opened the door to the house.

"You got a bucket?" Zayt asked.

"Under the sink. I'll get the mop."

Later, as Bradley poured them each a glass of juice, he said, "I've gotten used to him so quickly. I can't imagine what I would do without him."

"He'll be back in a couple days."

"You didn't happen to leave any of the poison food in the sandpit, did you?" Bradley asked.

"No, I didn't want anything or anyone to get into it," Zayt replied.

Bradley showed slight disappointment.

"But I had a feeling you might need it, so I did keep this." Zayt pulled a baggie half filled with meat from his jacket pocket.

Bradley looked at his watch.

"Want to take a ride?"

"Let's go."

Bradley took the toll road toward the Longfellow Bridge that took them across Charles River and onto the campus of Massachusetts Institute of Technology. He parked the truck at the Department of Chemical Engineering facility on Ames Street.

Early morning classes had begun. Zayt followed Bradley through the halls to the doorway of Professor Andrew Forsythe. Bradley didn't knock.

"I knew you'd be here," Bradley stated as he pushed the door open.

"Well, Maestro Whitman. To what do I owe this distinct honor?" Professor Forsythe stood and approached. A short man with white hair and happy face shook Bradley's hand.

"Professor, I'd like you to meet my friend Zayt. Zayt, this is one of the most intelligent and unimaginative people I know," Bradley laughed. "It's good to see you, Professor."

Zayt and the professor shook hands, and he waved him to take a seat. Zayt seemed uncomfortable in the academic surroundings.

"What brings you to see me, Maestro." Forsythe asked.

Bradley nodded his head toward Zayt, who pulled the baggie from his pocket and handed it to the professor.

"I need to know what's in there, Professor. And the clock is ticking."

Forsythe opened the bag, sniffed it, closed it, and handed it back to Bradley.

"Who got poisoned?" he asked.

Bradley was not surprised.

"My dog."

"It's hemlock. It looks like someone doesn't like your dog, Maestro."

"Excuse me for one moment, Professor."

Bradley dialed the veterinarian. Once he got her on the phone, he told her the substance Rusty ingested had been identified as hemlock.

"Knowing that allows us to treat him more effectively. Thank you," she said.

Bradley thanked her and hung up the phone.

"Thank you, professor. The vet says it will make a substantial difference in his treatment."

"So, when are you going to be my guest lecturer, Maestro?"

"As soon as my life becomes manageable, professor. Thank you for your help. I'm afraid I must go meet a colleague."

"I hope your dog does well, Bradley. Come see me when you have more time."

The professor smiled.

"Nice to meet you, sir," Zayt said.

"You, also."

Heading back to the truck, Zayt said, "Why does he call you Maestro?"

Bradley chuckled, "He used to say my research papers read like a symphony. He said they turned chaos into cohesion."

"Wow. I really don't understand academics," Zayt grinned.

Bradley's phone rang. He saw it was Derek.

"Hey, Derek."

"Bradley. Juliette Berryman is dead," Derek stated.

Bradley stopped his chair, lowered his head, and with his free hand rubbed his temples. Zayt stopped with him.

"Jesus. How?" Bradley asked.

"Stabbed. Same guy, same MO."

He had hoped he had been wrong, that he overreacted. But the truth was, he hadn't figured it out quickly enough. "I'm coming in," Bradley said and hung up the phone.

"Son of a bitch," Bradley yelled.

Zayt lifted his brows.

"The woman from the fraud case. She's dead," Bradley explained.

"Let me guess. Stabbed in the face?"

Bradley nodded.

Bradley called Mara.

"Hello?"

"Mara, it's Bradley. We're going into the office instead of meeting at my house. If you're already on your way, turn around. I'll see you there soon."

"Alright. I'll be there in twenty minutes."

"Zayt, what are you doing today? I'd like you to come to the office with me. I want Derek, my boss, to meet you."

"Alright. Let's do it."

"Thanks." Bradley bowed his head. "And thanks for this morning, man. I don't know what I would have done without you. No matter what happens, you did everything you could to save his life."

"No problem, dude. The dog deserves a break, putting up with all your maestro shit," Zayt smiled.

RETREAT, MY ASS

"Carl, I need a badge for my friend, Warrick Gaines," Bradley said.

"What's up, Bradley? Two days in a row without Agent Rusty? That ain't cool," Carl said.

"Someone poisoned him this morning, Carl. He's at the vet's."

"Holy shit. Sorry, Agent Whitman. I didn't know. I sure hope he's okay."

"Thanks, Carl. We're kind of in a hurry."

"Got it. Here you go, Mr. Gaines."

"Thank you, Carl," Zayt said.

"I'm not sure I'll ever get used to all your names, Agent Whitman," Zayt said while they rode the elevator.

"Same here, Mr. Gaines."

The elevator doors opened to Nick hollering into the phone.

"I want it in my hands in thirty minutes," he bellowed, then slammed the phone into its cradle. He saw Bradley.

"Jesus, Bradley. Can you believe this shit?" he yelled. He nodded at Zayt. "What are you doing here?"

"Hitching a ride," Zayt said.

Nick puffed his chest. Bradley held up his hand.

"Easy, Nick. Is Derek in his office?" Bradley asked.

"Yeah, last I knew he is." He stared down Zayt. Zayt didn't budge.

The elevator opened, and Mara walked off. She saw the commotion between Nick, Zayt, and Bradley.

"What the heck is going on?" she asked.

"Juliette Berryman was murdered last night," Nick blurted.

Mara's eyes widened as she brought her hand to her mouth. She looked to Bradley. He looked directly at her and lowered his eyelids in confirmation of her unspoken assumption. Her questions were many. *Why is Zayt here? Does Nick know about the casino case? And why would they target Juliette now?*

"I've got to talk to Derek. Zayt, let's go," Bradley announced. Both Nick and Mara appeared confused with Bradley including Zayt.

"Hazel, I've got to see Derek," Bradley said.

She announced Bradley, then told him to go right in.

"Zayt, give me a minute to talk to him."

Zayt nodded and sat in one of the chairs against the wall outside of Derek's office. He nodded to Hazel. She smiled back.

"What happened? How did you know he killed her?" Derek asked.

"I didn't. I hoped he hadn't but realized it could be a possibility."

"How did you figure that?"

"He poisoned my dog. He poisoned Rusty. He left food laced with hemlock at the base of the sandpit ledge where Rusty goes every morning."

"Jesus. Is he dead?"

"No, but it's not good. Luckily, Zayt found him when he was out for his morning run. Otherwise, he would be dead."

"That still doesn't tell me how you knew."

"Zayt and I were talking about how they made this personal and ..."

"Wait, you talked to him about this?" Derek asked.

"Only what he already knows—which is a lot, by the way. Anyway, when we talked about this being personal, it finally struck me that it's been personal from the beginning, from before I knew about the casino project. And yesterday I found a link between the Berryman money laundering case and Eastern Entertainment Alliance. They didn't want us talking to Juliette Berryman at all. Not because of her fraud, but because of her money laundering."

"But why now? Why did they wait until now?" Derek asked.

"To buy time, I'm guessing. They would want to retrieve their money, and I'm willing to bet they destroyed all paperwork regarding Berryman Home Healthcare in KIC's records. That's the company they used for payouts. And they probably didn't know for sure we were on to that part of her business. Ultimately, they didn't want to take a chance. They've been trying to throw us off track since we searched her office."

"What does this mean?" Derek asked.

"This means you'd better bring Sharon Stakes and Catherine Leeks in right now. Call it protective custody or whatever. They're next on the chopping block."

"Okay, we'll bring them in."

"Derek, I'm going to need help on this."

"Yeah, we'll bring Nick up to speed. And Jim."

"I need someone else. Someone I trust and who is in a position to help me in ways they can't." Bradley eyed Derek.

"Who did you have in mind?"

Five minutes later Hazel heard Derek on her intercom.

"Send the gentleman in, Mrs. Hadley."

Zayt walked through the door. Derek came from behind the desk to shake his hand.

"I've heard a lot about you, Mr. Gaines. May I call you Zayt?" Derek asked.

"Yes, sir. Nice to meet you."

"Call me Derek. This will be an informal relationship." Derek watched for Zayt's reaction. He didn't get one.

"I understand."

"It seems Bradley trusts you. I'm sure you don't know this, but that is quite a statement. Bradley has never trusted anyone. Not when it comes to the important things."

"Except you, Derek," Bradley grinned.

"I stand corrected. But only because he's known me since he was twelve years old. He seems to think you are invaluable to this investigation. And because you are intimately involved with some of the details already, he wants to keep you in the loop."

"I would very much like that myself, sir, ah, Derek."

"I will have to run a background check on you. And I will decide what information he can share. You will not be privy to sensitive materials."

"I understand."

"Why? Why would you want to be involved in this?"

"Because two of my friends are dead and one is in the hospital."

Derek looked at Bradley then back to Zayt.

"I didn't realize you knew Miss Powers."

"I wasn't talking about Miss Powers. I meant Rusty."

Derek smiled. "Ah, now I get it," he said as he recognized Zayt and Bradley held similar compassionate guardian instincts.

Bradley and Zayt glanced at each other in confusion.

"Get what?" Bradley asked.

Derek smiled. "Nothing. Give Bradley and me a minute alone, would you, Zayt?"

Zayt stood. "Thank you, Derek." He closed the door behind him.

"Alright. But we have to keep this quiet. I'm serious about having the final say on what you can tell him. And you don't make any moves or decisions without running them by me first. No heroics, Bradley. Am I clear?"

"Yes. Clear."

"I'll arrange for Stakes and Leeks to be picked up within the hour. Juliette Berryman's murder might just scare them enough to talk. Get with Nick on interrogation strategy. And don't forget, we still have a 3:30 meeting today with Rome and Philbin."

"Nick might be hard to handle today. He put everything he had into the Berryman case," Bradley said.

"Well, it's not over yet. Remind him of that."

Bradley joined Zayt outside Derek's office, and Bradley led him to his nearly empty desk in the main office.

"Do you ever work here?" Zayt asked.

"Not often. Only when a case involves top secret material and can't leave the premise. I get more done from my home office than I ever would here."

Right on cue, Nick thundered into the room.

"What the hell did you do with those financials, Jansen?"

Jim Jansen jumped to his feet and shoveled piles of paper around on his desk until he found what he looked for. He ran them over to Nick, who swiped them out of his hand.

"Give me another minute, would you, Zayt?" Bradley asked.

Zayt watched as Bradley approached Nick and spoke quietly to him. Then Nick followed Bradley into one of the interrogation rooms.

Mara joined Zayt at Bradley's desk.

"I didn't expect to see you this morning, Zayt. What brings you here?"

Zayt wasn't sure what, if anything, he should tell Mara. Suddenly he felt what it would be like to weigh every conversation you had. *It's got to be hard*, he thought.

Mara raised her brows and widened her eyes.

"We had some stuff to do this morning, and Bradley said he had to stop here for something," Zayt said.

"Stuff and something?" She grinned. "Okay, I won't pry. Do you want a coffee? I'm going to get one."

"Do they have any juice?" he asked.

"Let's go see."

Five minutes later, Bradley and Nick returned to the main office. Both noticed Mara and Zayt's absence. Bradley went to his desk and pretended to look for something, but he kept an eye on Nick. He worried that Nick would not hold his composure. Bradley sympathized with him.

He knew what it was like to feel robbed, to feel like someone snatched your victory just before the end of the race only to tell you to start again from the back of the pack. He knew the pity one could bestow on oneself when months, sometimes years, of preoccupation to earn that victory yields nothing, not even a slight wiggle of the toe. And he knew how much harder it is to emerge from that pity place once ensconced in it rather than keep oneself from sinking into it in the first place. For all the gruff exterior Nick presented, the passion for his work took him to both extremes. If he could learn to stay away from the edges, stay more centered while not losing his passion, Bradley knew he could do amazing things.

Bradley heard Mara's laugh coming from the hallway. She and Zayt turned the corner together, each smiling and carrying a paper cup. Bradley saw Nick scowl at the sight.

Bradley dialed a number on his phone.

"Family Pet Services. How can I help you?"

"Hi, this is Bradley Whitman. I'm calling to see how Rusty is doing."

"Oh, yes, Mr. Whitman. Rusty is breathing comfortably. The doctor is with another patient now, but I would be happy to have her call you when she has a moment."

"Yes, please. Thank you." Bradley hung up.

Zayt and Mara reached the desk.

Having overheard Bradley, Zayt asked, "Well?"

"He's breathing okay. She'll call with an update when she can."

Mara tilted her head. "Who? Who's breathing okay?"

Bradley glanced at Zayt. "You didn't tell her?"

"No. I didn't know if I should. I wasn't sure . . ."

"Yeah, I get it," Bradley said. "Someone poisoned Rusty this morning. They put hemlock-tainted meat where they knew he would find it. If Zayt hadn't found him so quickly, he would probably be dead."

"Oh, no. Is he alright? Is he . . . is he going to . . ."

"We don't know. The doctor couldn't really say. So far, he's fighting. Mara, we're going to meet in the conference room in fifteen minutes. We've got to bring Nick and Jim up to speed."

"Okay, I'll gather my notes." She started to walk away, then stopped. "I hope he is okay, Bradley."

Bradley smiled. "Thanks, Mara."

"What do you want me to do?" Zayt asked.

"I want you in there, if that's alright."

"Nick isn't going to like it."

"It's not up to Nick."

Zayt noticed a determination in Bradley he had not seen before.

The conference room held a large oak oval table twenty feet long and five feet wide surrounded by black, low-backed, padded swivel chairs. The windowless room had multiple monitors on each wall, a white board in one corner, and an empty refreshment cart in the other.

At one end of the table, Nick and Jim sat on one side with Mara and Zayt across from them, and Bradley eased his chair to the head of the table. The small gathering gave the room a grander feel. Derek entered. Each of them looked up, surprised. Bradley had not expected Derek to join them but was happy he had. He began to move his chair so Derek could sit at the head of the table, but Derek motioned him to stay put and took a seat beside Nick. Bradley saw it as an opportunity, and he took advantage of it.

Bradley began. "Okay. Everybody here has a small piece of this puzzle. We're here to put those pieces together. First, we're going to lay out everything we have, so be patient. We'll have plenty of time for questions when Agent Thompkins is finished."

Mara's eyes flew open wide. She snapped her head to face Bradley. Then she glanced at Derek, who sported a thin, almost undetectable grin. Bradley nodded for her to begin.

With quivering hands, she picked up her stack of notes, straightened them, and tapped them on the table to align them. Then she cleared her throat.

"Nine days ago, a woman named Elise Bowman was murdered in Revere . . . " Mara laid out the facts of the murders and the assault on Shea Powers, the December train derailment, and the connections to the Juliette Berryman case. She dissected the corporate structure of Eastern Entertainment Alliance. She discussed the murder cases that used the same modus operandi in three separate states involving EEA. She detailed wire transfer transactions that matched payouts to KIC Laundry Services and the early morning murder of Juliette Berryman.

"Also, this morning," she continued, "Agent Whitman's dog, Rusty, was deliberately poisoned. We can assume this action to be another personal message to Agent Whitman, much like the Shea Powers assault." She turned to Bradley. He smiled and nodded. She took a deep breath and leaned back in her chair.

"Thank you, Mara," Bradley said. "So, you see, as Mara has so competently laid out, someone has made this personal. And that's where they made a mistake. I didn't understand until this morning. The murders weren't only about the casino. Neither was the assault on Miss Powers. They were a warning not only to us, the FBI, but to Juliette Berryman. They knew we were talking to her, and someone didn't like it.

"Why?" Bradley eyed the blank faces around the table.

"Because she knew them," he continued. "She could identify him or her or them. They have gone to great lengths to keep their identity secret, but for some reason, they needed Juliette Berryman in their confidence. My guess is our killer, our message man, is also a courier. Juliette had to receive the cash from someone, someone the organization trusted. And ultimately, I do believe this to be an organization. Their reach encompasses too many diverse disciplines for it to be an individual."

Bradley sat back in his chair.

Derek stood. "Thank you, Bradley. Right now," he said, "agents are bringing in Sharon Stakes and Catherine Leeks,

Juliette Berryman's accomplices. We need to find out what—and who—Juliette Berryman knew. Thank you for your briefing, Agent Thompkins." Then Derek left the room.

Mara glared at Bradley. He smiled back.

Nick shifted in his chair before he spoke. "I don't get it."

"What is it you don't get, Nick?" Bradley asked.

"Why is he here?" He pointed to Zayt.

"That's not really your concern, Nick. Everybody in this room has a role to play. Concentrate on yours."

"Which is what, exactly?" he scoffed.

"You and Jim are going to interrogate Stakes and Leeks. Start your interrogation the same way you planned to for Juliette. Ask about the laundry, like we talked about. Get them comfortable with normal, easy questions. Then do whatever you have to do to find out about the guy in the black SUV. They would have almost certainly seen him over the years. Use Juliette's murder to scare them if you have to. Tell them they are probably next on his list to die and we'll have to put them back on the street if they don't talk. We need a name, description, anything you can get.

"Mara," Bradley continued, "the special election for the empty council seat is coming up in two weeks. Get me a report on the candidates. Find out who is aligned with whom, especially pertaining to the casino vote. Get pictures, newspaper articles, whatever you can. Dig deep.

"Zayt and I are going back to the hospital to talk to Shea Powers," Bradley concluded. "We'll meet back in the office at 2:30."

Nick left the room in a huff, clearly not happy about Zayt's presence. Jim followed Nick.

"How could you do that to me?" Mara turned on Bradley.

"Do what?"

"You didn't give me any warning I would be handling the briefing—and in front of Agent Richards? I wasn't prepared. You threw me in the ring without a cape."

"You did great. What's the problem?"

"I could have done better. I could have been more succinct or more detailed. I don't know," Mara worried.

"You did great. Derek was impressed. I could tell."

"He was? Really? I was so nervous," she said. "I've never done that before."

"Look, you spent all day with those notes yesterday. I knew you could handle it. Otherwise, I wouldn't have asked you to," Bradley replied.

"You didn't ask me," Mara pointed out.

"She's got you there, dude." Zayt grinned as they left the room.

Bradley wanted to check on Shea's condition, so he and Zayt headed to the hospital. On the way Zayt turned to Bradley and asked, "Why am I here? What can I do that the FBI can't?"

Bradley chuckled. "You just answered your own question. There's a lot the FBI can't do in certain situations. If I have to do something a little, let's say, outside the box, I want someone I can trust backing me up. I don't want to put another agent in a position to lose their job."

Zayt's face collapsed, and Bradley chuckled again.

"Don't worry, dude. I would never ask you to do anything illegal." Then, thinking about it, he added, "Not totally illegal, anyway."

Bradley smiled.

Zayt rolled his eyes at the thought.

"What did the doc say when you asked to speak with Shea?"

"Ah. I didn't talk to her. I don't think we have time to wait for her doctor's permission to talk with her. I may have to push Shea a little," Bradley said, unhappily.

"Alright, but you're on your own if she catches you."

"Some backup you are." Bradley grinned.

At the hospital, they found Shea sitting up in her bed. Either her bruises had begun to fade, or someone had used makeup to lessen the visual impact. Her dirty blonde hair brushed and pulled back into a ponytail gave her the appearance of a teenage girl.

Bradley rolled into the room, and Zayt followed.

"Hello, Shea." Bradley smiled.

"Hi."

"Do you mind that we came to visit?"

Without moving her head, Shea looked toward Zayt but said nothing.

"Oh, this is my very good friend, Zayt. I know he looks scary, but he's one of the good guys, Shea."

"It's nice to meet you, Shea," Zayt said softly with a smile.

"Hi," she responded.

"You look much better. How do you feel?" Bradley asked.

"Okay, I guess. It hurts when I move or cough or something." She winced as she shifted in her bed.

"Shea, I'm really sorry, but I need to ask you about that day. It's very, very important that we find the person who did this to you."

"Mr. Whitman, I don't think I can help you. I don't remember too much about it."

"Bradley. My name is Bradley. That's alright. Just tell us what you do remember. You said you were coming to see me."

"That's a weird name."

Bradley looked confused.

"Bradley?"

"No, Zayt," Shea said. "I never heard that name before."

Zayt pulled a chair beside Bradley and sat.

"It's a nickname I got in Afghanistan. We all had nicknames."

"What does it mean? I mean, what does it stand for?" Shea asked.

Zayt hesitated. "Vasily Zaitsev was a Russian sniper during World War II. He was an expert rifleman who established new and effective military tactics still used today," Zayt said, somewhat practiced at appeasing people's curiosity.

"Are you as good as he was?"

Zayt paused again.

"Yes."

Silence. Then Shea spoke.

"He had a black SUV, a big one. I couldn't see his face too well because he wore a black hoodie with the hood over his head. I know he was white 'cause I could see his hands."

"What about his voice? Anything unusual about it?" Bradley asked.

"No, not really. Normal, I guess." She stopped for a moment, closed her eyes, then remembered. "He's not from around here. He didn't talk like us."

"Did he have an accent?"

"Yeah, he did." Her eyes widened, then squinted. "But I don't know what kind. I never heard it before. It was weird." She shook her head. "I don't know. I'm stupid. What do I know? I got in the car with him. How stupid do you have to be to do that?" Shea began gathering the bed sheets in her fists, pulling them loose from the tucked-in sides. Tears streamed down her face.

"Hey!" Bradley initially raised his voice, then proceeded gently. "You are not stupid. You are smart and talented, and you have a great memory for details. The map you drew for me has been a big help."

Shea shook her head again. "No, it was stupid to get in the car. I deserved to get beat up."

Zayt stood from his chair as all six feet of him towered over Shea. He stepped in front of Bradley, leaned down, and wrapped his arms around her. She sobbed for several minutes before reaching her arms around Zayt and letting her emotions explode. Careful not to make any large or sudden movements, he gently rocked her, all the while whispering something to her.

Bradley stayed quiet and watched. Three minutes passed.

Shea stopped crying, wiped her eyes, and smiled at Zayt. "Thank you."

"Back at you," Zayt replied.

With a tilt of her head, she said, "He speaks slowly and deliberately. He pronounces every word like it's the most important one. And he doesn't have a Boston accent."

"That's good, excellent, Shea. What about his hands. Can you close your eyes and picture his hands?" Bradley asked.

She did. Bradley and Zayt watched as she scrunched her face and her eyes darted back and forth behind her eyelids. She clearly remembered something.

She opened her eyes.

"Do you have a pen?" she asked.

Bradley pulled a pen from his chair pocket.

"Give me your right hand."

Bradley held out his right hand, and Shea twisted it so the fingers pointed up with his thumb closest to his body. On the web of skin between the thumb and forefinger, she drew three small dots that formed a triangle about the size of a dime. One dot on top, two below.

"He had a tattoo." She smiled a thin smile.

Bradley reached for her hand and gently kissed it.

"You are amazing."

Bradley gave her a moment to enjoy triumph before moving on.

"Now, Shea. Can you remember anything he said? You said he spoke slowly. What did he say when you told him to stop at my house?"

Shea lowered her head and started to tremble. Bradley reached for her hand again and held it.

"He said . . . he said, 'Don't worry. The gimp will get his soon.'"

She sobbed.

"It's okay, Shea. You're doing great. Take a minute if you need to. Did he say anything else?"

Shea took deep breaths to try to stop sobbing. Zayt reached for tissues and handed them to her. She took the tissues and held on to his hand, the three of them forming their own triangle.

"He said . . . 'You are young and . . . stupid. Therefore I'll let you live. How— . . . However, I may get carried away.'"

A fierce shudder shot through Shea's body, and Zayt jumped to his feet and took hold of her. His arms wrapped her again, and he whispered into her ear. They embraced for several minutes.

It pierced Bradley's heart. He wished he, too, could jump from his chair and embrace her pain, pull it from her soul, and replace it with comfort and peace. He had not been quite sure why he wanted Zayt with him when he visited Shea. Now he knew. He had seen the pain in Zayt's eyes when he could do nothing for Mamma Lise and Joe Gaffrey. He had known Zayt would be able to comfort Shea in a way he couldn't. Bradley envied that.

DECEPTION

"What did you say to her?" Bradley asked Zayt as they headed back to the office.

"To Shea?" Zayt asked.

"Yes, to Shea. Who else would I be talking about?"

"I said a lot of things."

"You know what I mean. How did you calm her down like that? It was quite impressive to see."

"I told her we had her back."

"That's it? We have your back?"

"I may have made a few promises," Zayt said.

Bradley was about to ask what kind of promises when his phone rang. He answered it using his truck's integrated phone system.

"Hello, Mr. Whitman. This is Dr. Hebert calling with an update on Rusty."

"Hello, doctor. How is he?"

"He is doing much better. He is breathing comfortably and, by getting to him as quickly as you did and inducing vomiting, the charcoal seemed to take care of the remaining poison in his system. I would still like to keep him overnight just to keep an eye on him, but he should recover fully."

"That's great news, doctor. Thank you. Thank you so much for everything. May I still come by and see him later today?"

"Of course. Any time before eight o'clock. I'm sure he will be happy to see you."

"And me, him." Bradley sighed. The call disconnected.

"Good news," Zayt said.

"Yeah."

Both were quiet for several minutes.

"We've got to end this thing. Now!" Bradley said.

"Are you even going to talk about what Shea said?"

"Of course. We've got some good attributes to start with. The tattoo will be easily identifiable. And the speech pattern should make him stand out."

"That's not what I'm talking about, and you know it. He said he's coming after you," Zayt said with concern.

"Yeah, well, we can use that to our advantage. Let's just keep that to ourselves for the time being, huh?"

"You're not going to tell Derek?"

"Not yet. He'd be forced to take me off the case, and I'd be forced to investigate behind his back. It would just hinder the progress."

"I'm not sure I like that much," Zayt said.

"No problem. I can drop you off in the sandpit before I head back to the office."

Zayt scowled.

"I didn't say I wouldn't go along with it. I just said I didn't like it."

"Alright, then. Let's get to work," Bradley said.

They arrived at FBI headquarters at 1:15pm. Mara was at her desk, deep into her computer. Nick and Jim were not in the office. Zayt followed Bradley down the hall. They stopped to peer into Interrogation Room A. Nick and Jim sat at a table with an older woman with perfectly styled silver hair, light-green pant suit, and pale-yellow blouse. If Bradley had not recognized her as Sharon Stakes, Juliette's immoral accomplice, he might have thought of her as somebody's grandmother.

They could not hear the conversation, but at that moment, they could tell things were heating up. Nick stood, pushed his chair back, placed his fists on the table, and leaned toward Stakes. Bradley noticed she did not flinch. That was not a good sign.

Once they got to Derek's office, Hazel asked them to sit and wait. She explained that Derek was on a call and could not be disturbed.

They sat in silence and watched Hazel work. She moved efficiently and quietly. When she opened or closed them, even her file drawers didn't make a sound. Bradley attributed that to the WD40 oil sitting on top of the cabinet. The taps of her computer keyboard were muted, and the coffee pot sat far enough away that it could not be heard brewing from where they sat. She had created a perfectly quiet, pleasant, and comfortable space for herself, and more importantly, for her boss.

A light blinked on her phone.

"Yes, sir." Pause. "Right away. Sir, you have Agent Whitman and Mr. Gaines here to see you." Pause. "Yes, sir."

"Can I get either of you anything? Coffee? Water? Juice?" she asked.

"Thank you, Hazel. Two glasses of orange juice would be great," Bradley said.

Hazel took papers off her desk and walked silently down the hall.

"How does she do that?" Zayt asked.

"Do what?"

"She's as covert as anyone I've ever worked with."

Bradley chuckled as Derek opened his office door.

"Come on in. How's Rusty?"

"Better. They're going to keep him overnight, but they think he will be okay," Bradley answered.

"That's great."

Bradley watched as Derek sat in his chair and rubbed his forehead just above his eyebrows with his right hand. His eyes looked murky and tired.

"Are you okay, Derek? You don't look so good," Bradley stated.

Derek removed his hand from his face and sat upright.

"I'm fine. Just busy, that's all. I've been on the phone all morning. Were you able to get anything out of Miss Powers?"

"Yes, some. Our guy is white with a three-dot tattoo on his right hand." Bradley showed Derek Shea's drawing on his hand. "He is demeaning to women. He has a peculiar way with words and how he speaks them, and he has some kind of accent, she couldn't say from where, but he is not from the immediate area. He drives a large black SUV, and in this case, wore a black hoodie. We already know he is roughly six feet tall with a boot size of thirteen."

"How is she?" Derek rubbed his forehead again.

"She's better. She's tough. I think she'll be okay."

Hazel lightly knocked on the door before entering. She delivered coffee to Derek and juice to Bradley and Zayt before returning to her desk.

"What's the plan?" Derek asked.

"We're meeting in the conference room at two-thirty. We'll form a plan, depending on what we've come up with. Then we'll meet with Rome, Philbin, and maybe Doyle here at three-thirty."

Derek stared straight ahead and nodded slightly. He clearly had other things on his mind.

"Or," Bradley continued, "I could handle the meeting with Rome and Philbin in the conference room. Why don't I see if they can come in at two-thirty, and I'll combine the two meetings?"

Derek looked up. "Yes, great. See if you can make that happen."

Derek's phone rang.

"Yes, Mrs. Hadley?" Pause. "Alright, put her through." Derek covered the phone with his hand. "I've got to take this call. Keep me posted."

Bradley and Zayt left the room and went to Bradley's desk. Someone had put a chair at the desk where there wasn't one before.

"Huh! Have a seat," Bradley said. "I don't think I've ever seen Derek so distracted. Something is going on. And it can't be good."

"I guess it wouldn't have been a good time to mention that you have a murderer gunning for you, then, huh?" Zayt said quietly.

"I've got the advantage. That bastard doesn't know that I know his intentions."

Bradley called Detective Rome and Agent Philbin and arranged for them to meet in the conference room at two-thirty instead of Derek's office at three-thirty. Bradley found himself worried about Derek. He hoped he would have another chance to talk to him before the day faded.

Nick and Jim walked down the hall with Sharon Stakes alongside. Jim took Sharon to the elevator while Nick approached Bradley and Zayt.

"How did it go?" Bradley asked.

"Won some, lost some. You got your confirmation on the laundry issue. They did not perform that service. I'm going to go write this up while it's still fresh. I'll be finished by two-thirty."

Nick never looked at Zayt.

"What did I ever do to that guy? I just met him for chrissake," Zayt said, exasperated.

Bradley chuckled.

"That's just the way Nick is."

They heard a gasp from the other side of the room. Mara jumped out of her chair and hurriedly moved to the printer. She stood and waited, tapped her foot, and moved her hand up and down as if to hurry the flow of ink. Once printed she ran out of the room.

"That looks promising," Bradley said.

In the conference room at two-thirty, Bradley sat with Zayt, Nick, Jim, Detective Rome, Agent Philbin, and Sergeant Doyle. Noticeably absent were Mara and Derek.

Bradley made introductions for those who hadn't met and began.

"Okay, here is where we were at this morning, for those of you who weren't here. We've discovered that the cases between the murders, the train wreck, and the casino project are also linked to a large home healthcare fraud case we have been working for many months. Unfortunately, we discovered this too late, and we found the recipient of the investigation murdered this morning by way of the same MO as the other killings. Also, the perpetrator made this more personal by poisoning my dog this morning. There is a lot of information to go through today. Things are happening quickly. But we have a bigger problem."

Bradley looked around the table.

"From the beginning, even before we knew these cases were connected, our bad guy or guys have been one or two steps ahead of us. Somehow, our information is getting to them. I'm urging everyone to be extra vigilant as to how you handle the evidence we gather in this case. I'm going to ask Agent Richards to have the IT guys run diagnostics on the in-house computers and my equipment at home. Detective Rome, I urge you to do the same with your department."

Rome nodded his head.

"Maybe we shouldn't have nonlaw-enforcement people in the room with us," Nick said while staring at Zayt.

"Give it a rest, Nick," Bradley barked.

Bradley briefed the newcomers on the latest material, including what he and Zayt had learned from their talk with Shea but left out the part about the killer's threat toward him. Then he asked Nick to report on his interrogation of Sharon Stakes.

"Stakes is a psychopath. She and Juliette Berryman made the perfect pair. She had no reaction when I told her Juliette had been stabbed to death. In fact, she almost smiled.

"Our first goal was to establish whether there was a legitimate reason for Berryman to pay fifty million dollars to KIC Laundry Services over the course of the years. There is none. Berryman Home Healthcare did not provide laundry services. We believe this is the money that Berryman laundered for another entity, receiving a handsome twelve percent fee for her troubles.

"Our ultimate goal today was to get Sharon Stakes to tell us who the contact is, which did not go well. She's not talking, and I don't think she is afraid of getting back on the street. She did say that Juliette would disappear for a couple of hours every Wednesday morning, but Sharon could not or would not say where Juliette went or who she met. We've got Catherine Leeks downstairs, and I'll be talking to her after this meeting."

"Thanks, Nick. At least we can lay the groundwork for the laundering connection. See if you can get information from Leeks regarding the guy with the tattoo and accent. He's the guy we want. If you absolutely need to make a deal, do it. Detective Rome? Sergeant Doyle? Anything happening in the murder investigations?"

Detective Rome spoke. "We can confirm, using area traffic cameras, a large black SUV was in the outlying area when both murders occurred in the sand pit. And we have a witness who saw a black SUV at the convenience store but said it had blacked-out windows. We may have a partial license plate number. The lab is working on that as we speak.

"We're analyzing the tire tracks from behind the warehouse where Miss Powers was beaten and the footprints from the sandpit, but I wouldn't hold much hope for any revelations there."

"Thank you, Detective. Agent Philbin, do you have any questions?"

"No. I just want to help any way I can."

"Thank you, Mark. I hoped we would have some news from Agent Thompkins, but it seems she is occupied. Detective Rome, I think it would be wise to put an officer on Miss Powers. It's possible that after speaking with her today we may have put her back in danger. Until we figure out how he's getting his information, I don't think we should take any chances."

"I'll get someone over there right away," Rome said.

"I don't want to scare Miss Powers. Could you use a female officer who might blend in?"

Rome thought for a moment. "Yes, I can do that."

Bradley took a deep breath.

"This thing is much bigger than any of us anticipated. We need to tread lightly but move quickly. We don't need any more dead bodies. We are dealing with an entrenched organization, and this is not their first roadshow.

"This same scenario has played out in Florida, New York, and Maryland, and who knows how many other places. We found the beginning of the rope. Now we need to unravel it.

"Philbin, I need you to look into those three previous Eastern Entertainment Alliance projects. Document all the similarities and find out who the main players were. See if you can find any others that we don't know about.

"Nick and Jim, you have Catherine Leeks. Make her talk. Detective, Sergeant . . . keep us posted on the results of the lab tests and anything else you find. Remember to keep all information confidential and only among the people in this room as well as Agent Thompkins and Agent Richards. Any questions?"

"When will we meet again?" Agent Philbin asked.

"I'll get back to you on that," Bradley said.

Philbin, Rome, and Doyle left the room.

"Where the hell is Mara?" Nick asked.

"I don't know. She grabbed something off the printer and ran out of the office. I'm sure there is a good reason she wasn't here. Let me know when you're done with Leeks. I have a feeling once this dam breaks, it's going to come at us fast."

After Nick and Jim left, Bradley turned to Zayt.

"We have a leak. It's the only explanation. And there's only two places it could come from—the Revere Police Department or our own FBI headquarters."

"Well, if you look at it from an outside perspective, it could also be me," Zayt said, stony-faced.

"Don't think I hadn't considered it. But it's not you."

"How do you know?"

"Because you didn't know anything about the Berryman case until today. I mentioned working a fraud case last night, but I never mentioned the name Berryman. And this all began with Berryman, not the murders."

"So, who do you think it is?"

"It's not Derek, and it's highly unlikely it's Nick. I don't know enough about Jim and Mara to count them out. And Philbin . . . well, I would like to take a closer look at him. As far as Rome and Doyle, I can't rule either of them out. How's that for a playing field?"

Looking over Bradley's shoulder, Zayt said, "Jesus, she's in a hurry."

"Who?"

Out of breath and very excited, Mara burst through the door.

"We've got them. I know who they are. I know who they are." She slammed a stack of papers on the conference room table.

"Slow down. Catch your breath, Mara. And, please, close the door," Bradley said.

Mara closed the door and sat in a chair between Zayt and Bradley. She took a few deep breaths but couldn't wait to tell her news.

"You asked me to check on the city council race. There are only two candidates left in the contest. One is a woman named Marci Gason. Her platform suggests the electorate replace a woman with a woman. However, she is pro-casino. Smart, right? Her opponent is a man named David Simms. His only message is the need to defeat the casino. Polls are showing Miss Gason with a slight lead over Simms."

Mara inhaled deeply and exhaled slowly.

"I figured I'd start with her, which paid off. Searching social media, local online newspaper websites, and chat rooms concerning the new casino, I found this."

She plopped a printed photograph in front of Bradley.

The photo showed a group of seven people sitting at a banquet table where one chair sat empty in front of a place setting. Someone obviously occupied the space but had left the table. The picture clearly had been taken during an event of some kind. People mingled in the background. Bradley instantly recognized one of the men at the table.

"That's Mayor Reynolds," he said, pointing to a dark-haired man on the far side of the table. He showed the photo to Zayt.

"That's right," Mara said. "And starting from his left you then have Webster Collins, Linda Poule, Henry Lipkan, an empty chair, Gil Bates, Hunter Leeden, and bringing you to the mayor's right side, Taylor Chang."

Mara stood triumphantly.

Zayt sat clueless.

Bradley tilted his head.

"I know those names. Collins, Poule, Lipkan, Bates . . . ," He recited them out loud mostly to remind himself where he had heard them before.

He slammed his right hand on the table.

"The companies under Kaishi & Jieshu. Those are the names of the CEOs and presidents."

Mara smiled.

"That's right. Webster Collins, the construction tycoon. His name appears as president of both Queen's Court Unlimited and King's Court Unlimited. Linda Poule, a television personality, is CEO of Eastern Entertainment Alliance. Henry Lipkan, healthcare management, is CEO of the Atlanta-based OC-CYX Industrial Corporation. Gil Bates, computer industry, is president of Mathematical Data Perception Enterprises out of Minneapolis. Hunter Leeden is a financial guy and

CEO of Billings Estate Industries. Which brings us to Taylor Chang, CEO of China-based, Swiss-owned Kaishi & Jieshu, a manufacturing company and at the top of the totem."

"Okay, okay." Bradley took a moment to think. "But what about Mayor Reynolds? How does he fit in with these people?"

"I'm so glad you asked," Mara smiled.

She slapped another piece of paper on the table.

"This just came in from Delaware. Look who is listed as the president of Revere Industrial Properties, LLC."

Bradley scanned the report, then smiled.

"Robert P. Reynolds, also known as Mayor Robert Reynolds."

"I don't get it. Is one of these people our murderer?" Zayt asked.

"Doubtful. But I'll bet my life they hired the murderer," Bradley said. "Mara, what about the last seat, the empty chair?"

"I don't know who sat in that chair, but I bet whoever it was will be listed as the owner of the last remaining company, the only company with information unaccounted for, KIC Laundry Services. I'm still waiting to hear from Delaware on that one."

"This is the organization. These are the main players. Now we just need to follow the money trail, and we'll have them," said Bradley.

"But what about the killer? He's still out there too, dammit," Zayt said, frustratedly.

Bradley looked to Zayt. "Nobody has forgotten him, Zayt. But there are two ways to find this guy. The first way is through the people who hired him, these people." Bradley stabbed his finger at the photo lying on the table.

"What's the second way?" Zayt asked.

Bradley stared at Zayt, and Zayt had a good idea what the second choice entailed.

"What? What's the second way?" Mara asked.

"Never mind, Mara. Keep digging. Find out who is missing from that photo. One more thing. This information stays with us three. Well, four. I'm going to fill Derek in. But we can't let this information get out. Can I take this photo, Mara?"

"Yes, I've got another copy."

Bradley explained to Mara about the leak within their group. He felt confident he could take Mara off the suspect list.

"Great work, Mara. Really great," Bradley said.

"Thank you." She smiled and raced back to her desk.

Zayt waited until Mara had left. "You're going to set yourself up, aren't you? Make yourself a target!"

"No. We are going to set him up."

"I don't like it. Orders are orders, Bradley. You don't break away from your team and go rogue. It's too dangerous, and it never works."

"It'll work. I just need you to back me up. This is the thing I told you about, the thing I can't ask my fellow agents to participate in."

"I don't know, dude. I don't know if I can do this. We can find another way."

Fear showed in Zayt's eyes. It threw Bradley off guard.

"What's the matter, Zayt? What happened?"

Zayt turned his head away.

"Nothing, dude. Never mind." He went quiet.

Bradley could tell Zayt struggled with a painful memory and felt bad about bringing it to the forefront, but it was the only way he could conceive of to capture the guy. And he had an obligation to Shea to do so.

"Don't worry, man. We got this."

"Yeah."

"Hey, I want to fill Derek in. Do you want to hang out? Otherwise, I can have an officer take you home or to my place. I don't know how long I'm going to be."

"I'm okay. I'll wait," Zayt said.

"You can hang out at my desk it you want. There's also the cafeteria."

"Yeah, I know the lay of the land, dude. Go ahead. I'm good."

Bradley rolled down the hall to Derek's office while Zayt pulled a chair for himself over to Bradley's desk.

Hazel informed Derek of Bradley's arrival, and Derek met him at the door looking unsettled and rumpled. Bradley had never seen him like that.

"Jesus, Derek. What the hell is going on? You look terrible."

"Goddam bureaucratic bullshit," he replied. "I've been on the phone all day taking heat from Director Davis, Governor North, Mayor Reynolds, and every other self-important asswipe in the state. Every one of them wants my head on a rail."

When Derek realized he had said all of it within earshot of Hazel, he composed himself, apologized to her, and shut the office door.

"I'm sorry, Bradley. You caught me at a bad time. I didn't mean to unload like that."

"No need to apologize. It's nice to find out that you are still human. So, what are they upset about?"

"They want to know how we allowed Juliette Berryman to get murdered right under our nose. How the mayor and the governor found out about the investigation in the first place, I don't know."

"We have a leak." Bradley blurted.

"What?"

"I've narrowed it down to either Jim Jansen, Mark Philbin, Detective Rome, or Sergeant Doyle."

"Jesus."

"There's more. We just got the report from Delaware. Mayor Robert Reynolds is listed as president of Revere Industrial Properties. That's the company buying up all the property surrounding the sandpit."

Bradley showed Derek the photograph of people sitting around the table with Mayor Reynolds.

"Every one of the people sitting with the mayor is recorded as CEO or president of at least one of the businesses under the Kaishi & Jieshu umbrella."

In deep thought, Derek spun his chair to the side and glanced down at the floor.

He turned back to face Bradley and said, "It's a failsafe."

"What do you mean?" Bradley asked.

"If everyone in the organization risks exposure, then no one can back out. They are all culpable. It's an old mob tactic. You know, make the new guy kill someone so he can be trusted. But in this case, each member has their name associated with part of the organization. If one goes down, they all go down."

"So the empty chair at the banquet may have belonged to our killer. Or maybe it belonged to Juliette Berryman. I've got Mara working on it. I want to talk to the mayor," said Bradley.

"We can't tip our hand."

"I won't. Let's have him come in for a briefing. Tell him you want to keep him in the loop of the investigation. He won't be able to resist."

"What would you hope to gain by bringing him in?"

"First, I'd like to see how he operates," Bradley asserted.

Second, I think we can make him a little uncomfortable, maybe enough to reach out to the rest of the organization."

"How will you do that?"

"I'll lie. I'll make it sound like we have more than we do. Make him squirm. And it may get the rest of the asswipes off your back."

Derek chuckled.

"I'll make the call. When do you want to do it?"

"Tomorrow would be good."

"I'll see what I can do."

"Derek, don't let them get to you, alright? Nobody can do this job better than you."

"Right. Get out of here." Derek managed a smile.

Zayt and Mara sat at her desk, both of them looking at her computer screen.

"Giving away FBI secrets, Mara?" Bradley smiled.

"Only the juicy ones, Agent Whitman." She smiled back.

"How are you making out with our eighth dinner guest? Any ideas?"

"Nothing yet," Mara replied.

"Do me a favor. Do a search including Juliette Berryman and Mayor Robert Reynolds. See what pops up," Bradley nearly whispered.

"Okay."

Mara's fingers flew across the keyboard.

"Here's an article about the dedication of the hospice unit in Revere. The mayor and Juliette attended, but not together. An election night article lists Berryman Home Healthcare as a contributor to the mayor's campaign along with some other major corporations. Not much else. But I can keep looking."

"Check the newspaper database too, please, Mara. Whoever sat in that chair will most likely be registered as president of KIC Laundry Services. Let me know as soon as you hear from Delaware regarding their corporate structure."

"I will. We should be hearing from them soon," Mara surmised.

"Zayt, can I talk to you in the conference room?" Bradley asked.

"Yeah, sure."

On the way, Bradley asked, "So, what's going on with you two, anyway?"

"Who? Me and Mara?"

"Yes, you and Mara. It seems the two of you have hit it off."

"What are you talking about? We hardly know one another. What else was I supposed to do? Sit alone in your corner over there?"

"I'm just saying. I'm not the only one who noticed."

"Noticed what? Who?"

"Jesus, Zayt, for a Navy Seal, you sure are oblivious to the people around you."

Zayt stopped walking. Bradley stopped in the hall in front of Interrogation Room A, where Nick, Jim, and Catherine Leeks were in deep conversation. He turned his wheelchair to face Zayt.

"What are you talking about?"

"I'm talking about Nick, man. You asked what you did to piss him off." Bradley bobbed his head toward Mara.

"Nick? And Mara?"

"Well, I don't think Mara knows it, but yes. You had Nick jumping out of his skin last night—and this morning."

Zayt laughed. "No kidding. Mr. Tightass himself. Well, he has good taste."

He walked into the conference room. Bradley followed and closed the door.

"We're trying to get the mayor in here tomorrow under the pretense of briefing him on the Berryman murder. I'm going to tell him that we have physical evidence that will lead us to the murderer. I'll make it sound like an arrest is imminent. Can I count on you to back me up?"

"Yeah. I'm good."

"Alright, I'll let it slip that I'll be alone at my house tomorrow night. We can set things up tonight and come up with a plan."

"Dude, you've seen how efficient this guy is. Whatever he has planned for you will be the same."

"I'm counting on it," Bradley said. "He's going to want to cut me like the others. That means he needs to get close. I don't intend to let him."

"Why don't you get Nick involved? I'd feel much better if we had this guy far outnumbered."

"I can't put him in that position. I'd be putting his career in danger. I won't do that to him."

Someone knocked on the door.

"Yeah, come in," Bradley shouted.

Nick walked in looking like the cat who swallowed the canary. A wide grin flashed across his face, and he had his swagger back in full force.

"She knows him. Catherine Leeks has seen him many times. We got a description. A little over six feet tall, light brown hair, almost blonde, cut military style, you know, like a flattop, and crooked teeth. He's got a few tattoos. His left forearm has a couple of Chinese or Japanese symbols. He has a dagger on his right forearm and three dots between his thumb and forefinger on his right hand. And he speaks slowly with a Midwestern accent. Juliette called him Joshua."

Bradley closed his eyes and pictured the man. Then his eyes flew open. He pulled the picture of the group of people sitting at the banquet table from his chair pocket. In the background stood a tall man. He looked uncomfortable wearing a suit. The camera captured him glancing at the gathering of people at the dinner table.

"Is she still in the interrogation room?" Bradley asked.

"Yeah," Nick said.

Bradley folded the photo in a way that only exposed the lone man. "Show her this man," Bradley said. "Just him. Don't let her see the rest. See if it's him."

Nick took the picture and left the room.

"This guy is definitely the paid muscle. He might be former military," Zayt said.

"Mara is gathering as much information as she can find on everyone at that table. Maybe that will lead to whoever is missing from the photo and put a name to this guy. I wouldn't be surprised if Joshua is not his real name."

Bradley grew quiet.

"What are you thinking?" Zayt asked.

"I'm thinking I have to get back to my place and get to work. I want to know everything I can about these people before I meet with the mayor."

Derek opened the conference room door.

"I hear you may have an ID on our guy," Derek said.

"We'll find out in a minute. Nick is showing Catherine Leeks a picture right now."

"We have a picture?"

"Maybe. There was a guy in the background of the banquet photo. He fit her description."

"The mayor will be here at one o'clock tomorrow afternoon. I told him he would be meeting with you. It's the only time he had available. Unfortunately, I have a meeting with Director Davis at the same time."

"No problem. I'm just going to feel him out. You know, give us an idea what we're up against."

Nick barged into the room.

"It's him. We got a positive identification. Once she finds out this is now a murder case, I think she will roll over completely."

"Offer her protection. Whatever it takes. Has she brought in a lawyer yet?" Derek asked.

"No, I've been focusing my questions on Juliette Berryman's murder and general business practices. She has no idea the position she is in."

"I want to do this right. No mistakes. Remind her she can have a lawyer present before you ask her any more questions," Derek told Nick. "Let's go easy with her, keep her comfortable. But start ramping things up a bit."

"Nick, ask her about the abacus," Bradley said.

"The what?" Nick asked.

"Juliette had an abacus in her office. The colors on the abacus correspond to the colors on the file folders. There is a connection there. I just haven't found it. Ask specifically about the green beads on the abacus. Let's see her reaction."

Bradley, Derek, and Zayt moved into the hallway where they could watch but not hear the discussion. Trying to appear casual, they formed a circle as if in their own conversation. Catherine Leeks never looked their way. They watched as she nodded her head. They assumed Nick had mentioned her right to have a lawyer present.

Then Nick said something that made her stiffen. Her eyes widened and her fingers gripped the arm of her chair. She turned her head and saw the three of them looking at her. Fear engulfed her face.

Nick and Jim left the room.

"She wants a lawyer," Nick said.

"Good," Derek replied. "Now we can hit her hard. Get her to a phone."

"What's with the abacus?" Nick asked Bradley.

"My theory is Juliette used it as a means of scheduling and recording transactions. It was her way of keeping track of things. The green beads had me stumped, but now I think she must have used them to keep track of the money laundering. I'm sure she had a more sophisticated way of monitoring the transactions, but the abacus gave her an account of her dealings with just one glance, and it didn't require a paper trail. I used a similar system when I was a kid."

"Well, it scared the crap out of her," Nick said.

"Now she knows that we know. I'll send you the report I wrote about that. It's not much, just in theory form, but she may be able to fill in the blanks," Bradley said to Nick. "You handled her well, Nick. Your uncle would be proud."

Nick's face softened.

"Okay, everyone back to work," Derek said.

On the way home, Bradley and Zayt stopped to visit Rusty. He was groggy and unsteady on his feet, but his bobbed tail wagged and his tired eyes gleamed. Bradley did not want to leave him there, but he knew it was best for the dog. He had also made a decision to ask the veterinarian to keep him for an extra night. He told the people in the office he could not be home with the dog and didn't want to leave Rusty alone. The next night would be a dangerous one and he didn't want Rusty getting hurt.

They happily obliged.

"Make me a promise, Zayt," Bradley said.

"That's never a good start to a conversation," Zayt replied.

"I'm serious. If anything happens to me, I need you to take care of Rusty."

"You don't even have to ask, dude."

"I figured as much."

Once home, Bradley and Zayt made their plan. Bradley strategically placed his Smith & Wesson Performance Center 1911 .45-caliber pistol in a holster attached to the underside of his desktop. He placed his .38 special Colt revolver in the firewood box. His Glock 9mm went into a kitchen drawer, and he kept his Glock .45-caliber in his chair pocket.

"Have you got a firearm?" Bradley asked Zayt.

"Are you asking as an FBI agent or the guy whose life will be in my hands?"

Bradley cast him a glance. "The second guy, the one who will remind you afterward that possessing an unregistered firearm in Massachusetts is a felony."

"Just joking with you, dude. I'm licensed and it's registered, just not to the address where I currently live."

"You do have a peculiar sense of humor," Bradley said.

"And you do have a lot of handguns," Zayt replied.

"My father gave me the Smith & Wesson when I graduated from the academy. The Colt was my grandfather's, and the .45 Glock was a gift from Derek. It's the one he used at the academy.

And I bought the 9mm as a gift to myself. It fits nicely in my chair. But I think I want a little more firepower at my fingertips tomorrow."

"So, how do you want to do this? Where do you want me?" Zayt asked.

Bradley reached into his chair pocket, pulled out a cell phone, and threw it to Zayt.

"I got it from the office," he explained. "The sliders will be unlocked. I'll call you when I'm on my way home. That way no one will see us together. You can come from the pit and position yourself somewhere near the backyard. He'll come in. I'll let him get close before I call for you. Then you come in and we take him without a shot being fired."

"What if he has a gun?"

"Then I might have to shoot him," Bradley said.

"Do we know if this thing works?" Zayt held up the phone.

Bradley called a preprogrammed number, and Zayt's phone rang.

"I put my cell number in there, too, just in case you're feeling lonely," Bradley chuckled. "Now, I've got work to do. You're welcome to stay. Help yourself to anything in the refrigerator."

"No. I think I'll look in on everyone down below. Call me in the morning just to let me know you're still alive. This guy may not want to wait until tomorrow."

"You be careful, too. Whoever our leak is, I'm sure he has mentioned your involvement. Sweet dreams," Bradley grinned.

It was too quiet. Bradley realized he hadn't been alone in his house for over a week and a half. Usually comfortable with being alone, just then he didn't like the feeling. He set his security alarm, something he never before felt compelled to do when he was at home and awake.

He moved to his office and delved into the lives of the banquet brigade. Derek had submitted the picture of Joshua to the facial recognition lab, but Bradley knew that any results could take days.

He sent Nick his report on the abacus theory among other information he though pertinent to Catherine Leeks's interrogation.

EXPOSED

Opting to get right back to work, Bradley skipped his morning workout. He had uncovered many connections between the banquet brigade, as he had come to call them, and their illegal activities. Not only was Juliette Berryman laundering money for them, but Bradley also believed that she supplied them with drugs stolen from her clients. She would most assuredly sell them at a low price, then the brigade would sell them on the black market through one of their own businesses, which then would require money laundering. Juliette made money on both ends.

Bradley found himself admiring Juliette's business acumen if not her choice of business. She was intelligent, shrewd, cruel, and relentless. It all but convinced Bradley that Juliette held the eighth seat at the banquet table. And he felt sure her name would appear at the top of the list of officers of KIC Laundry Services.

The next morning, Bradley checked in with Zayt before heading to the office.

"Yeah?" Zayt answered.

"Has it been so long since you answered a phone that you forgot how?" Bradley asked.

"Yeah."

"How's everything there?"

"Quiet. You?"

"The same. I'm leaving for the office soon. I'll call you when I'm on my way home. I'm going to try to lure him here after eight. I wouldn't expect anything to happen until after nine."

"Alright. Good luck, dude."

"Yeah, thanks. You, too."

"Good morning, Carl," Bradley said.

"Good morning, Agent Whitman. How is Rusty doing?"

"He's doing much better, thanks. He's still at the vet's, but he should make a full recovery."

"That's good news. Here, I made something for him." He handed Bradley a badge that looked like official FBI identification with Rusty's picture and name, *Agent Rusty Whitman*, written across the top. The tag had a string attached through it to slip over Rusty's head.

"Well, that's perfect, Carl. Thank you. Where did you get his picture?"

"I took it with my cellphone the last time he was here. I wanted to show his picture to my kids. They loved him," Carl replied.

"Rusty's going to love it." Bradley shook Carl's hand and placed the badge over his head so it hung down onto his chest.

Bradley had noticed Derek's car in the lot out front, so he passed Nick and Mara, the only others in the office at that hour, and went straight to Derek's office.

It was too early for Hazel, so Bradley knocked on Derek's door.

"Come in," came Derek's voice.

"Good morning," Bradley said.

"Good morning. What are you doing here this early? And what the hell is that around your neck?"

Bradley showed the badge to Derek.

"Carl made it for him."

Derek rolled his eyes. "Looks like I need to have a talk with Carl."

"Oh, leave him alone. He didn't use the official badge. See? There's no watermark or seal. It's all in fun."

"So, what are you doing here? Your meeting with the mayor isn't until one o'clock."

"I figured it would be easier to coordinate if we were all in the same building. Information is coming in fast."

"What information?"

"Can I brief you later, Derek? I want to be thorough."

"Then why did you come in here?"

"I just wanted to see how you're doing."

"I'm fine. You don't need to worry about me," Derek said.

"How's Cate?"

"Huh! Angry at me. She says I'm running myself into the ground."

"Maybe she's right. Maybe you need to take your wife on a nice cruise or something. Relax, have some fun."

"You? You are lecturing me on working too hard? On how to enjoy my life? The guy sitting here wearing a dog's tag? When is the last time you had a date, one that didn't walk on four legs?"

"Alright. Maybe I'm not the best one to give advice. But I know Cate, and if she is worried, I'm worried."

"Let's just finish this thing. Then, maybe, I'll think about it," Derek grinned.

Bradley left Derek's office, went to his desk, and booted the computer. He checked with Mara and Nick, and each updated the others on what they had learned. Mara had researched the history of each brigade member and worked on cross referencing their activities. Nick explained his strategy for

Catherine Leeks. He would spend most of the day with her and her lawyer.

Bradley decided not to mention that the mayor would be coming in. He didn't want to have to explain himself, and he certainly didn't want to give them the opportunity to listen to his conversation with the mayor. It had worked out perfectly that Derek would be in a meeting with the director and Nick would be in interrogation. He could easily come up with something to keep Mara busy.

"Anything from Delaware yet?" Bradley asked Mara.

"Nothing. I'll make another call today, see if I can hurry things along."

"And I assume we haven't heard anything from facial recognition either?"

"Nothing."

The office filled with agents and employees while Bradley, Mara, and Nick continued their research. Jim had arrived, and Nick tasked him with organizing the massive amount of paperwork that had been generated by the investigation.

The morning raced by as Mara made good progress with her inquiries and briefed Bradley as she discovered new connections. With Nick's handling of Catherine Leeks, Bradley felt confident they would eventually have the evidence they needed to put an end to the brigade's enterprise.

Derek stopped by Bradley's desk on his way to the director's office.

"I'm going to be a few hours. I'll call you later. You can fill me in on your talk with the mayor."

"Good luck with Davis. Don't take any of his shit," Bradley grinned.

"Right."

Bradley handed Mara a list of items he wanted her to explore. Busy work.

"Could you check on these as soon as you're done with whatever you're working on?" he asked her. He wanted to keep her at her desk.

All eyes turned to the elevator when Mayor Reynolds and his three-man entourage stepped onto the eighth floor. Bradley quickly moved to greet them and show the mayor into Interrogation Room B. He noticed the mayor glance into Room A where Catherine Leeks sat with her attorney. The mayor's eyes betrayed recognition.

"Please, Mr. Mayor, come right in. We won't be interrupted in here. If your associates would like to sit in the conference room, they are more than welcome."

"They'll be fine in the hallway." Bradley felt a twinge of satisfaction knowing that it would put pressure on Catherine Leeks to seek protection with the mayor's men just a few feet away.

"My name is Agent Bradley Whitman. I am the analyst in charge of the Juliette Berryman murder. I'm here to answer any questions you have. Can I get you some coffee? Or water?"

"No thank you, Agent Whitman. Let's get to business. I understand that the FBI had brought Mrs. Berryman in for questioning regarding her home healthcare business."

"Yes, that is correct, sir."

"And now Mrs. Berryman is dead."

"Yes, sir. Unfortunately, that is true."

"Well? How did this happen? By all accounts Mrs. Berryman was an upstanding member of our Commonwealth and our community. Her services are revered in the highest regard."

"Yes, I understand, sir. Please, let me explain. The Federal Bureau of Investigation received a report from the state citing client complaints that Berryman Home Healthcare, LLC, had billed clients for services not rendered. We opened an investigation based on those complaints."

"And?"

"Well, sir, we did find some discrepancies in her records to suggest the complaints could be justified. However, we had only begun our investigation when Mrs. Berryman was brutally murdered."

"And what have you found out about her murder?" the mayor asked.

"Well, sir, I can tell you that we have linked the murder to two others in the area. Of course, we have not made this information public, and we must ask for your complete cooperation in keeping this between us."

The mayor shifted in his chair.

"I see. What murders are they connected to?"

"We've had two homeless people murdered in the last week, sir."

"And how do you know it is the same murderer?"

"He has a signature, a routine, if you will. He's rather sloppy that way."

Bradley noticed the mayor tense slightly.

"Are you close to catching this murderer?"

"I'm convinced we will have him in custody tomorrow," Bradley stated matter-of-factly.

The mayor cleared his throat.

"That's good to hear. I hope you are as competent as you are confident, Agent Whitman."

"Yes, sir, I am. But I didn't need much expertise for this. The murderer left physical evidence at the Berryman scene. Something unintended. I am expecting the lab results later tonight. We know him to have a military background or at least mercenary, and expect his fingerprints to match those in our database. Frankly, sir, I don't think he's too bright."

The mayor pursed his lips and shifted again in his seat.

"Excellent news. I want you to keep me apprised of the situation. This is a very high-profile case, and I don't want the public to panic. I want you to call me as soon as you are certain you have the identity of the murderer. I will need time to prepare a speech to placate my constituents."

"Yes, sir. As I said, I expect that report by nine o'clock tonight. We have people working around the clock on this. Here is my home number. I'll be there after eight o'clock tonight. Feel free to call me for an update."

Bradley handed the mayor his business card.

The mayor stood. Bradley held out his hand to shake the mayor's.

"Thank you, Agent Whitman. I look forward to speaking with you tonight. I have no tolerance for violence in this city."

"Yes, sir, I understand. Thank you for coming in, sir," Bradley smiled.

The mayor left the room, and his entourage followed him into the elevator. As Bradley rolled back to his desk, all eyes in the room followed him. He felt a heaviness in his gut. There was no turning back.

"What the heck was that about?" Mara asked as she reached Bradley's desk.

"We want to keep the mayor informed, don't we? Be cooperative, share information?"

He flashed her a roguish smile.

"If you say so. I spoke with a woman at the Delaware Division of Corporations. She has run into a roadblock trying to access the paperwork for KIC Laundry Services. She hopes to have the information by the end of the day, but it is Friday and people tend to knock off early there. I told her it was vital we have the information before the weekend. She said she would do her best."

"Okay. We work with what we have. We will need to comb through the financials of not only these individuals, but their businesses, spouses, and children. We'll attack it the same way we did with Berryman, only on a larger scale. I want you to take the lead on that."

Mara's mouth dropped open.

"I . . . I don't . . . I've never . . ."

"Mara, you can do this. You just spent days spilling over complicated and cumbersome data, and you had no problem analyzing it. You understand how to do it one step at a time. Be thorough and detailed. I'll be available any time to help if you need me. Start with Mayor Reynolds."

"But . . ."

"Go. We have a lot of work to do." Bradley shooed her away, pleased with himself for his part in her growth as an analyst.

It was almost four o'clock before Nick and Jim finished with Catherine Leeks and her attorney. Poised and triumphant, Nick strolled out of the room. Catherine's eyes appeared vacant, and her movements lacked energy. Her lawyer showed no emotion. Bradley knew they had her. Jim showed them to the elevator where another agent waited to accompany them out.

"She's agreed to protective custody for full cooperation," Nick announced as he arrived at Bradley's desk. "This morning, the grand jury voted to indict Sharon Stakes and Catherine Leeks. Leeks took the deal."

"How much does she know?" Bradley asked.

"Enough. She talked about Juliette's obsession with the abacus. Leeks doesn't know exactly how it worked, but she knew what she used it for. She used it like you said, to keep track of scheduled fraudulent activities and how much money she would need to account for. That's what scared Leeks, that we knew about the abacus."

"Sometimes you just have to exaggerate which cards you hold," Bradley smiled. "What about the money laundering? Do you think she has useful information about that end of the business?"

"I don't know. We haven't played that hand yet. But if I had to guess, I don't think she was part of it. Sharon Stakes is our best bet there," Nick said.

"I agree. Leeks doesn't have nearly the bank account that Stakes or Berryman had. It would stand to reason she wasn't involved. But let's not deal her out yet."

"Is Derek back yet?" Nick asked.

"No. His meeting with the director must be taking longer than he thought."

"What was the mayor doing here?"

"We need to deflect suspicion. So, I was playing nice," Bradley said.

"Well, it freaked Catherine Leeks out, I'll tell you that. I think she thought we were going to hand her over to the guys in the hallway."

"Added bonus," Bradley laughed. "I'm going to go to the hospital and check on Shea Powers. Then I'm heading home. Enjoy your weekend. It may be the last rest you have for a while."

"Yeah. You too."

Bradley wished Mara a nice weekend and, glad that Derek hadn't returned sooner, left the office. He didn't look forward to lying to him about the meeting with the mayor.

He dialed Zayt's temporary phone on the way to the hospital.

"Yeah?" Zayt answered.

"'Hello, Bradley. How is your day going?' That's the proper way to answer a telephone," Bradley insisted.

"I know a colorful way to say goodbye," Zayt replied.

"I'm sure you do. I'm going to the hospital to see Shea. We're all set for tonight. I told him I would be home after eight. He's antsy. This is going to happen tonight. Is there anything you need?"

"Yeah. Someone to knock some sense into you. I still don't like it."

"It'll work. It's the best way. He thinks I'm an easy mark."

Zayt stayed silent.

"What? What is it you want to say but aren't saying?" Bradley asked.

"Dude, you're a chicken in a coop, and this guy, Joshua, is a wolf."

"Well," Bradley cleared his throat, "it's a good thing I have a wolf hunter on my side. I'll call you later."

Bradley showed his badge to the female officer outside Shea's room and asked if there had been any activity. The female officer reported nothing unusual.

Shea smiled when Bradley came through her door.

"Well, you're looking much better," he said.

"I feel good. I can move a little without those shooting pains. Dr. Weaver said they are going to move me to a regular room tonight. I don't need the machines anymore."

"That's great, Shea. I'm happy for you."

Shea's expression shifted to worried.

"What am I going to do when I get out of here, Mr. Whitman?"

"I told you, call me Bradley. Don't you worry about that. We'll figure something out. Just put your efforts into recovering. Leave the worrying at the door."

"Bradley? Thank you. Thank you for visiting me and caring about me."

Shea teared up.

"No need to thank me. I've enjoyed every minute. You are an exceptional person, Shea. Don't let anyone tell you otherwise. I knew it from the minute I met you."

Shea burst into full-blown tears. Bradley reached for her as best he could, and she slid herself over to the edge of the bed and crawled into his arms. Bradley felt years of self-doubt and fear course through her body. He recognized the feeling. He did not let her go until she felt ready. She wiped the tears from her eyes and laughed.

"I'm sorry. I don't know why I did that."

"Because you needed to," Bradley said.

Doctor Laney Weaver walked into the room.

"Well, Shea. You're looking much better today," she said.

"Oh, my God. I'm a mess," Shea laughed.

"Yes, grown men often make me cry, too," the doctor joked.

Bradley grinned. "Wow, okay. I guess that's my cue. I'll come by and see you tomorrow. Don't worry about anything. We'll figure it out."

"Thank you . . . Bradley," Shea smiled.

"Nice to see you, Doctor Weaver."

"And you, Agent Whitman."

Shea slapped her palm to her forehead.

"Ugh. I keep forgetting you're an FBI agent."

Bradley laughed as he left the room.

Ten minutes went by before Laney Weaver left Shea's side. Bradley waited for her by the bench near the ICU entrance.

"I thought you'd left," she smiled. "You are very good with her. I think you are one of the reasons she is responding so well." She sat next to Bradley.

"She reminds me of someone I knew a long time ago. She's had some tough breaks, but she's strong."

"And how about you? Has your guilt subsided?"

"My guilt? I don't . . . ," Bradley was about to dispute the notion but thought better of it. He sighed. "No. It hasn't."

"You are a nice man, Bradley Whitman."

"Then how would you feel about joining me on Sunday for an afternoon dinner with some people I know," Bradley asked.

"This Sunday? I planned to do my laundry. But I suppose I do have to eat. What time?"

"I can pick you up at noon. Do you like dogs?"

"I love dogs."

"Well, then. Rusty and I will see you on Sunday. Where shall I pick you up?"

They exchanged phone numbers, and he took down her address. He had not planned to ask her out, but the opportunity arose, and on that day, he had a strong feeling that life should be lived in the moment.

He paraded a boyish grin all the way to his truck, then dialed Zayt's phone.

"Well, hello, Bradley. So nice of you to call. How is your day going?" Zayt answered.

"Now, there you go. Was that so hard?" Bradley laughed.

"Yeah."

"I'm leaving the hospital now. Where are you?"

"Outside your house."

"What? Why?"

"I don't want this guy getting ahead of us."

"Jeez, you Seals are crazy. I'm going to stop and see Rusty. Then I'll be home."

"Roger that."

Bradley made his visit with Rusty short because he couldn't stand the thought of leaving the dog there, even though he knew it was the right thing to do. Rusty had gained most of his strength back and wanted to go home.

"Tomorrow, buddy. I'll come get you tomorrow."

Bradley sure hoped that would be the case.

He surveilled his surroundings as he drove down Industrial Drive. There was never much activity on the road, but he saw none at all. He wasn't sure if that made him feel safer or more vulnerable.

He parked his truck in the lean-to and, before descending to the tarmac, checked his .45 Glock. With enough daylight still to see into the dark corners of the lean-to, he saw no lurking figure. Knowing that Zayt had been there most of the day, he felt confident he would find no one inside the house, but he proceeded carefully in spite of his assurance.

Once he disarmed the alarm, he unlocked the back sliders, looked out back, and saw no one. He didn't know where Zayt hid, but he could feel his presence. The clock showed 7:20 pm.

Inside, Bradley booted his computer and camera screens, checked the firearms he had placed the night before, and tried to relax.

He watched his cameras from all angles even though he knew it was too early for Joshua to show. The few blind spots he had on his property began to annoy him. He promised himself he would take care of those if he survived the night, which he fully intended to do, he told himself. He went over multiple scenarios in his head: waiting for Joshua by the desk, in the kitchen, by the fireplace, or closer to the sliders where Zayt would enter when needed.

The tick of the clock grew louder as each minute passed and the sun faded into the night. Sounds that normally go unnoticed deafened him: the icemaker in his freezer dropping cubes into the bin, the whir of the computer sounding like a sandstorm, and the quickening of his heartbeat resembling rainfall on a plastic roof. He had been in stressful situations before but never as vulnerable as this.

This would make a great psychological study, he thought. He felt for his Glock.

DEREK

Derek returned to the office at five o'clock. A few agents remained at their desks, including Mara. He still had an entire day's paperwork to finish, so he settled in at his desk.

By seven-thirty, he had had enough. He was about to leave for the night when he realized he had never called Bradley to see how he made out with the mayor. He looked at the clock and thought he would wait until tomorrow.

Then he remembered he didn't have to. He walked into the room where they listened to the interrogations and worked the recording machine. He played back the recordings for Interrogation Room A and listened to Nick's interview with Catherine Leeks. He appreciated Nick's technique, but he was too tired to listen for long. He played back the only Room B recording for the day.

Derek listened to the conversation and admired how easily Bradley could put someone at ease. Bradley apparently made the mayor comfortable by playing down the Berryman investigation, saying they had just begun and really didn't have anything.

Further, Bradley agreed with the mayor about Juliette Berryman's standing in the community but explained they were obligated to investigate.

Derek was surprised to hear Bradley reveal that they had connected the Berryman murder to the homeless murders.

He listened further.

BRADLEY: We've had two homeless people murdered in the last week, sir.

MAYOR: And how do you know it is the same murderer?

BRADLEY: He has a signature, a routine, if you will. He's rather sloppy that way.

"What?" Derek yelled. He played it back, thinking he heard it wrong.

BRADLEY: He's rather sloppy that way.

"What the hell?" Derek roared, speaking to no one.

MAYOR: Are you close to catching this murderer?

BRADLEY: I'm convinced we will have him in custody tomorrow.

"Are you out of your fucking mind?" Derek bellowed.

MAYOR: That's good to hear. I hope you are as competent as you are confident, Agent Whitman.

BRADLEY: Yes, sir. I am. But I didn't need much expertise for this. The murderer left physical evidence at the Berryman scene. Something unintended. I am expecting the lab results later tonight. We know him to have a military background, or at least mercenary, and expect his fingerprints to match those in our database. Frankly, sir, I don't think he's too bright.

"No, no, no, no. You didn't do this, Bradley. Shit!"

MAYOR: Excellent news. I want you to keep me apprised . . .

BRADLEY: Yes, sir. As I said, I expect that report by nine o'clock tonight. We have people working around the clock on this. Here is my home number, I'll be there after eight o'clock tonight . . .

"Goddamit!"

Derek ran out of the room and to his office. He retrieved his Glock from his desk drawer and looked at his watch. It read 7:53, and Bradley lived twenty minutes away. He ran down the hall where he came face-to-face with Mara, whose eyes showed panic.

"Agent Richards. I just got . . ."

"No time, Mara. Come with me. Hurry."

The two reached the elevator. Derek spewed words Mara couldn't understand. His face ashen, Derek moved at a pace she could barely keep up with. They ran to his car, and his tires squealed as he left the parking lot.

"He set himself up, Mara. Bradley set himself up as a target. I don't know if we're going to get there in time.

"Oh, my God. Why would he do that? Sir, you need to know. I found out who the missing person at the banquet is."

THE PLAN

Zayt watched from a neighboring abandoned business property as a vehicle drove by, a white sedan that then parked on the side of the road in front of Bradley's home. Looking as if he were lost, a man carrying a folder left the vehicle. Once he got within twenty yards, Zayt recognized him. Zayt stayed in the shadows and walked toward the left side of Bradley's house.

"Hey," Zayt called. "What are you doing here?"

"Oh. Hey. I've got my reports for Agent Whitman." He started to walk to the door.

"No, wait. I'll take them. You can't go in there now," Zayt said.

The man approached Zayt.

"I don't know. I think I should give them to Bradley myself. This is sensitive stuff."

Zayt, exasperated, reached out for the folder. "Just give it to me."

"Okay."

Zayt felt a pinch in his stomach, then his body muscles went into full cramp, and he fell to the ground. Unable to move, he realized the man had tased him and there was nothing he could do. Before he regained control, the man bound Zayt's hands behind his back with a plastic tie. He then used a second plastic tie to bind his feet. The assailant ran a rope between the two plastic ties, leaving Zayt lying on his stomach with his knees bent and his feet sticking straight up. He finished by shoving a cloth in Zayt's mouth.

Zayt then saw another figure walk toward him from the shadows of the building next door. He recognized the man as Joshua. Joshua stood over Zayt and said, "We are much alike, therefore, I won't kill you. However, your friend will feel enough pain for you both."

Zayt's wild eyes grew big as he struggled to loosen the ties. He tried to yell, to warn Bradley, but the cloth soaked up his voice as sand does the water. Zayt watched as Joshua rounded the back side of Bradley's house.

Bradley watched as the car parked by the street. *What's he doing here? Why is he walking to the side of the house? He must be talking to Zayt.* A minute later, after hearing no skirmish or threatening activity through the thin, insulated wall, he watched Agent Mark Philbin walk from the side of the house to the front door and ring the bell.

Jesus, his timing sucks, thought Bradley. Only slightly leery, he placed his hand by his side within reach of his Glock, then opened the door.

"What are you doing here, Mark?" Bradley asked.

"I have those reports for you. I thought you would want them before the weekend, so I figured I'd drop them off."

"Yeah, okay. Great. But you've got to go— now!" Bradley said.

"What's the hurry. It's Friday. How about a beer or something?" Philbin said as he made his way into the room.

Bradley knew then that it wasn't right, but it was too late. The back slider opened, and Joshua walked through the door. His attention diverted for only a second, Bradley reached for the Glock in his chair pocket, but Philbin had already pulled his service pistol and pointed it at Bradley's head.

"Hands up, Whitman. No sudden moves." Philbin reached into the chair pocket and retrieved the Glock before Bradley could get it.

"I knew it had to be you," Bradley said as he raised his hands.

"We duped you right from the start, Whitman. You and your buddy, Richards."

"You didn't fool anyone, Philbin. You're still the loser I took you for."

Philbin's nostrils splayed, and he bared his teeth like an animal about to attack. He took a step toward Bradley, put his free hand around his throat, and squeezed.

Bradley gripped Philbin's arm. His upper body strength allowed him to wrestle Philbin's hand from his throat with little trouble.

"You are a failure at everything you do, Philbin," Bradley pressed.

Philbin swung the grip end of his gun and connected with the left side of Bradley's head. Blood trickled down, covering Bradley's ear and running down onto his shoulder.

Lightheaded, Bradley looked at Philbin and grinned.

Joshua finally spoke. "Go away. He's mine now."

Bradley detected a Midwestern accent, Minnesota he guessed. He slowly backed up and turned his chair toward Joshua, bringing him closer to the firewood box and his .38 special Colt.

Philbin reluctantly retreated and stood in the front doorway.

"That was pretty . . . sloppy . . . leaving your friend out there to die alone. I would have thought an FBI agent would be more . . . bright," Joshua laughed like a hyena, high-pitched and crazy.

Bradley's heart fell into his gut. *Zayt, I'm sorry*, he thought. Forced to recover quickly, he said, "Well, Joshua, it looks like you needed the FBI to do your dirty work this time." He shot Philbin a look of disgust.

Hearing Bradley use his name incensed Joshua. "I don't need anyone. I've been doing fine on my own all these years."

"About eight years now, isn't it?" Bradley inched his way toward the firebox.

"Oh, Agent Bradley Whitman, you are sorely mistaken. I go back further than eight years," Joshua sneered, countering with his use of Bradley's full title to suggest his own superiority.

"Minnesota. Am I right?"

The fireplace almost lay between them now.

"Very good, Agent. It is nice to know someone appreciates my work."

"You've perfected it since that kill. A thirty-three-year-old woman found stuffed in the closet of her apartment. The authorities didn't find her for weeks. You didn't slash her throat. She struggled. A lot. She was your first, wasn't she?"

Bradley was close to the box. He just needed to angle his chair so he could reach the revolver.

"You don't really think I'm sloppy and stupid, do you? And you know I didn't leave any evidence behind at that bitch Berryman's house. You knew there was only one chance to catch me. So, you set me up. Well, you tried to set me up. But I'm always a few steps ahead, Agent."

Bradley tweaked his chair to the left and waited for the right moment.

"It looks to me like you do need backup. Otherwise, why would he be here now?" Bradley bobbed his head toward Philbin.

That made Joshua angry.

"Get out!" he screamed at Philbin and turned his attention towards the door. "Get out, you fool!"

Bradley reached for the wood box and took hold of the revolver. Joshua ducked behind the fireplace as Philbin and Bradley fired at each other simultaneously. Philbin fell backwards out the front door. Bradley froze momentarily until Joshua rounded the fireplace, positioned himself behind Bradley, and grabbed Bradley's right arm. Struggling for control of the gun, Bradley felt the blade slice into his right bicep. His grip on the gun faltered, and it fell to the floor. Joshua slowly slid the knife from Bradley's arm, kicked the gun toward the front door, and smiled.

"I never liked that guy," Joshua laughed.

Bradley used his left hand to put pressure on the slice in his arm. A large puddle of blood formed at the base of his chair. Lightheaded, he stared at it as he thought something wasn't right but he couldn't figure out what.

Joshua circled his chair and stood in front of Bradley. He took control of the chair's joystick and moved Bradley back and forth through the puddle of blood.

Joshua chortled a macabre, ghastly sound like a pack of fisher cats on a fresh kill.

As if a new toy for a child, Bradley's chair took Joshua's attention. Bradley slipped his hand under the arm of the chair to flip the power switch off. That angered Joshua. He growled as he dragged the heavy chair away from the fireplace, rocking it violently from side to side, Bradley bobbing back and forth with the chair until the chair spilled him onto the floor in front of his desk.

Bradley's head hit the floor first. He became dizzy and disoriented. Laughing, sneering, Joshua stood over him, and Bradley thought he saw white foam drip from his mouth.

"My mother put up more of a fight than you," Joshua said.

Bradley used his good arm to drag himself closer to the desk. *Just keep moving, Bradley. Don't stop.* The words played over and over in his head, words his mother spoke often during his physical therapy sessions as a child. He repeated it over and over as he inched his broken body toward the corner of the room.

Joshua watched, amused. "They should have killed you as a baby," he said, then laughed at the thought. "What good are you to anyone? Go ahead. Crawl and hide. I'm about done with you."

Bradley felt himself losing consciousness. He fought with everything he had. *Keep moving, Bradley,* but he could go no further.

Joshua straddled Bradley's body. "You are useless. Therefore, you will die. However, no one will miss you."

He raised the knife and held it with both hands over Bradley's face.

Screaming as the pain from the wound in his bicep felt like a fire in his chest and side, Bradley reached with his right hand for Joshua's left arm.

Joshua released the grip with his left hand, repositioned the knife in his right hand, and held it high above Bradley's head.

Bradley reached back with his left hand searching for the weapon under the desktop, slid the Smith & Wesson out of its holster, turned his head to the side to avoid the blade, and fired the gun.

Two more shots sounded. Bradley didn't know where they came from.

It's time now to die, he thought.

He lost consciousness.

Bradley heard voices speaking quickly, loudly, but they didn't make any sense. A nonstop beacon from the lighthouse annoyed him as he tried to sleep. Too loud. Just let me sleep. He floated in a sea of water, warm and comfortable, the sun beating down on him. He felt his feet splash through the clouds. No, that's not right. It's water. No, it's as light as air. I'm soaring. I'm flying. I'm free.

He wanted to see. He tried to open his eyes, but they felt heavy, sealed. *Keep trying, keep moving. Keep moving.*

He jumped to his feet. The cold steel floor sent a chill through his body beginning with his toes, spreading through his arches, around both heels, and shooting up through his legs. His torso stiffened, and his back arched.

And then there was darkness.

AFTERMATH

Light seared his eyes, so he squinted to minimize discomfort. Slowly, he lifted his lids and focused on her face. She looked down on him and smiled.

"Hello, Bradley," she whispered.

"Hello, Laney." He struggled with the words and didn't recognize his own voice. It sounded harsh and dry.

"Don't try to speak. Give it a little time," she said. "You are at Mass General Hospital. They had to operate. The bullet shattered your fibula, the small bone in your lower leg. You had a tube down your throat. That's why it is sore."

Bradley's eyes darted as he recalled what happened. He shook his head from side to side.

"No. I was stabbed, not shot," he strained.

Laney Weaver brushed a lock of hair from his face. A look of concern replaced her smile.

"You were shot and stabbed. You also have a deep contusion on the left side of your head and a large bruise on the right side. You lost a lot of blood."

Blood, Bradley thought. The pool of blood under his chair. There was too much. That is why it didn't make sense. He tilted his head back into his pillow and closed his eyes hard, as he remembered more details.

"Zayt?" His eyes shot open in panic.

"He's fine. He's out in the hall with everyone else. They've been here all night."

Bradley's body began to tremble. The thought that he had gotten Zayt killed had almost paralyzed what was left of him. Finding out that his friend was alive and unharmed released a tremendous amount of tension and self-loathing, so much that he could not immediately control his emotions.

Laney placed her hands on either side of his face. He leaned his head into her hand and reached with his uninjured arm, placing his hand on her forearm. "I'm alright."

He took a deep breath. It felt like a razor scraped his throat.

"Derek. I need to . . . " He swallowed hard. Laney gave him a cup of ice water with a straw.

"Just a little. Sip a little at a time," she cautioned. "You can see him soon."

"Now. I need to . . . " His eyes conveyed his sense of urgency.

"I think you should wait just a little while."

He reached his hand for hers and squeezed it as though a plea, then shook his head.

"Okay," she conceded. "But I'm staying in the room."

He nodded.

Laney opened the door to the corridor outside Bradley's room. Bradley heard her tell Derek that he was awake and wanted to see him.

"Hey." Derek stood beside the bed.

"Hey," Bradley's voice scratched. Hoping to get his voice back, he labored to swallow.

"Joshua?" he asked.

"He's dead."

"How?"

"One bullet to the face, yours; two to the back of the head."

Bradley's head jerked. He remembered hearing other shots.

"Who?"

"Me."

Confusion showed on Bradley's face.

"How did . . .?" his voice trailed off.

"I listened to your interview with the mayor before I left the office." Derek's face grew stern then softened to concern.

"I'm sorry," Bradley looked him in the eyes.

"We'll talk about it later."

"Philbin. He's . . . ?" Bradley swallowed again.

"We know. You shot him in the chest. He's listed in critical condition here at the hospital."

"Zayt?"

"He's fine. They tased him and tied him up. He's pretty pissed off. And he feels responsible for what happened to you."

"My fault," Bradley said.

"Yes. It was." Derek grew stern once again. "Your parents are here. Your mother won't leave until she can see you. Cate is outside, too. She sends her love."

Bradley's eyelids fluttered. He drifted off before he could respond.

When he woke, his mother sat holding his hand, and his father stood at the foot of the bed.

"Hey, Mom," he whispered.

She stroked his hair with her right hand while holding his left hand tight with her other.

"Hello, sweetheart." Tears filled her eyes.

"I'm sorry, Mom," he said. A small tear slid down the side of his cheek.

She handed him the cup of water and wiped the tear away. He took a small sip.

"Hey, Dad." He looked toward the large man at the foot of his bed.

"You gave us quite a scare, Bradley. We almost lost you. Your mother has been frantic."

"I know, Dad. I'm sorry," he rasped.

"Don't talk, Bradley. Laney said you should give your windpipe a chance to heal," Lynn, his mom, said.

Bradley grinned when Lynn called Laney by her first name.

"She's great, isn't . . . ?" Before Bradley could finish, Lynn placed her finger on his lips.

"Shhh," she smiled. "And, yes, she is great. Now, no more talking from you."

Bradley nodded.

"When I told Doctor Weaver that you were supposed to come to dinner on Sunday, she laughed. She told me you invited her for afternoon dinner with . . . quote . . . some people I know?"

Bradley smiled.

"I do hope you planned to give us warning so we could put our best foot forward," Lynn said.

Bradley nodded.

There was a knock on the door.

"Come in," Lynn called.

Laney came through the door accompanied by two male nurses, one pushing a wheelchair.

"Time to get up," she insisted.

Bradley's eyes widened.

"What? Did you think we were going to let you lounge around here all day?" she grinned.

"That's right, Bradley. It's time to get moving and keep moving," Lynn said.

Hearing those words, Bradley felt a tenderness in his heart and the will to persevere.

"What time is it?" he asked.

"Nine in the morning," the doctor said. Then turning to Lynn and Doug, she countered, "You two should get some rest. He's going to be busy for a while."

"Whatever you say, doctor," Lynn smiled. "We'll be back in a few hours."

"Take my keys. Go to the house and get some sleep," Bradley offered.

"We can't do that, son. The police and FBI still have the house locked down. We are staying with Derek and Cate. They insisted," Doug replied.

"Oh. Right." Bradley hadn't thought about that. His place must look like a war zone.

The cast on his leg made things awkward but not prohibitive. The strength in his right arm only slightly diminished, he found it painful to use, and the contusion on his head resulted in a slight concussion, but unless symptoms persisted, his medical team found no cause for alarm.

Laney came to check on Bradley.

"How are you feeling?" she asked.

Bradley pushed himself up in bed, arranging the pillows so he could sit up straight. He used his fingers to fix his hair and licked his lips to wipe away the dryness.

"I'm doing great," he smiled. "How are you?"

"Me? I'm a little disappointed. I really looked forward to having dinner tomorrow with some people you know." She feigned a pout.

"You're not going to back out on me, are you? Just because of a little gunshot hole, knife wound, and split skull?"

"You really are a charming man, Bradley Whitman. And your parents are wonderful. I do hope you had planned to warn me I would be meeting them at dinner."

"I did. I just wanted to wait until you couldn't back out," he laughed.

"I would love to have dinner with all of you. But unless you plan to have dinner here in the hospital, I suggest we reschedule. Besides, you need to rest."

"No, Laney. I don't. I need to live," he said as he reached for her hand.

A tear strolled down her cheek. "I wasn't sure you were going to make it. When your heart stopped, I thought we lost you."

"My heart stopped?"

"Yes. They had to use the defibrillator on you. I thought your parents would have told you."

"No." Bradley's mind flashed back to the sensation of cold steel running through him, his body arching, and the feeling that he had jumped. He continued, "They didn't."

"That's one of the reasons you need to stay in the hospital for another night, to monitor your heart. Besides, you need to rest and regain your strength."

At three-thirty Sunday afternoon, Bradley rolled out of the hospital in one of their bulky, uncomfortable wheelchairs. Doug had pulled their SUV to the curb, and the passenger door lay open.

"Ready?" Doug asked Bradley.

"Two days stuck in this place. I'm more than ready."

Swiftly and easily, Doug lifted Bradley and the two, working together, maneuvered him into the passenger seat.

"It's been a while since we had to do that," Bradley said.

"Like riding a bicycle. I just didn't realize how much I missed it," his dad said.

Bradley could sense the nostalgia oozing from the moment. Lynn sat in the back seat as she had done for so many of his teenage years.

"Derek said the authorities are done with your house," Doug stated.

"Um, Mom, I don't think I want you to go in there," Bradley said.

"Bradley, whatever we face, we face. That's what family is all about. We face things together," Lynn said.

"Mom, I know you are a strong person, but I don't think this is something you should see."

"The discussion is closed, Bradley. Your mother and I have already talked about it."

"Okay. But I don't know what we're going to find."

They pulled into the driveway, and Bradley saw Zayt standing by the front door with Bradley's chair. Zayt used the joystick to bring it to Doug's SUV. Bradley opened the car door.

"Zayt, man. It's good to see you."

"Dude, you scared the shit out of me."

"Same here, man. I thought you were dead. Joshua told me you were dead."

Doug came around to lift Bradley out of the truck and into his chair. Bradley finally felt at ease. He hadn't understood why he didn't feel complete. It was his chair. His chair made him complete. The realization astounded him.

He worked his way to the front door and opened it. Rusty came charging toward him and stopped short of jumping on his lap but bounced on his hind legs as if he wanted to.

"Rusty, buddy. Come on up!" Bradley gladly instructed. He hugged the dog and stroked his neck. "You look good, buddy," he said to the dog. "How're you doing?"

Bradley looked to Zayt for the answer.

"They said he's doing great. He shouldn't have any long-term effects."

"Long-term effects from what?" Lynn asked.

"He was poisoned a couple days ago. He's been at the vet's," Bradley said.

"Oh, my goodness. Well, let's go inside and get introduced to your new housemate, the poor thing," Lynn said.

Bradley hesitated but moved inside. He surveyed the room and found himself shocked. Nothing looked out of place. It was clean, fresh scented, and more organized than he would normally keep it. He glanced at Zayt.

Zayt shrugged his shoulders. "It looked like this when Mara dropped me and Rusty off. She drove me to pick him up at the vet's. An RPD officer watched the place until we got here."

Derek, Bradley thought.

Lynn stood with her hands on her hips and her head tilted to look the short distance down to Bradley.

Sarcastically, she said, "Well, yes, Bradley. I can see why you wouldn't want us to come inside."

"Derek must have had the cleaning crew in here, Mom. He wouldn't have wanted you to see the aftermath of what happened any more than I wanted you to see it. Anyway, Rusty, meet Mom. Mom, meet Rusty."

Rusty sat in front of Lynn and looked up with his heart-melting eyes.

"He's beautiful, Bradley. And so well behaved." She petted Rusty. "He reminds me of Roscoe, the dog you had as a boy."

"Mom, Roscoe was a mutt. Rusty is a Doberman Pinscher, probably purebred."

"He's a dog, isn't he?" she laughed.

Doug reached his hand out for Rusty to smell and get acquainted. Once they had all met, Bradley wanted to get his parents out of there.

"Listen, Mom and Dad, I'm a little tired. I'm going to lie down for a while. Maybe you could come back for dinner tonight around six-thirty or so?"

"Oh, honey, of course. We'll head back to Derek and Cate's and see you later. We'll bring something for dinner," Lynn said.

After they left, Zayt turned to Bradley and said, "Well, I better get going so you can rest."

"What? No. We need to talk. And we need to get hold of Derek, Mara, and Nick and find out what's going on."

"Dude, you just lied to your mother."

Bradley groaned. "Zayt, I sure would have missed you if you died, man."

"Same here." They clasped hands, the way two people would if engaged in an arm-wrestling competition.

"I'm sorry I put you in that position. I could have gotten you killed," Bradley said.

"And I'm sorry I wasn't there when you needed me," Zayt responded.

REPERCUSSIONS

Bradley dialed Derek's cell phone.

"What are you doing? Where are you?" Derek snapped.

"I'm at home. Zayt's here with me," Bradley said.

"Well, go to bed or something. The doc said you needed rest."

"I wanted to thank you for having my house cleaned. I didn't want my parents to see it."

"I didn't want that either. Lynn would have forced me to fire you, and she would be right to do so. But I am suspending you. You fucked up big this time, Bradley."

"Joshua already had me on his hit list, Derek. I just made it happen on my terms, not his."

"Don't start with the excuses, Bradley. You lied to me. You looked me in the eye and lied to me. I can't work with you if I can't trust you," Derek barked angrily.

Bradley felt a hole in his gut.

"I know. You're right. I'm sorry."

"I've heard it before. Not too long ago, in fact. Grow up, kid, or you're out." Derek meant every word. The episode had scared him enough that his initial thought *had* been to fire Bradley. It was Cate who talked him out of it.

Bradley softened his voice like he did when scolded as a young boy.

"Alright, Derek."

"I have to go. We're busy here. I need your notes on the case. Everything you've got," Derek said.

"Give me another day or two. Let me help finish this and then I'll go away for however long you need me to. Quietly."

Pause. "No push-back? No argument?" Derek asked. He knew it would be difficult to wrap the case up without Bradley's input.

"None."

The phone went silent. Then, "Online meeting in twenty minutes. I just sent you the link. But, Bradley."

"Yes?"

"After tomorrow, you're out. For six months." Derek hung up.

Bradley slowly pulled the phone from his ear. He had never had to deal with Derek's wrath before. Not really. He hated that he had lied to him, and he didn't like the position he had put him in. Bradley knew he had gone way too far. He had known it when he came up with the plan, but he did it anyway. He found himself wondering why.

"Jesus, that didn't sound good," Zayt said.

"No, it wasn't. Looks like I'll be out of work for a while."

"How long?" Zayt asked.

"Six months."

"That could work to my advantage," Zayt said.

"What do you mean?"

"I have an idea. I want to run it by you. But not right now. Soon," Zayt said.

"I'm intrigued. But I have a conference call in twenty minutes, and I don't think Derek would be happy if you sat in on it."

"Nope, I'm on his shitlist, too," Zayt said.

"Come back for dinner. Mom always makes too much food."

"Look who's talking. Later."

Bradley logged into the meeting a minute before its scheduled start. Mara waited. Bradley could tell she sat at her office desk.

"Hey, Mara."

"Bradley," she smiled. "I didn't expect you in this meeting. How are you feeling?"

"I'm doing great, thanks. Listen, I don't want to make a big deal about this, okay."

"Alright, I understand," Mara said as Nick showed up on the screen. He called in from home. Bradley could see Nick's apartment kitchen in the background.

"Shit, Bradley. I didn't expect you to be here. You okay? I mean, Jesus . . ."

"Yeah, Nick. I'm fine. We'll talk about it another time, okay? We have work to do."

"Sure, Bradley."

Jim, Detective Rome, Sergeant Doyle, and Derek all chimed into the meeting at the same time. Derek sat at his office desk, Jim called in from home, and Rome and Doyle shared a screen from the Revere Police Department.

"Holy crap, Bradley, you crazy bastard," Jim said.

"Jesus, Bradley. You're lucky to be here," Rome proclaimed.

"Luck, I tell you. Pure luck," Doyle stated.

"Alright!" Derek yelled over them. "Schedule the Agent Whitman admiration conference some other time. We have work to do." Derek clearly had no intention of disguising his anger.

Bradley's chin sunk to his chest.

"Mara, give us the rundown on where we are with evidence against these people," Derek snapped.

"Well, Agent Whitman has a better understanding . . .," Mara began.

"I want to hear from you, Agent Thompkins."

Derek was one wrong word from an explosion.

Bradley knew Mara would look toward him for encouragement, and he didn't want to make Derek angrier by making eye contact with her, so he kept his head down until she began her update.

"What we currently have is a group of eight individuals, all holding positions of authority and all connected by one umbrella manufacturing corporation registered in Switzerland and located in China. The name of the corporation is Kaishi & Jieshu, which, by the way, loosely translates to The Beginning and The End.

"There are eight businesses or corporations under that umbrella," she continued. "Each one lists a different CEO or president, depending on its corporate structure. All of those people can be seen in this photograph, minus one. You will notice their names printed below the photograph."

Mara's face disappeared from the screen and the Banquet Brigade appeared.

"We have identified the eighth individual," she continued, "the one who presumably sat in the empty chair, as our own Agent Mark Philbin who is currently in the hospital after an attempted murder on Agent Whitman Friday night in his home. The other suspect in the attack is known only as Joshua. He can be seen in the background of the picture. He was pronounced dead at the scene of the Friday night murder attempt."

She took a deep breath when her voice began to quiver.

Bradley kept his head down and did not look at anyone.

Mara continued.

"Put simply, we need to produce overwhelming evidence that these eight individuals conspired to commit multiple murders in at least four states and engaged in illegal activities such as money laundering, black market drug sales, intimidation tactics, and other fraudulent activities."

Mara looked to Derek for a cue as to whether to continue. He nodded.

"We believe the evidence will be available in their financials, and we are working on that. However, it may take years to unravel, and we can assume the suspects will simply disappear the closer we get to unveiling their organization."

Derek cleared his throat. He spoke in a monotone.

"Thank you, Mara. Mara will take the lead on the financial end of the investigation. Nick, I want you and Jim to find a way to connect these suspects in a more personal way. They likely meet periodically to discuss business. Find out how often and where they do. Detective Rome and Sergeant Doyle, thank you for all of your help to this point. We will share any information we uncover regarding the sandpit murders. However, we must keep the rest of this investigation in-house. I'm sure you understand."

"Yes, I do," Rome said. "Thank you, Agent Richards. If there is anything the Revere Police Department can do to help, please ask."

"If you would excuse us now, Detective, Sergeant? We have more to discuss," Derek said.

"Of course." Detective Rome and Sergeant Doyle disconnected from the meeting.

"Okay," Derek said. "Let's hear your thoughts on how best to go about this."

Bradley always admired and respected Derek's willingness to ask for others' input into a situation. But even though Bradley would usually be the first to speak, he wasn't sure it was a good time for him to do so, so he sat back to let the others voice their opinions.

No one spoke. The silence felt awkward and contrived. Bradley could feel the tension reach out and grab him by the throat. And he could see Derek's face change from unhappy to outraged.

"What? Nothing? No one has a fucking brain today?" Derek slammed his hand down on his desk. "Am I the only . . ."

Mara, Nick, and Jim had never seen Derek lose his temper. Never. Bradley had only seen him that angry once before. He knew he had to do something.

"Derek!" Bradley shouted.

Derek's tirade stopped abruptly. He breathed heavily. The heat radiating from his infuriated face could have cooked an egg.

"I know who Joshua is," Bradley said.

It was suddenly quiet again. Derek calmed himself, wiped his brow, and sat back in his chair. The others waited for Bradley to continue.

"Mara, do you have the list of murders that we received from the FBI database search of stabbing MOs handy?"

"Yes, I have it here." She rifled through one of the piles on her desk. "Here."

Bradley continued. "About ten years ago, there was a thirty-three-year-old victim found stuffed in a closet in Minneapolis, Minnesota with stab wounds to her face but not to her neck. Can you find it?"

Mara combed the report.

"Here it is. Patricia Mooring, age thirty-three. Single mother of one child, found approximately two weeks after her death."

"What was her child's name?" Bradley asked.

"Charles. Charles Joshua Mooring. Born in Minneapolis, Minnesota, twenty-seven years ago." Mara's mouth dropped and her eyes drew together. "It was right here all this time."

"Joshua was seventeen years old when he killed his mother. His first murder. I imagine if we look back into his childhood, we'll find a history of violent acts toward small animals and possibly against other children. Does it say who his father is?" Bradley asked.

"No. Not on this paperwork," Mara answered.

Derek jumped into the conversation sounding more like himself, calm and in control.

Bradley's expression turned pensive.

"Find out, Mara. Get a complete history of Charles Joshua Mooring and . . .," Derek interrupted himself. "What is it, Bradley? I know that look. What are you thinking?"

"Mara, do you have the mayor's file in front of you?" Bradley asked.

Mara pulled a file from her drawer and opened it.

"Yes," she said.

"How old is Mayor Reynolds?"

"He's forty-nine."

"Where was he born?"

"St. Paul . . ., Minnesota."

Bradley smiled. "He's worked hard to rid himself of the midwest accent. Mara, where did the mayor live twenty-seven or twenty-eight years ago? He would have been about twenty-two years old?"

"He would have been in college, correct?" Mara asked.

"Most likely," Bradley answered.

"Oh, my God," Mara gasped. "Mayor Robert Reynolds got his degree in political science from the University of Minnesota. He attended the school from the age of eighteen and graduated at age twenty-two."

"And how far from the college did Patricia Mooring live? She would have been about fifteen years old?"

They could hear the keys on Mara's keyboard. And then Mara's face beamed.

"Patricia Mooring's father was, and still is, a professor at the University of Minnesota. She grew up in a house on the outskirts of campus."

"Mara, get the hospital records and any information you can on both the parents and the child. Nick, you and Jim concentrate on the mayor. I want his life story, his friends, the college clubs he belonged to, everything." Derek was back in form. "That's it, get to work. Bradley, hang on for a minute."

Mara, Nick, and Jim signed off.

"Bradley, how do we link the others?" Derek asked.

"The grand opening for OC's Slots & Entertainment is in Ocean City, Maryland in four months. Get the guest list and see if our brigade will be attending together."

"Brigade?" Derek questioned.

"That's just what I'm calling them. Anyway, I'll check the previous events and see if they attended those together also. But, more importantly, we need to link the money laundering deposits to KIC Laundry Services. Once we do that, we can see how the money got distributed. Because Mark Philbin is registered as president of KIC, we have cause for a search warrant for the business records. That should be done today."

"I'll call the district attorney now," Derek said.

"If we can show that money made its way from KIC to any of these other people, we should have enough to go to a grand jury. And, we still have Catherine Leeks and Sharon Stakes. I think we can do this, Derek. I really think we can nail these people."

"Alright, get to it," Derek said.

Then, "Wait. No. I'll have Mara do it."

"Mara has too much to do already. Come on, Derek. You said I had another day," Bradley reminded him.

"I refuse to let you kill yourself on my watch, Bradley," Derek snapped.

Derek disconnected.

Bradley picked up his phone and dialed Mara's number.

"Hello," she answered.

"Hey, Mara. Could you do me a favor?"

"Anything, Bradley. What do you need?"

"Wait a few minutes, then go check on Derek. Find an excuse to see him."

"Alright. But what do you want me to do?"

"Just make sure he's alright," Bradley sighed.

"Okay, Bradley. Do you want me to call you back?"

"No need. Thanks, Mara."

He hung up the phone and sat back in his chair. He closed his eyes and thought about what Derek said. *I refuse to let you kill yourself on my watch.*

Bradley thought about how close he and Derek were, as close as brothers, or at least how Bradley perceived brotherhood. *Derek knows me better than anyone else,* Bradley thought, *including my own parents. He's a level-headed man. Does he really believe I was trying to kill myself?*

The text alert sounded on his cell phone. It came from Mara.
Derek said to go to bed!

Bradley chuckled. "I can't fool him," he said out loud, with only Rusty there to hear him.

No, you can't, a voice in his head responded.

AWARENESS

Rusty ran to the door, but it wasn't until Bradley heard the knock that he woke from his unintended nap. He still sat in his chair in front of the computer.

"Come in. It's open," he yelled.

"Bradley, my word, why would you leave the door unlocked? Hello, Rusty. Sweetheart, you look awful. Do you feel alright?"

Lynn ambled through the door. "Did you take your pain medication? Goodness, you look terrible."

Doug walked behind, his arms loaded with bags.

"Mom, I'm fine. You just woke me, that's all. I've hardly had a chance to open my eyes."

"You slept in your chair?" She frowned. "Bradley, you really must learn to take care of yourself."

"Hi, Dad," Bradley grinned.

Bradley noticed that Doug had left the door open. He moved toward it to close it but then saw Cate. His face brightened and so did his mood.

"Cate, it's so good to see you." He reached up for a hug.

Cate reached down and held on to Bradley like she would never let him go again. Bradley felt her body tremor. She was sobbing.

"Hey. It's alright. I'm okay, Cate."

She wouldn't let go.

Bradley felt her tears moisten his shoulders. He had difficulty holding on to his own emotions. Cate had a way of exposing Bradley's core, and sometimes it scared the hell out of him.

She let go, wiped her eyes, and kissed him on the cheek.

"You aged me, Bradley Whitman, and you are going to pay for that. Sheila made me promise to give you that kiss. She and David send their love," Cate said.

"How is your lovely sister, Cate? Are they still living in the lap of luxury in their large, lavish lair in Hollywood Hills?" Bradley grinned.

Cate giggled, "You haven't lost your flair, Bradley. Yes, they are still in Hollywood Hills, and she desperately wants you to visit soon."

"Well, I will soon have some time on my hands," Bradley said.

Cate's eyes showed alarm as she gazed at Bradley and slightly shook her head from side to side.

"Oh, why is that, Bradley?" Lynn asked.

Bradley looked at Cate.

Swiftly, Cate said, "Oh, are you planning to take a vacation?"

Bradley then understood that Derek had not told Bradley's parents the full story of what happened. They didn't know that Bradley had arranged for Joshua to seek him out. And they didn't know that Bradley was about to be suspended.

"Yes, Cate. I've been thinking about it for a little while," Bradley lied.

Rusty jumped up and ran to the door, his tail wagging to signal that Zayt had arrived.

"Come in, Zayt," Bradley yelled.

Zayt entered, and Rusty jumped up to greet him. Surprised by all the activity, Zayt stood at the door.

"Well, come in. Nobody here is going to bite you. Well, maybe Cate." Bradley winked at her.

"Zayt, this is Cate, Derek's wife. Cate, this . . ."

"Bradley, we met last night. At the hospital," Cate reminded him.

"Oh, yeah, I guess you would have." Bradley began to realize just how many people his actions had affected. A grey cloud enveloped his brain.

Doug and Lynn unpacked aluminum trays of food. Lynn turned on the oven and asked Bradley where he kept his wine bottle opener.

"Who else are you expecting for dinner, Mom? The 25th Marine Regiment?"

"There's nothing wrong with leftovers, Bradley. You shouldn't be cooking for a while. So, tell us about the vacation you've planned."

"Ah, well, I haven't planned anything, Mom. I am just thinking about taking some time off," Bradley said as he nodded to Zayt. "Zayt and I talked about going on a fishing trip, right Zayt?"

Zayt's eyes shot open. "Uh huh."

"Maybe even camp out somewhere, right Zayt?"

"Uh huh."

Doug listened to the exchange between Bradley and Zayt. Bradley could tell he didn't believe it. He tried not to look his father in the eye.

"How can I help you, Lynn?" Cate asked.

"I'm going to get some fresh air," Bradley said and headed to the sliders.

"I'll come with you," Zayt said.

"Me, too," Doug said.

Once outside, Doug asked, "What's going on, Bradley?"

He knew there would be no sense in lying.

"As of tomorrow, I will be on suspension from the bureau."

"What? Why?" Doug asked.

"Because I didn't follow procedure, Dad. I messed up."

"Well, can't Derek do something? Suspension seems awful drastic for not following a procedure."

"It's Derek who is suspending me. And he is right to do it. I put too many people in danger, Dad. I screwed up, and someone died. I was just lucky it wasn't one of us." After saying the words aloud, Bradley finally acknowledged the severity of his deception.

Doug stood silent. He looked hurt, as if someone kicked him in the gut. When he spoke, he did so softly and empathetically.

"I suspected," Doug said.

"Suspected what, Dad?"

"You put yourself between that man and everyone else, didn't you?" Their gaze met, and Bradley saw a sense of failure in his father's eyes.

"Just like you did when you were twelve years old and you put yourself between Duke Montalvo and Cate," Doug continued.

Bradley looked confused. "I was twelve, Dad. I did what I thought I had to do. We talked about that."

"And the drug addict at the pharmacy? How many times, Bradley? How many times have you put yourself in danger? I can recall a few more in your teen years that your mother told me about. How many more don't I know about? How many more have you hidden?"

Zayt stepped back, distancing himself from the conversation. He walked around the side of the house to give them privacy.

"Dad, I don't know . . ."

"You're still that young boy, aren't you, the one who thinks he's only worth something if he's out saving the world."

"That's not true." Nothing in the conversation felt real. Bradley felt as if he were floating in water and something pulled at him from below to sink him to the depths.

"And it's my fault," Doug said. Tears formed in his eyes. He looked in the direction of the sandpit but saw only a blur. "It's my fault, Bradley. I'm sorry. I should have been there for you. I never should have gone back on active duty after your illness."

"Dad, this is crazy. What are you talking about? You've been the best father in the world."

Bradley felt himself drowning.

"No, Bradley, I haven't. I wasn't there. And even when I was, I wasn't. We should have had this conversation a long time ago, but I was unsure—and afraid. Maybe if we had, you wouldn't have put so much pressure on yourself."

Doug turned back toward Bradley.

"What I'm trying to say is sometimes we all feel helpless and sometimes we all feel like Superman. The truth lies somewhere in the middle. For all of us, Bradley. You are not alone. We all have our own limitations."

Doug wiped his face and knelt on the ground to face Bradley. He held Bradley's face between his hands and looked him square in the eyes.

"Listen to me. You are much more valuable to this world than you believe, Bradley. And you won't be able to save it if you're dead. And if you continue to put yourself in these positions, you will come out on the losing side. And for what purpose? To prove what? What we already know. That your life has meaning. You are not the helpless six-year-old boy in the backyard. You have a lot to offer. You make this world a better place. You make this world a safer place. But you don't need to do it alone. And you don't need to die to prove that you lived."

Bradley sat still, stung by his father's words. Thoughts and memories rattled in his brain like his favorite carnival ride, the Scrambler. Each car nearly collided with the next and the next and the next, spinning out of control with no switch to turn off the ride. Pounding grew louder with each memory: Montalvo writhing on the ground, a knife-wielding drug addict in a pharmacy, a man with a gun in a dark alley, and a double-teamed assault in his home. And there had been more, a lot more. They all came back to him in his scrambled state. But the pounding receded as he acknowledged each one until it was quiet once again, and he found himself buried in his father's chest, rocking back and forth, sobbing uncontrollably.

Lynn and Cate stood at the sliders holding each other close, and Zayt stood behind them when Derek came through the door.

Cate turned and ran to him, tears streaming down her face. She led him to the sliders where Bradley still clung to his father. She didn't need to explain what was happening.

Derek lowered his head, not wanting to intrude on Bradley's private moment. He walked to the refrigerator and reached for a beer. Then, surprising himself, he said, "Zayt, you want a beer?"

Astonished that Derek offered, Zayt said, "Yeah. Thanks, Derek."

The two sat at the kitchen table, Zayt on the stool, Derek in the webbed lawn chair.

"It's been a long time coming. He'll be alright," Derek said.

"I'm sorry for my part in this," Zayt said.

Derek nodded and hesitated before he went on.

"Bradley has this intense need to protect the people around him. Sometimes it gets away from him and clouds his judgement. I think he beats himself up because he thinks he is

. . . ineffectual. Of course, that's total bullshit, but he can't help how he feels. I can usually see it coming, but I missed it this time. He's gotten better at hiding it."

Derek lowered his head and narrowed his eyes. Then, barely above a whisper, he said, "Maybe even from himself."

Zayt sat quiet but nodded his head in response.

"Here's the thing, Zayt." Derek gave Zayt a piercing look. "I get the impression you and Bradley are very much alike, and that worries the hell out of me."

Zayt reciprocated with concentrated eye contact.

"You're right, Derek. We are very much alike. Which means I will do everything in my power to protect him, even if it means protecting him from himself."

After giving Zayt's comment consideration, Derek reached across the table and held out his beer. Zayt lifted his bottle, and they tapped the two longnecks together.

DINNER

When Bradley woke the next morning, something felt different. After the fog lifted from his sleepy eyes, he noticed Rusty lying on his bed, his head resting on Bradley's left leg, the one without a cast.

"Hey, buddy," Bradley smiled. "What are you doing up here?"

Rusty lifted his head and angled it toward Bradley's face. Bradley reached down and caressed him.

"It's good to have you home, pal."

They lingered in bed longer than normal, both appreciating the fact that they could. Bradley pondered the conversation he had with his father the night before.

He wasn't used to seeing his father in such a vulnerable state. Never through his childhood had he and his father talked about making mistakes or feeling inadequate, useless, or helpless.

They had talked for over an hour in the backyard, just the two of them. During his adult life, Bradley's internal bouts of self-loathing would come and go, but he never admitted to feeling powerless to his father until the previous night. He barely admitted it to himself.

After their talk—and tears—Bradley saw himself clearer than he ever had before. The grey cloud that always hovered over him thinned to a wispy fog. He began to see that his feeling of ineptitude sometimes drove his desire to overcompensate for his constraints. Even more startling stood the revelation that Derek may have been right. Maybe beneath his confident and poised charade lay an unconscious desire to end his life in the guise of saving others.

Staring at him with his chocolate eyes and calming gaze, Rusty observed Bradley.

A deep internal warmth rushed through Bradley's whole body. Startled that he felt the sensation in his feet and legs, he lifted himself up to a sitting position and looked at his lower body. Rusty lifted his head.

"Huh, that was weird."

Rusty cocked his head.

"Did you feel it too?"

Rusty tilted his head to the opposite side.

Bradley grinned.

"Time to get up, Rusty. We've got some living to do."

Doug, Lynn, Derek, and Cate arrived at five o'clock with a set of four dinner-table chairs and bags of food.

"What's the matter?" Bradley laughed. "You don't like my furniture?"

"I didn't want to have to sit on the weight bench to eat my dinner," Lynn smiled.

Bradley received hugs from Lynn and Cate as Doug and Derek carried the chairs to the table.

"Consider it an early birthday present," Lynn said.

Doug and Bradley firmly embraced. So powerful was their grasp that Bradley once again felt the sensation of internal heat through his body, a feeling he hoped he would have to get used to. When they released, Bradley saw a look of pride in his father's eyes.

Derek approached to shake Bradley's hand, but instead, Bradley pulled him in for a hug.

"Can we talk? Outside?" Bradley asked Derek.

"Alright."

Derek took the webbed chair from the kitchen and brought it outside. He placed it in front of Bradley.

"Derek, I know I've said this before, but I am sorry. I think I finally understand what you've been trying to tell me. I haven't been honest with you—or myself. You've protected me all these years, and I just kept pushing." He paused. "I want you to know that I'm going to do everything I can to change, to appreciate what I've got, and not dwell on what I don't have. I love you, Derek. You're like a brother to me."

When Derek started to speak, his voice cracked. He cleared his throat and said, "You are my brother, Bradley. And I will always protect you. I love you, too."

Derek stood and leaned over Bradley, himself initiating the hug.

"But," Derek said, "you are still suspended."

He smiled.

"Yeah, I know. I deserve it."

"Before we go back inside, I want to let you know we got a copy of Charles Joshua Mooring's birth certificate. His mother's name is Patricia Mooring and the father's name is listed as R. Reynolds. How did you know?"

"Research. I remembered seeing something about Minnesota in the mayor's biography. What about Philbin?"

"He's going to pull through. We got the search warrant for KIC Laundry. I've got a team in there today. Their walls are tumbling. You did great work."

"We did great work," Bradley said.

While having their conversation, Bradley watched as tension drained from Derek's body, the tension Bradley had created. He vowed right then never to be the cause of it again.

"Let's get inside. Cate wants to drill you about Doctor Weaver before she gets here," Derek chuckled.

She arrived at six o'clock. Bradley met her at the door before she had the chance to knock. Rusty sat by his side.

"Hello," he smiled.

"Hello." she returned the smile. "This is an interesting neighborhood you live in. It suits you."

"I don't know if that's good or bad," Bradley laughed. "Come in. This is Rusty."

"Hello, Rusty. You are a handsome boy, aren't you?"

Laney walked into the house, and the aroma of Italian food consumed her.

She inhaled deeply. "Something smells delicious."

"It's lasagna," Cate said. "Lynn has been teasing me with it since yesterday. Her sauce is divine. Hello, Doctor Weaver."

"No doctor. It's Laney, please."

"Laney it is," Cate said.

"It's actually Bradley's recipe, Laney," Lynn spoke. "He's a much better cook than I am."

"Mom, please." Bradley felt slightly embarrassed and nervous.

"Well, it's true, isn't it?" Lynn said.

Doug, Derek, and Cate all said yes before breaking into a collective laugh.

"Let me show you around," Bradley said to Laney.

They moved to the other side of the room near the office area. Rusty followed.

"Thank you for coming," Bradley said. "It means an awful lot to me. I know it can't be easy meeting my family on our first date."

"Bradley. What wasn't easy was when you almost died in my emergency room. And then I met your parents and your friends, and I knew you would fight. I knew you would fight for them."

"It was they who fought for me, Laney," Bradley spoke somberly.

"I don't understand," she said.

"I'll explain it to you later, when they go home, and we can be alone."

Bradley took her by the hand.

"It's a date."

SIX MONTHS LATER

Bradley and Zayt sat in Bradley's backyard and surveyed the tentless sandpit. Large equipment scattered through the area as excavators, dump trucks, and bulldozers performed a construction dance. A cement truck poured its contents into one of the many rectangular wooden frames within the pit's boundaries.

"Are you going to miss your camp?" Bradley asked.

"A little, I guess. There's some self-satisfaction living off the grid."

"What do you think Mamma Lise is thinking right now?"

Six months earlier, after Bradley and Zayt survived Joshua's attack and Bradley got suspended, Zayt approached Bradley with an idea. He had already confessed to Bradley that he knew where Mamma Lise had hidden the money her insurance company searched for. What Bradley didn't know was that she still had a large sum stashed away, though not enough to implement Zayt's vision. Zayt wanted to build a community of tiny homes to house the homeless, especially veterans. He enlisted Bradley's help.

With the casino project dead, the sandpit became the logical location for the project. With the help of Shea and her real estate license, they petitioned the City of Revere to agree to a thirty-year lease with an option to renew. It took three months before the city council, with its newest member, voted to approve the lease. The ground-breaking ceremony for the

REACH program, Revere Enhancement and Community Housing, took place the day before.

After months of negotiations, consultations, and fundraisers, Zayt's vision lay before him.

"Mamma Lise would say, 'Take care of yourself, so you can take care of others,'" Zayt had said.

The slider doors opened behind them, and Derek appeared. Wearing his new red service-dog collar, Rusty followed him out the door and sat between Zayt and Bradley.

"What are you doing here?" Bradley asked. "It's Sunday. Shouldn't you be home with your wife?"

"Hello to you, too," Derek shot back. "Hi, Zayt. Cate's inside with Laney. They're probably chatting about you.

"I stopped by, Bradley," he continued, "to make sure you remember that you have to work tomorrow. Vacation is over."

"What do you need me for? You served justice for Councilwoman Bates's murder, and the newspapers say former Mayor Reynolds will undoubtedly go to jail with the banquet brigade to follow. With Philbin and Sharon Stakes behind bars already, I'd say you are doing fine without me. Besides, I kind of like the real estate business. Shea, Zayt, and I are forming our own company. We're going to call it Rebel with a Clause Realty. Getting suspended was the best thing that ever happened to me. I found my calling. And I have you to thank for it, Derek."

Derek's face dropped. He shifted his eyes from Bradley to Zayt, back and forth. "What? No . . . you?"

"Jesus, Derek. Watch your blood pressure. I was just kidding. Of course, I remember I'm back to work tomorrow."

"One of these days, Bradley, I swear you're going to make my head explode. I can't believe . . . " Derek continued to mutter.

Bradley responded in kind, raising his voice to overpower Derek's mutters. "How could you think I was serious . . ."

Zayt inserted his curiosity. "Rebel with a Clause? Where did you come up with that? Did you really just make that . . ."

Their playful banter followed them into the house, leaving behind the hum of heavy equipment shaping the sands, forging new opportunity and promise.

ACKNOWLEDGEMENTS

To my family and friends who constantly encourage me to burst through my comfort zone—you are the light shining on my darkness, the courage conquering my fears, and the love overshadowing my loss.

A special thank you to my sister, Paula Francis, for her valuable input and contributions to my stories. She never seems to tire of my interruptions. And to my sister-in-law, Mary Johnson, who has the unenviable task of reading my first drafts— you have encouraged me from the start, and I thank you.

Wonderful readers, I am honored and humbled that you put your faith in me, and I promise to continue to try my best to live up to it.

For proofreading this work, thank you, Richard Bruno, for giving your utmost attention to these pages.

Thank you, Mary-Ann DeVita Palmieri, for your excellent copy editing. I know my characters and story are safe in your hands.

And as always, to my publisher, editor, and good friend Marcia Gagliardi of Haley's Publishing—I would be lost in the dimness, stuck in the sand, and wallowing in my words if it weren't for you. I thank you, and Bradley thanks you.

ABOUT THE AUTHOR

Christine Noyes

photo by Paula Francis

You can't always plan where life will take you. That is certainly true for Christine Noyes. Growing up in Shrewsbury, Massachusetts, as a tomboy, she spent her youth building forts, playing sports, and enjoying the perceived innocence of the 1960s.

Not having a clear vision of what her life should be, she went where she was most comfortable, to the kitchen. Beginning her work life as a cook at her grandfather's restaurant at the age of eleven, she spent the next several decades re-inventing herself, becoming an accomplished chef, a sales representative, an entrepreneur, and now a writer and illustrator. She never chose her professions. They chose her.

She married her husband and soulmate, Al, in 1989. They moved to Orange, Massachusetts, where, after Al's passing, Chris remains today with thirty years of wonderful memories to keep her company.

When not at her keyboard, she can be found in her kitchen: back to her roots and love of cooking.

from the next Bradley Whitman novel
Meet Your Maker by Christine Noyes

ACTION

Barely missing the woman who pushed a double-wide stroller and grazing a parking meter, the black Dodge Charger careened around the corner and skipped over the curb as it made its way from Salem Street past the Old North Church and onto Charter. The driver slammed the brakes, forcing the car into a rubber-grinding spin that spewed clouds of noxious fumes into the street. The menacing vehicle stopped, facing the wrong way on the one-way street, and sat idling. A Massachusetts Armored Transportation truck headed toward the car and picked up speed with no intention of slowing down. The vehicles played a game of chicken, and neither looked like it would give in. A collision became imminent.

"Cut!" a voice yelled over a bullhorn. "Okay, we got it. Let's re-set for the crash scene."

The driver of the Dodge unfastened himself from the safety harness, removed his helmet, and walked through hordes of cameras, crew, and equipment toward the man holding the bullhorn. He sat in a chair that read, Director.

"Is it ready?" the director asked.

"All set," the driver replied.

"Ready on the set."

Cate watched in fascination. She had never before been on a movie set. Filming of movies in Boston had inconvenienced her before, but she had never seen the action as she did now with her sister Sheila. As a producer of the film, Sheila's husband, David, invited Cate and her husband, Derek, to watch the filming. But to Cate's frustration, Derek could not get away from work.

"I'm sorry, Sheila. Derek is wrapping up a big case. He's worked ten straight days. I thought, it being Sunday, he may have been able to join us, but you know how my life is. I didn't just marry Derek. I married the Federal Bureau of Investigation."

"Well, Cate, David is over there working, too. I married him and the Hollywood movie industry." They both half-heartedly laughed.

"At least I get to see you. I've missed you so much," Cate smiled. "Let's go get ourselves a glass of wine and catch up. I want to hear all about the twins. There's a great place a couple blocks from here, right on the harbor."

"Perfect. I'll tell David."

Cate watched her sister as she found David in the crowd of movie personnel. Sheila hadn't aged a bit, she thought. She wore her beautiful blonde hair shorter these days, but Cate thought she looked more lovely today than in their younger years. Motherhood agreed with her, Cate thought. A stitch of sorrow pinched her heart.

"Onward."

Sheila wrapped her arm around Cate's. "Sisters afternoon awaits. Let's go spend all the money that our menfolk are making," Sheila laughed. They hadn't gone more than a block and a half before they heard the unmistakable sound of metal crashing metal and a perfectly timed pyrotechnic explosion: Hollywood magic.

Their drinks in hand, Sheila filled Cate in on her two boys. "They're seventeen, and they think they own the world. Max has his whole life mapped out. We just don't know if it will play out on the East Coast or West Coast. He's applied to both Stanford and MIT."

"What does he want to do? I mean, what does he want to major in?" Cate asked.

"I was afraid you were going to ask me that. He wants to major in geophysics."

"Huh?" Cate said.

"That's exactly what I said," Sheila laughed. "Okay, let me see if I can get this right. It has something to do with the physics of the earth and . . . its environment in space."

"Wow." Cates eyes opened wide. "How about Alex? What's his plan?"

"Alex's plan is a bit more grounded, literally. He's decided to take a year off before he goes to college and backpack across the country, maybe even go to Europe. They are both adventurers in their own way."

"And you two are okay with Alex backpacking?"

"Yeah. We think it will be good for him. He's a wonderful writer, you know. And what a great experience it will be. I'm a little jealous."

"Well, I'm happy for all of you," Cate smiled, but Sheila could see the sadness behind Cate's praise.

Sheila placed her hand on Cate's. "They miss you and Derek, of course."

"Well, I'm rooting for Max to come to MIT," Cate said with a smile that did not quite reach her melancholy eyes. Until recently Cate had not regretted her and Derek's choice not to have children in their earlier years. When they finally decided they wanted to start a family, it proved more difficult than expected. After two miscarriages and her well into her forties, Cate and Derek found it too painful to try again. Sheila wished to lighten the mood. "So, does Bradley have any idea that David and I are in town?"

"I don't think so. Derek has gotten much better at misleading people since we met. I taught him that," Cate laughed as she lifted her goblet to tap against Sheila's. "I can't believe it's been eighteen years since we all met on that cruise. I can't wait to see everybody at Bradley's party tonight. They're all coming, right?"

"As far as I know, yes. Holly and John are going to pick Mike up and meet us at our house at five-thirty. Bradley thinks his parents are just taking him out to dinner for his birthday, but Lynn and Doug made reservations for all of us at the Envoy Hotel. First, we'll have drinks on the rooftop lounge at six-thirty, then dinner at eight o'clock."

"What about Bradley's new lady friend, Laney? Am I going to get to meet her tonight?"

"She's hardly new. They've been together for well over a year. Yes, she's going to surprise him there. She made some excuse about having to supervise the hospital emergency room tonight to throw him off track. You are going to love her, Sheila. They are so good together. I've never seen Bradley this happy."

"I've never known Bradley not to be happy," Sheila replied.

Sometimes Cate forgot how little of her life she shared with Sheila. The distance between their living quarters lent to a distance in communication, and that felt unsettling. She thought it best not to mention Bradley's battle with feeling inadequate. Besides, that might all be in the past. Instead, she replied, "We all have our moments. Oh, and you're going to get to meet Zayt and Shea."

Sheila's expression indicated a lack of recollection.

"They are Bradley's REACH business partners and my coworkers. I told you about them when I started volunteering there. Zayt is a former Navy Seal, and Shea used to be a real estate agent. Now Shea manages the housing portion of the business."

"You'll have to fill me in. I think the details get lost somewhere in Middle America during transmission from Massachusetts to California. Sometimes my attention span is that of a six-year-old," Sheila giggled.

Mildly annoyed that her sister paid little attention to something so important to her, Cate explained the Revere Enhancement and Community Housing program to Sheila.

"It was Zayt's idea. As a former homeless veteran himself, he knew firsthand the plights of the homeless. With Bradley and Shea's help, Zayt locked into a lease agreement with the City of Revere for the old sandpit behind Bradley's house, raised the funds, and built a community of tiny homes complete with a community center and kitchen. It has been an enormous success. I manage the kitchen and community center, Shea does the housing, and Zayt is security and enforcement. By enforcement, I mean no drugs or alcohol. Of course, sometimes that rule must be bent in order to help in the long run."

"Cate, I had no idea how big this project was. I pictured you volunteering at a one of those homeless shelters somewhere in the middle of Boston. I would love to see the community. Maybe there's something David and I could do while we're here."

"Great. I can't wait to show you around."

"How are Holly and John? And their daughter . . . ?"

"Grace. Her name is Grace, Sheila. Holly says everything is going really well. She is so excited David bought the movie rights to her client's novel. I asked her if she were going to come to Boston for any of the filming, and she said would only come here to see you and David. She's not much of a city girl."

"That's sweet. I'm so happy for her. Hey, I still need to get a gift for Bradley. Did you come up with any fantastic ideas?"

"He's impossible to buy for unless it's something for his kitchen. Or his dog," Cate laughed.

"Okay, so let's go find either a Williams-Sonoma store or a Petco."

At four o'clock, Derek emerged from his private office and headed into the bullpen, the shared open-office space of his FBI agents. Cate had told Derek to make sure Bradley left for home early enough to get ready for dinner. On the far side of the room, Bradley sat huddled at his desk with Agent Mara Thompkins as they sifted through endless financial statements.

"I thought you said your parents were taking you out to dinner tonight," Derek yelled across the near empty office.

Bradley momentarily looked up from his computer screen with a sour expression and then sank back into his screen.

"Yeah, well, I think I'm going to call and cancel. We're mired down in this mess," Bradley said.

Derek froze.

"Ah, you can't do that," he said, his eyes wide and his face troubled.

"Huh?" Bradley looked up again. "Why not? It's just dinner. They'll get over it. I'll go visit them this weekend or something."

He hunkered back down.

Derek knew he couldn't spoil the surprise or Cate would never let him hear the end of it.

"You know, you can be one selfish son-of-a-bitch, Bradley Whitman."

This time Bradley held Derek's gaze. "What are you talking about?"

"Your parents have been looking forward to this for weeks. What the hell is the matter with you? Lynn will be crushed if you cancel. And Doug will be pissed off at me."

"It's only dinner," Bradley stated emphatically.

"It's your parents," Derek countered equally emphatically. "Besides, I'm leaving in a half hour. I want both of you out of here before I go. It's Sunday, for chrissake." Derek moved his pointed finger between Mara and Bradley. "Pack it up."

Wondering if either one of them would listen to him, Derek walked back to his office.

"He's right, you know," Mara said. "Your parents would be totally disappointed if you cancel on them. Especially your mother."

Bradley liked Mara. The youngest agent in the bureau, she had excellent organizational skills, and he found her unwavering in her determination to be the best at her job. They had on occasion worked closely together and knew each other's inclinations.

"It really sucks that all my coworkers know my parents and always take their side."

"It's of your own doing. If you hadn't gotten yourself shot and stabbed a while back, I wouldn't even know you had parents," Mara chuckled. "I might have thought you were hatched."

Alright, alright. Let's wrap this up and go home. Derek seems like he's in a lousy mood, and I don't want to escalate it."

Twenty minutes later Bradley backed his electric wheelchair away from his desk, took the elevator down eight flights to the main lobby of Chelsea FBI headquarters, and out the front door to his custom Chevy truck. The driver and rear passenger doors had been replaced by a one-piece panel. Bradley used his key fob to unlock the wide door and initiate its opening. The panel automatically pulled straight out, stopped, beeped, and lowered a wheelchair platform. Bradley expertly backed onto the lift and rode the mechanism up to floorboard height. The apparatus beeped again before the platform slid Bradley into place behind the steering wheel.

The vehicle safety system would not allow the truck to start if Bradley did not strap in properly, so he hitched his seatbelt before starting the engine.

Bradley loved his truck. His truck meant freedom. He thought back to his younger days when someone, usually his mother, had to drive him around in a specially equipped van. He hated that. But his mother never complained. Derek is right, he thought. My parents would be hurt if I canceled our birthday dinner celebration. How the hell did I become a thirty-year-old man?

"John, we're picking my father up at four-thirty. Have you even started to get ready yet?" Holly yelled from the bedroom.

She put the finishing touches on her new outfit, the one she had bought specifically for this night. Earlier that day, she had her hair styled, her nails done, and, once home, spent a great deal of time on her makeup. She hadn't pampered herself like this since her wedding day and she enjoyed every minute of it.

On the cruise where they met eighteen years before, it was Cate and Sheila who taught her about coddling herself. Holly had been shy and anxiety-ridden at the age of twenty-four and she had never learned how to wear makeup properly or do her nails. Her mother had died when she was just a child, and she felt much too timid to ask anyone for help. But Cate and Sheila took her under their wings and taught her everything she knew about fashion and making an entrance. And the last is what she intended to do tonight. Not because she wanted the attention, but to show Cate and Sheila how much they had helped her and how much she appreciated what they had done.

"Do I need to wear a tie for this thing?" John yelled back.

"If you do, you'll be the only one."

"Got it. No tie," John said as he strolled into the bedroom. "Wow! You look . . . wow!"

Holly smiled and playfully turned in a circle to showcase her new dress. She wore a deep-purple-lace, high-waist asymmetrical design, the skirt lower in back than front with a cami top. Her mother's pearls hung on her slender neck. Her opened-toed lilac shoes boasted a four-inch heel, and a white lace wrap lay waiting on the bed beside her. Her once golden brown hair had slightly darkened, and she wore it shoulder length, curled beneath her chin.

Holly felt intoxicated, and all it had taken was a dress and a little indulgence.

"Thank you, honey. You look . . . casual," she laughed.

"Five minutes."

Five minutes, Holly thought. I've been at this all day. She laughed at herself.

Holly didn't care about appearances. She never had. Her priorities lay in honesty, sincerity, and loyalty. Her father taught her those values a long time ago. The two of them shared a wonderful relationship. Holly grew from a young, self-conscious child to a woman of confidence. She could have worked for any large publishing firm in the country but chose to open her own small publishing company in the college town of Amherst in west-central Massachusetts, where she met John. She knew almost from the minute they met she would spend the rest of her life with him.

They met when she was a guest lecturer at the University of Massachusetts. Her boss was scheduled to speak but sent Holly in her place. The Introduction to Professional Writing students she spoke to seemed receptive to her talk. After class, a handsome man, somewhat older than the students who surrounded him, stayed behind waiting for his chance to converse with Holly. Because he was the only one in the room who audibly laughed when she addressed them, she suspected he would drill her on several controversial statements she had made that went against typical publishing standards. She stood ready to take his shots.

"Hello. My name is John."

"Hi. I'm Holly."

"That was an interesting take on the current state of big-house publishing. Who is it you work for again?" he asked.

Holly laughed. "Parrot Publishing. And yes, I meant what I said. The future of publishing won't take place in the castle but in the barn. Metaphorically speaking, of course. I couldn't help but notice your reaction. I didn't intend for it to be funny. Unfortunately, I think the idea got lost on the rest of the group, anyway."

"I'm sorry if I offended you," John said, "but it was unexpected. I teach a society and literature course, and I've been saying the same thing for years. Not quite as eloquently as you, though."

"Well, thank you. I hope my boss is as receptive. Better yet, I hope she never hears a word of what I said."

Holly giggled.

"Can I buy you a cup of coffee?" John asked.

And that was it. The tall, handsome professor had won her heart by laughing at her lecture. They married two years later, and Grace arrived two years after that.

"Okay, I'm ready, how do I look?" John twirled around to mock Holly's showcasing.

Holly laughed and took his hands in hers. "Perfect," she said as she reached up to kiss him.

"How much time do we have?" John softly teased.

"Not enough," she giggled.

The chauffeur pulled up in front of Cate and Derek's Medford home at 5:25 p.m. Sheila and David hadn't rung the doorbell when Derek opened the door. The movie production company had hired a limousine service for the duration of filming in Boston, so David had suggested they take advantage of it and all drive to the restaurant together.

"Right on time. You are nothing like your sister, Sheila," Derek pronounced. He and Sheila laughed.

"I heard that," Cate yelled from the kitchen.

"David, how did the filming go today? Sorry I missed it," Derek said.

"Surprisingly well. We only had twenty-seven death threats for shutting down Salem and Charter Streets. Bostonians are quite civil. First they tell you how they are going to hurt you before they actually try to do it," David snickered.

"Yes. We are still Puritans at heart. If we are going to break the rule of piety, we must be forthright about our intentions," Derek chuckled.

"Good to know," David laughed and shook Derek's hand. "It's good to see you. I hear you've been pretty busy."

"Just the usual. Things should be calming down soon."

"That's what he always says. Then, boom. A bigger case comes up, and we start all over again," Cate quipped as she walked into the living room.

The doorbell rang.

Derek threw up his hand. "Thank God for the doorbell!," he exclaimed as he opened the door to Holly, John, and Mike.

"Oh, Holly, you look gorgeous," Sheila screeched.

"You do. You look amazing. Damn. I might have to go change," Cate declared.

"Oh, please. You two always look stunning. It took me all day to look like this," Holly laughed. They hugged as the men shook hands, and exchanged banter all the way to the limousine.

"The plan is for us to be there before Bradley, Lynn, and Doug arrive. They'll meet us on the rooftop lounge," Cate said as she stepped into the car. "Mike, sit back here between Sheila and me so we can catch up."

"You girls are as beautiful as ever," Mike said.

The two women giggled.

"I think you are the only person in the world who still thinks of us as girls, Mike!" Sheila pointed out.

"I can't help it. You haven't changed a bit in all these years. Except for getting more beautiful."

"Derek? Are you hearing this? This is the way you talk to a woman," Cate said.

"Okay, I'll try it out on Mara tomorrow, but I'm not sure how it will go over," Derek joked.

The limo exploded with laughter as the chauffeur pulled away from the curb. Eight minutes later, just before crossing the channel on Seaport Boulevard, they waited for the traffic light to turn green. They were less than two minutes away and right on schedule.

"Bradley is going to be so surprised to see all of you," Cate smiled. "I can't believe we . . . "

They felt the heat first then heard the ear-shattering blast. The back end of the limousine violently jumped into the air, then came down hard, bouncing multiple times. Cate's head hit the roof as the explosion threw her out of her seat. She hurtled forward and her blood-soaked crown contacted the dividing wall separating driver from passengers.

Mike and Sheila's bodies collided, both then thrust to the scorching floor. Mike sprawled on top of Sheila as the odor of her singeing flesh instantly permeated the scene. Holly and John, who had been seated on the passenger side of the u-shaped sitting area shot into the air and forcefully struck their heads while broken glass from the windows behind them pierced their skin like pellets fired from a shotgun.

The blast propelled David and Derek, who had sat opposite Holly and John, out the side windows and into the street, where they landed almost eight feet away from the smoldering limousine.

The driver's head cracked the front windshield. He lay motionless across the front of the car. All lost consciousness as flames shot from the back end of the vehicle.

COLOPHON

MVB Verdigris is a Garalde text family for the digital age. Inspired by work of sixteenth-century punchcutters Robert Granjon, Hendrik van den Keere, and Pierre Haultin, MVB Verdigris celebrates tradition but is not beholden to it. Created to deliver good typographic color as text, Mark van Bronkhorst's design meets the needs of today's designer using today's paper and press. A full-featured OpenType release with an added titling companion, it's optimized for the latest typesetting technologies, too.

Garalde: the word itself sounds antique and arcane to anyone who isn't fresh out of design school, but the sort of typeface it describes is actually quite familiar to all of us. Despite its age—born fairly early in printing's history—the style has fared well. Garaldes are the typefaces of choice for books and other long reading.

www.ingramcontent.com/pod-product-compliance
Lightning Source LLC
Chambersburg PA
CBHW050123030726
47505CB00007B/2015